P9-APU-991

MURDER FOR THE PROSECUTION

MURDER FOR THE PROSECUTION

Blair Hoffman

Carroll & Graf Publishers, Inc.
New York

Copyright © 1993 by Blair Hoffman

First Carroll & Graf edition 1993

Carroll & Graf Publishers, Inc.
260 Fifth Avenue
New York, NY 10001

Library of Congress Cataloging-in-Publication Data
Hoffman, Blair
    Murder for the prosecution / Blair Hoffman. — 1st ed.
        p.   cm.
    ISBN 0-88184-995-2 : $18.95
    1. Courts—California—San Francisco—Fiction.   2. San Francisco
(Calif.)—Fiction.
    PS3558.O34476M87   1993
    813'.54—dc20   93-21931
                                                                         CIP

Manufactured in the United States of America

To Peggy

Wife, friend, partner, and chief assistant in charge of plot development

MURDER FOR THE PROSECUTION

Foreword

This is fiction. I know from personal experience that the San Francisco criminal division of the attorney general's office is a highly professional, mutually supportive, and extremely competent law office. However, an organization that is highly professional, mutually supportive, and extremely competent is not a good setting for a murder mystery. So I had to invent the one portrayed in these pages. Some of the difficulties and frustrations experienced by my characters, however, do reflect reality. It is equally obvious, I trust, that my fictional characters bear no resemblance to their real-life counterparts, all of whom I respect greatly. For example, it should go without saying that the real Chief Justice of California is utterly unlike the one who appears in a cameo role in this story.

I have exercised poetic license in several respects for the sake of the story. I am fully aware, for example, that as a result of the 1989 earthquake, the criminal division and the appellate courts no longer share the same building, although they did for many years. I hope the reader who can spot these inaccuracies will forgive them.

Chapter 1

The hand knocked gently on the office door. No answer. Carefully, with infinite patience, the hand turned the doorknob just below the sign reading, "Martin Granowski, Deputy Attorney General," and opened the door. As expected, no one was inside. Noiselessly, the feet stepped inside the office. The hand closed the door. The person walked directly to a cardboard box next to the large, cluttered desk. The box was labeled, *"People v. Morton,* exhibits."

The hand reached into the box and pulled out a .357 magnum pistol. Attached to the pistol was a tag from the preliminary hearing labeled "People's Exhibit No. 7." The hand reached into the box again and pulled out a plastic bag with a similar tag labeled "People's Exhibit No. 13." Inside the bag were eight live .357 caliber hollow point cartridges. Then the hand removed a third item bearing a similar tag labeled "People's Exhibit No. 8." It was a silencer.

The intruder quickly screwed the silencer to the barrel of the handgun. Next, three of the cartridges were inserted into the magazine. Was it lack of expertise or merely nerves that caused so much fumbling? Finally, everything was ready. The person inspected the finished product. Perfect. The hands placed the loaded gun into a case file containing transcripts that the intruder had brought for the purpose. The person walked quickly to the door, opened it silently, and looked up and down the hallway. Nobody in sight.

Carrying the file with the gun as if it were merely a new case with transcripts, the person walked to the end of the hall and around the corner to the left. This hallway was quite short and rather isolated. On the third door on the right was affixed a sign reading, "Rachel Brandwyn, Deputy Attorney General." The door, normally open, was closed. The person carrying the file knew why, and was confident that Brandwyn was inside. After checking to see that no one was in sight, the person strode to the door and knocked. One hand was inside the file, gripping the gun, ready for business. A voice inside said, "Come in."

Rachel Brandwyn was a deputy in the San Francisco branch of the criminal division of the California attorney general's office. She was scheduled to have oral argument in the California Supreme Court that Tuesday morning in early May. It was a death penalty case—*People* v. *William Jones*, a serial killer. Jones had been convicted of four first-degree murders, with special circumstances of rape murder, multiple murder, and, as to two of the murders, torture. His attorneys raised 46 issues on appeal in a 523-page brief. It was up to Rachel to try to uphold the convictions and the death sentence. Oral argument would begin at nine o'clock. It would be her fourth Supreme Court argument.

She had worked at her home in the Marina district of San Francisco until ten-thirty the night before, rereading the briefs and the major cases, and preparing her oral presentation. After a night of broken sleep, she awoke at five-thirty with facts, arguments, cases, answers to anticipated questions, swirling in her mind. Although she knew the contents of the eleven-thousand-page record as well as anyone could, she felt the inevitable fear that she would not know the answers to the questions the court asked. While she was brushing her teeth, she thought of one part of the record she wanted to reread.

She arrived at her office at 7:30 A.M., and continued preparing. To avoid interruptions, she closed her door. The part of the record she reread said exactly what she remembered it said. *Relax*, she told herself. *You know this case inside and out.* Relax. Fat chance. No matter how prepared she was, and in the Supreme Court she was able to prepare at length despite her heavy caseload, she always had the nagging doubt that there was something else she should do.

Shortly after eight o'clock, as required by court rules, she went to the courtroom two floors lower in the same building and checked in with the Supreme Court clerk. The clerk, a plump man with graying hair and a slightly wrinkled business suit, told her that hers would be the first of three cases to be argued that morning. Argument would begin promptly at nine o'clock. Next to the clerk, a bailiff was starting to prepare the tape recorders to record the arguments. He glanced up and smiled at Rachel. He remembered her from her previous appearances.

Rachel said a perfunctory hello to opposing counsel, who was already at his table on the left side of the podium rereading his notes. Then, rather than wait around and get more and more nervous (no matter how many times you argue in the Supreme Court you always get nervous), she decided to return to her office for one last reading of her notes. There was no use returning to court until just before nine. When she left the courtroom, the clerk said, "Don't be late."

As she walked down the hall to her office, she nodded to several colleagues who were in their offices. She again closed her door. For the zillionth time she went over her intended opening remarks. She had them memorized by now, and hoped the judges would allow her to get through them before the inevitable barrage of questions began. She tried to think of more possible questions from the judges, and more possible answers. After a half hour or so she heard a knock on the door. This irritated her, for everyone knew she had oral argument in a few minutes, and the closed door was an obvious sign that she did not want to be disturbed. Nevertheless, she said, "Come in."

The person who had knocked walked briskly into Rachel's office and closed the door, one hand at the ready inside the file. Rachel gave a sign of recognition, and started to stand up. Suddenly, she stared at a hand holding a .357 magnum with a silencer pointed at her midsection. A finger was around the trigger. Two tags that appeared to be evidence tags were hanging from the weapon. The gun looked enormous to Rachel. Her instinctive reaction was to gasp, and to fall back down into her government-issue black plastic-covered office chair.

No words were spoken. The finger pulled the trigger, there was a muffled spit, and blood spurted from just under Rachel's left breast. One second later, there was another spit, and blood flowed from her abdomen. Rachel was unable to scream; she could only slump back in the chair. The intruder walked to her quickly, thrust the head up, and calmly, oh so calmly, pointed the gun between her eyes, about four inches away. The trigger was pulled again, and a third spit was heard, or actually not heard by anyone but the shooter. A hole appeared about one-half inch above the eyes, slightly to the right of the midpoint between them. Rachel jerked slightly, then did not move. The eyes, still open, were looking upward.

The killer, no longer visibly nervous, grabbed a rag that had been placed in the file for this purpose, and efficiently wiped everything that could contain fingerprints. The gun, the silencer, and the plastic bag that had contained the bullets, all still bearing the evidence tags, were placed on the desk. The police would soon enough figure out where the murder weapon came from. No reason to make it hard for them. The killer had no more connection to that weapon than many others.

The killer then stepped to the tall file cabinet in the corner of the office behind the door, opened the second drawer from the top, and delicately searched through the manila folders and other documents inside. Not finding what was sought, the killer pondered for a moment what to do, then reluctantly reclosed the cabinet. The rag was used to wipe off all portions of the cabinet and contents that had been touched, and then was put back into the case file.

With everything taken care of, the person stepped to the closed door. An ear pressed to the door heard no sounds from the hallway. The hand opened the door quietly, and the head peered out carefully. No one in sight. Quickly, the person stepped out and closed the door. The feet walked down the hall in the opposite direction from which they had come. The hands carried the file. The feet took a roundabout route back to their office. On the way, the rag was tossed into a wastebasket. Inside the office, the person placed the file on a table, next to seven other files and a mass of other documents. The person sat down, took a deep breath, then thought, *That wasn't as hard as I expected it to be.* The thought was exhilarating.

It was 8:54 A.M.

Chapter 2

The silence could be heard clearly throughout the crowded courtroom. The big clock high above the back teak wall clicked over to 9:03 A.M. The bailiff continued to make sure the recording system was in order. The clerk looked around nervously, glancing repeatedly at the empty seat reserved for the deputy attorney general who was to argue the *Jones* case. The defense attorney on the other side pored through his notes, ready to start his argument as soon as Rachel appeared. He had a three-ring binder with about twenty-five pages of notes, neatly paginated and organized into topics with eight divider tabs. He was practicing flipping from section to section, hoping he would be able to do it as smoothly when he was actually being asked questions.

In a row immediately behind defense counsel sat nine attorneys from large private firms, either the attorneys who would actually argue the two civil cases scheduled to follow the *Jones* case, or their associates. The six male attorneys were all wearing dark business suits, red ties, white or light-blue shirts, black socks, and black shoes. The three female attorneys were all wearing conservative wool flannel single-breasted suit jackets with matching skirts, and a single strand of pearls and small gold earrings. Each carried a designer purse as well as an expensive monogrammed briefcase. Their dark high-heeled shoes looked brand-new, but that was easily explained by the fact that they all carried in their briefcases a pair of running shoes which they wore to and from work. All the attorneys had huge briefcases stuffed to the brim with briefs, notes, transcripts, and, in one case, antacid tablets. Two of the attorneys were passing notes back and forth. None made a sound.

Behind these attorneys were the rows of seats open to the public. One reporter for an afternoon newspaper from the small town in the San Joaquin Valley where the murders had occurred glanced at his watch. He had an 11:00 A.M. deadline to get his story in, and he did not need any delay in the argument. Two other veteran court reporters, notebooks open and pens at the ready, exchanged knowing glances as if to say, "No one is ever late to a Supreme Court argument." The clock clicked to 9:04 A.M.

Many spectators were in the audience. In the second row from the back, Deputy Attorney General Martin Granowski stared at the geometric design on the high ceiling. It was not like Rachel to be late to something as important as this court appearance, but Martin was too busy thinking about his upcoming "Silencer Killer" trial to worry about her absence. He wanted to watch the argument, but even the Supreme Court could not take his mind off his own case. Among the three victims of the Silencer Killer was the nephew of a secretary in the Mendocino County district attorney's office, which was why the attorney general was prosecuting the case. It was the biggest case in Granowski's career, and trial was scheduled to begin in three weeks. This week he was organizing and reviewing the exhibits in his office.

Other deputies attorney general were scattered throughout the courtroom. William Kelly, a new deputy who had started work a couple of months earlier, contemplated his fingernails. His brand-new black wing-tip shoes were pinching his feet. Could he take them off for the time being? After careful consideration, Bill decided not to. He had come down to watch his first Supreme Court argument, and it seemed inappropriate to be in his stocking feet. He had been told that Rachel Brandwyn was "dynamite" at oral argument, and he could learn from watching her. Why was she so late?

Next to Bill was Beret Holmes, another young deputy. She was examining the huge gold seal of the State of California that towered above the justices in the front of the courtroom. Beret had seen a few Supreme Court arguments, and had argued several cases in the court of appeal. She, too, was looking forward to learning from Rachel's argument. Rachel was supposed to be so conscientious and reliable. Why was she so late?

On the right side of the courtroom was a group of fifteen sophomores from Lowell High School who had come to watch the judiciary in action. Before the judges had entered the courtroom, the clerk had explained to them the process of Supreme Court oral argument. The seven judges would come in and sit in a row in the front, below the state seal. The clerk would call the cases, then counsel would argue the first one, a death penalty case called *People* v. *Jones*. The clerk described the facts of the *Jones* case, which piqued the students' interest briefly. He explained that because the defendant had already been convicted after a long trial, and was now appealing the case, there would not be any witnesses, only legal arguments based on the transcripts of the trial and the legal briefs on file. The judges would probably ask the attorneys a lot of questions. So far, the students were less than impressed with the proceedings. They were wondering why there was such a long period of absolute silence. More importantly, they were wondering how long they could stand it.

The seven justices were sitting in stony silence on the podium in front. Chief Justice Wilkins was in the middle, with three justices on each side. The more senior the justice, the closer he or she got to sit to the Chief. The court had entered, had been announced by the clerk, and had sat down. The clerk called the name of each of the cases to be argued that morning, and the attorneys announced their presence. Although Rachel Brandwyn had checked in earlier, she was not there when her case was called. Since hers was the first case, the Chief simply had everyone wait quietly until she showed up. Thus the silence.

The clock clicked to 9:05 A.M. The Chief became increasingly irritated. *I'm going to have to find her in contempt of court for her tardiness,* he told himself. The thought cheered him. The Chief liked finding people in contempt and fining them—attorneys, parties, witnesses, spectators, court reporters, even on one occasion that he particularly relished, a lower court judge. He told himself that he had not found anyone in contempt for months, although it had really only been a matter of weeks. On the last occasion, he had cited a court reporter for contempt because she had not prepared a lengthy transcript in time. He fined her five hundred dollars, which he now thought might have been too lenient. These thoughts eased the silent passage of the minutes.

While the Chief was contemplating such pleasant matters, the clock clicked to 9:06 A.M. Five minutes since he called the case. Suddenly, a man wearing a business suit burst into the courtroom from a side door. In an oddly high-pitched voice he shouted, "Rachel's been murdered!"

* * *

A few minutes earlier, Elizabeth Cronin, the secretary for the attorney who headed the criminal division in San Francisco, carried a new case file to be assigned to Ramon Aguilar, who had an office down the hall from Rachel. She thought it was odd that the door to Rachel's office was closed. Rachel normally kept it open when she was not inside. Wasn't she supposed to be in court by now? Then Elizabeth saw a liquid, a red liquid, seep from under the door. What was that? Elizabeth knocked on the door, quietly at first, then more firmly. No answer. Tentatively, she opened the door a crack. Still no reaction. Then she opened the door all the way. She screamed at what she saw.

The shout about a murder jolted the Chief Justice from his reverie. His first reaction was of outrage that someone had violated the sanctity of his courtroom without his permission. His second thought was of disappointment. If Ms. Brandwyn had been murdered, he probably couldn't cite her for contempt. Then he remembered that he was responsible for the courtroom proceedings. Nothing must interfere with Supreme Court business.

Several people in the audience, including three reporters and the deputies attorney general, got up and ran out of the courtroom. The students from Lowell High School woke up abruptly. *Is this what the judiciary is all about? Maybe this isn't so boring after all.* The bailiff ran to the interloper to see what was going on. Suddenly, in a commanding voice, the Chief Justice ordered the clerk to call the next case. The clerk did.

As the courtroom emptied of spectators, five rather confused attorneys hurriedly assembled their briefs, notepads, and briefcases, and approached counsel's desk. One quickly consulted with her two associates, then stepped to the podium. She took a deep breath, tried to adjust the microphone to her height, gave up, cleared her throat, then said the magic words, "May it please the court, my name is Sandra Barmore, and I represent the plaintiff and appellant, Partech Consolidated Hydrotech Products, Incorporated." She proceeded to discuss whether the Code of Civil Procedure section 398.364, subdivision (a)(7), transfer of venue applies to a third-party assignee credit transaction when the first and second parties had not consented to either the assignation or the transfer in writing until three days after the statutory limitation period had expired. At least three million dollars lay in the balance.

Frederick Olson, the chief of the San Francisco criminal division, sat in stunned silence when he heard the news. He was dismayed. How could he cope with losing a deputy attorney general at this time? Who would do the work of his division? Although most (not all) criminal cases were tried by local district attorneys' offices, the attorney general's office represented the prosecution in all criminal cases in all appellate courts throughout the state. This was a big job and getting bigger all the time. Because of recent budget cuts, Olson's division had nine vacancies out of forty-seven authorized legal positions. A hiring freeze prevented him from filling any of the vacancies, although he had several qualified applicants he wanted to hire. The number of appellate cases increased far faster than the number of attorneys to absorb them. Because of this, there was an ever-increasing number of appellate briefs his division had to write that remained unwritten. It was known as the "Backlog," with a capital "B."

There were now seven briefs due for each attorney. Several attorneys, like Martin Granowski, who had a triple murder case to try, were on special assignment and not available to write briefs. The situation was bad enough to begin with. And now this. Rachel Brandwyn was one of Olson's most productive attorneys. If she was indeed dead, he could not expect any more work from her. The Backlog would not shrink, but would grow even faster. How would he get by?

Maybe, Olson told himself, the murder would be a significant enough event that he could get an exemption from the hiring freeze and replace her. If he did, who would he hire? He started reviewing in his mind the applicants one by one. There were some excellent possibilities. The low salaries (compared to the large private firms) that the state offered did not entirely discourage good applicants. But they would not wait forever for the state to start hiring again.

These thoughts were interrupted when one of his attorneys asked him what they should do about the *Jones* case. Oral argument was supposed to have begun fifteen minutes ago. Chief Justice Wilkins would be furious about the delay. Olson turned his mind back to business. He ordered the attorney to go to court and request that the case be put over until the June calendar. He later learned that the Chief Justice granted the request. The Chief reluctantly concluded that the sudden murder was arguably good cause for the continuance, and that it would not look good to impose sanctions on an office that had just lost one of its best and most productive attorneys.

After sending the attorney on his way, Olson contemplated briefly who should be reassigned the *Jones* case. It would be a big job for a new attorney to get on top of it by June. Then Olson had a terrible thought. Suspects! Unless the murder were solved quickly, and somehow he doubted that it would be, there would probably be suspects in this crime. Possibly among his staff. How could he expect high productivity from attorneys who were mur- der suspects? And what if one of them was actually the murderer? Could Olson expect the actual murderer to continue writing ap- pellate briefs after he was caught? Probably not. That might cre- ate another vacancy. Eventually. Would he be able to fill it? When? The more Olson thought about it, the worse the situation appeared.

As William Kelly climbed the stairs back to the attorney general's office, he could not help but think of the lawyers' league softball game scheduled for that evening. Although new to the office, Kelly had been conscripted to be the softball team coach when he admitted to a liking for the sport and a modicum of talent. He had exactly ten people—the minimum number—lined up to play to- night, including Rachel. She played—used to play—a good sec- ond base. If she was dead, who would replace her? He noticed that Beret Holmes was just ahead of him on the stairs. "I wonder if she plays softball," he asked himself inconsequentially. "It can't hurt to ask."

Chapter 3

Officer Theodore French of the California State Police had never before been involved in a murder case. He generally handled building security, not major crimes. But he was the first officer of any kind on the scene, and had to take charge until some more experienced officer from the San Francisco Police Department could replace him. After assuring himself that Rachel Brandwyn was quite dead, he sealed off her office, and left it alone. He was trained and experienced enough to know that the best thing he could do with the crime scene and potential physical evidence was nothing. He was, however, intrigued by a pistol on the desk that appeared to have an evidence tag affixed to it. It took all of his training and all of his experience to resist the temptation to look at it closer. He then turned his efforts to trying to calm Elizabeth Cronin, who was still screaming.

Within a few minutes, officers from the San Francisco Police Department arrived. Evidence technicians, photographers, and criminalists began doing their jobs, taking pictures of everything in the room from all directions, checking all possible surfaces for fingerprints, gathering blood samples, searching for stray hairs, threads from clothes, a stray button, and anything else the killer might have left behind. They searched carefully for bullets and bullet holes and any other evidence. The body was eventually covered and removed for the autopsy. The cause of death was obvious, but something useful might be learned.

Two homicide inspectors, Alexander "Sandy" Petersen and Roman Tarkov, arrived to take charge of the investigation. Petersen was a thirty-two-year veteran of the police department, eleven years in homicide. He had seen everything, and had investigated just about every kind of homicide there was, from execution-style drug killings to his most recent case, the murder for hire of a ten-year-old girl who had been strangled to prevent her from testifying against a man who had raped her. Petersen had had to take a three-week vacation after solving that case to recover his equilibrium. It had been his first vacation in four years, and he had only been back on the job for two days. He firmly believed in legwork and old-fashioned investigation as the secret to success—he had interviewed 137 people in four states in the murder-for-hire case before getting his first break. Although Petersen was willing to try any technique to solve a serious crime, he was generally disdainful of modern scientific methods.

After four years in the department, Tarkov was a rookie in homicide. He had a bachelor's degree in criminal justice, and was continually taking refresher courses, eagerly studying the latest scientific techniques, including those still on the drawing board. So far, he had found an occasional fingerprint, but he had not yet solved a case by scientific means. He was determined to do so soon. Tarkov had been Petersen's partner for six weeks, and admired him as a hard worker who had achieved great success over the years. Tarkov was, however, frustrated that Petersen's enthusiasm for science was not quite as great as his own.

Everyone hoped that at least one blood sample would prove to have come from the killer, although since there was no evidence of a struggle, it seemed unlikely. The killer had evidently taken his or her victim by surprise. Tarkov insisted that the area be searched thoroughly, excruciatingly thoroughly, for semen stains or any other bodily fluids. Petersen indulged Tarkov, although with little hope. The crime did not appear to be sexually motivated. But ever since Tarkov had read of a murder in England that had been solved by analyzing bloodstains for their DNA content, he dreamed of solving a crime that way himself. If there was any possible source of the killer's DNA in the office, it would be found. Inspector Petersen was not holding his breath. His instinct and his long experience told him that this killer was too smart for that.

With the physical investigation well under control—all the officers were trained professionals and required little direct supervision—Petersen and Tarkov started interviewing possible witnesses. They first spoke with a shaken Elizabeth Cronin, and learned only that she opened the door to Brandwyn's office and saw the body. They then decided to interview the head of the criminal division, Frederick Olson.

* * *

"The murder weapon was apparently a .357 magnum that was an exhibit in a criminal case called *People* v. *Morton.* Do you know anything about that case?" Inspector Petersen started the questioning in Olson's office in the southeast corner of the building. The office was spacious, but far from luxurious. It had a large desk that, like much of the furniture in that government building, had been built by inmates at San Quentin, the state prison just north of the Golden Gate Bridge in Marin County. The floor was covered by linoleum, with two throw rugs that Olson had supplied himself. Olson sat behind the desk in his padded chair. The inspectors sat in smaller chairs in front of the desk. Tarkov was taking notes.

"Well, I don't know. That is, yes, we are prosecuting a murder case named *Morton.* But there can't be any connection. Can there?"

"Does the *Morton* case involve a silencer?"

"Yes. He is nicknamed the Silencer Killer. How did you know?" Within a split second, Olson answered the question himself. "You mean, the same silencer was used to kill Rachel Brandwyn?"

"So it would seem. Who is prosecuting the case?"

"One of my best trial attorneys, Martin Granowski. He can't possibly be involved in the murder. He went down to watch the Supreme Court argument at the time of the murder. At least I think he did. He and Rachel were close friends. In fact, he has relied on Rachel's advice throughout the *Morton* prosecution. The idea that he would use the weapon in that case to shoot her is absurd. Why would he do that? It would make him an obvious suspect."

"He certainly *is* an obvious suspect. In fact, right now, number one. I think we had better get this Mr. Granowski to see what he has to say. Roman, go get him and bring him in here in five minutes." Tarkov left the room. "In the meantime, Mr. Olson, can you tell me whether anybody you know had any reason to want Rachel Brandwyn dead?"

"No, absolutely not. She was one of my most popular attorneys. Everybody liked her, including the secretaries. She got along with everyone. I can't imagine anyone wanting to kill her."

"And yet somebody did, and in no uncertain fashion. Did she

ever quarrel with anybody you know? Was she in debt? Having an affair? Insult anyone professionally?"

Olson pondered the questions at length. "Everybody quarrels sometimes, but I can't think of anything specific. As the head of the San Francisco criminal division, I never heard any complaints about her whatsoever."

"If you should think of anything, let me know. Here is my card." Petersen handed it to him. "Also, purely as a formality, I need to know when you arrived at work this morning and where you were at all times until the body was discovered."

"Certainly." To his chagrin, Olson began to sweat. As an appellate attorney for sixteen years, Olson had listened to tapes and read transcripts of literally hundreds of interrogations. He should have been at ease, should have known exactly what to expect. But here he was, a possible suspect himself, as he instinctively realized. Reading a transcript in an appeal, and being the person interrogated in real life, were two quite different matters. It was less theoretical now. Olson found himself less detached.

"Let's see," he began. "I arrived from the BART train around quarter to eight this morning." BART was the Bay Area Rapid Transit system that Olson took to work every day. He lived in Burlingame, in the peninsula south of San Francisco, and drove between his home and BART's southernmost station in Daly City. "I went to my office to review the stack of new cases to be assigned to my attorneys. I do this every week at this time. I look at the size of the transcripts, review the issues, and decide which of my supervising attorneys to assign each case to. The supervising attorneys then assign the cases to the attorneys on their teams . . ." Olson paused, then added somberly, "It is not pleasant when there are so many cases to give to so few attorneys. I was still engaged in this task when I heard of the murder."

"You were in your office the whole time?"

"Yes."

"Alone?"

"Most of the time." Olson obviously understood the significance of the question. *They can't really suspect me, can they,* he wondered. *They must understand that I am trying to reduce the Backlog, not increase it by killing off my most productive workers.* "My secretary, Elizabeth, arrived around twenty to nine. We engaged in small talk for about fifteen seconds, then I gave her some files to take to the assigned supervisors. She entered my office two or three times to get more files before she accidentally discovered the murder." He stopped to concentrate. "No, it was four times. Let's see. She picked up the files for the Atkins team—he was Rachel's supervisor—then for two other teams, then finally one file for the Aguilar team. Aguilar's team is really overloaded, and can't take many more cases. Elizabeth was never gone for more than a few minutes at a time."

"I guess that does it for you then. You're sure you saw no one else?"

"No, but I'm sure Elizabeth will confirm everything I have just said." The interrogation was much harder on Olson than he cared to admit. Imagine him, a career prosecutor, indeed the chief of the San Francisco branch of the criminal division of the office of the attorney general of the State of California, being grilled like a common suspect.

Just then, Inspector Tarkov arrived with Martin Granowski in tow.

Tarkov told Granowski to sit in a chair in front of the large desk. He took out a tape recorder and his pad of paper. "Do you mind if we record this conversation, purely as an investigative convenience?" he asked Granowski.

"No, of course not. I want to help in any way I can." Unlike Olson, Granowski appeared self-assured. He was an experienced trial attorney.

"Are you aware that the murder weapon in your *Morton* case, the .357 magnum marked as exhibit seven, was also the murder weapon in this case?" Both Inspectors Petersen and Tarkov peered intently at Granowski.

For a split second, doubt seemed to flicker in Granowski's eyes, then it disappeared. He lifted his right hand from the arm of the chair, placed it on his lap, then put it back on the arm. "No. What do you mean? How should I know? That's impossible."

"Is it?" asked Petersen.

"But the exhibits are in my office. In a box." He shifted his weight from the right chair arm to the left, and scratched his left shoulder. Then his eyes widened. "Oh, my God. You mean somebody took the gun from my office and shot Rachel with it?"

"You tell us."

Granowski paused to think. "I was working on the case until nine-thirty or ten last night. I took some of the exhibits in and out of the box a couple of times. I'm sure the gun was in it when I left."

"Was there only one firearm?" Tarkov resumed asking questions. He leaned his buttocks against the desk and bent forward at the waist until his face was only about two feet from Granowski's face. A veteran detective had once told him that an effective interrogation required you to get into the interviewee's face. Tarkov had never found the technique particularly effective, but at least it looked good. He considered it unfortunate that they could no longer shine a bright light into the face.

"Yes, Morton killed everyone with the same gun. It was effective."

"Very," agreed Tarkov. "What about the silencer? Was there only one silencer?"

"Yes." Then, for a brief moment, Granowski's eyes again widened in comprehension. Tarkov could see white all the way around the pupil. "You mean, he used the silencer, too?"

"Why do you say 'He?' "

"I don't know. I guess it could be a she. I don't know who did it, if that's what you're driving at."

"We aren't driving at anything. We just want the facts." Tarkov loved interrogations. This one was perfect; it reminded him of something, of what he did not know. "When was the last time you saw the gun, the silencer, and the bag of live cartridges?"

"You mean, he used the cartridges in the box, too?" Granowski knew the answer as soon as he asked the question. The killer was efficient. If he used part of the murder package that was conveniently available in Granowski's office, he would use it all. The inspectors stared at Granowski silently. Olson stood and paced nervously behind his desk.

"As I said," continued Granowski, "the exhibits were all in order when I left last night. When I came to work around eight-thirty this morning I didn't notice anything out of the ordinary."

"Did you look?"

"No. Why should I have? I didn't know I would be grilled about the exact contents of the box. But if anyone had removed the gun, I think I would have noticed."

"What were your exact movements from the time you arrived this morning until the body was discovered?"

Granowski should have expected the question, but did not. "Surely you don't suspect me of the crime? I wouldn't be so foolish as to use a gun everyone knew was kept in my office. That would make me an obvious suspect. Besides, I had no motive. I liked and respected Rachel. Ask anyone."

"We will. In the meantime, this is a mere formality. What were your exact movements?"

"Like I said, I arrived around eight-thirty. I walked to my office, saying good morning to Michelle Hong—that's another deputy—on the way. I stayed there a few minutes reading through my notes on one of the preliminary hearing transcripts, then decided to go to the courtroom early to watch Rachel's oral argument. I was there when I heard the news."

"What time did you leave to go to the courtroom?"

"I don't know. Maybe twenty to nine."

"Who might have seen you leave?"

"Just about anyone. I made no attempt to conceal my movements. Everyone knew I wanted to watch the argument."

"Who did you see in court and who might have seen you?"

Granowski thought for a moment. The question was crucial to his alibi. But he drew a blank. "Jesus, I don't know. I was so preoccupied with my trial that I simply didn't notice who else was there. But I'm sure several deputies also went to watch the argument and can vouch for my presence."

"Were you sitting next to anyone?"

"No, I was alone."

Tarkov jotted down some notes, and moved to another subject. "How many exhibits were in that box?"

"There are over a hundred exhibits in the case total, but only maybe fifteen or so in that box—mainly diagrams, photographs, and reports. I always kept the gun and silencer covered with documents so they would not be in plain sight. I'll show you the box if you want."

Petersen resumed the questioning. "We will. What security arrangements did you have for the gun?"

Granowski sat quietly for a moment, reluctant to respond. He knew that the answer would make him appear incredibly careless. Olson stared out the corner window at the traffic six stories below.

He had worked hard to get a reputation as an efficient, reliable administrator. Granowski's answer would inevitably damage that reputation. The people in Sacramento, who were in charge of the attorney general's office statewide, were looking for an excuse to replace him as chief in San Francisco. Would this give them that excuse? His office did mainly appellate work. Transcripts and briefs, not .357 magnums and silencers, were its primary stock in trade. How was Olson to suspect that a gun, a silencer, and plenty of bullets might be neatly packaged for a killer in one of the offices?

Granowski finally responded. "None, really. I mean, like I said, I kept the gun covered with documents. But that's about it. Oh, and I always kept my office door closed when I was not in it. I closed it when I went to the courtroom this morning."

"Did you lock it?"

"No. I, uh, I guess I should have, shouldn't I? I was just going to have the gun for a few days. Also, our receptionist keeps out all unauthorized personnel." Granowski brightened. That might be the excuse. No one not allowed in the area had access to the gun; people allowed in the area were obviously not security risks. Olson did not find solace in this comment. He knew how notoriously lax the receptionists were. The standing joke within the office was that while the receptionists were carefully checking the credentials of some high government official from outside San Francisco, a bum would be allowed to simply walk in to use the restroom. Olson would need a better excuse for the murder than the diligent security provided by the receptionists.

Petersen turned to Tarkov. "Roman. Check out the floor security arrangements." Tarkov made a note. Olson winced. To Granowski, Tarkov said, "So you're telling us that anyone allowed in the area could simply open the door to your office when you are not there—that is, *anytime* the door was closed—walk in, and help himself to a .357 magnum, a silencer, and a bag of perfectly good bullets."

"Yes. Or rather, no. Only someone who knew they were there and knew how to use them."

"Did anyone else know they were there?"

Granowski paused again. This answer would also not make him look good. "Only a few of the attorneys in the office. Well, actually, several." Olson sat down and put his right hand over his eyes. His future looked less promising with each answer.

Tarkov turned to Granowski. He had long since forgotten his ploy of keeping his face close to Granowski, and had begun to wander about the office. "What do you mean by that?"

"Everyone knew that I was prosecuting the *Morton* case, and that the exhibits were in my office. A few people came in to look at the exhibits."

"Mainly the gun, I take it." Petersen was well aware of the public's fascination with handguns in general and murder weapons in particular. Lawyers, even criminal prosecutors, were not immune.

"And the silencer," Granowski stated the obvious. After a moment he added ruefully, "And the bullets."

"You showed the entire package to anyone who asked?" The inspectors assumed Granowski's silence was agreement. "And how to put everything together?"

"Yes." Denial was useless. "It actually isn't that hard to load the gun and screw on the silencer. People were curious."

"Which people?"

Granowski thought for a moment. Obviously, those he named who could not establish a confirmed alibi would become suspects. It's called means and opportunity. "Let's see. There was Rachel herself. She was very curious, and came into my office within an hour after my investigator gave me the exhibits. In fact, after she screwed on the silencer and loaded two of the bullets, she said that one could kill quickly, quietly, and effectively with it. How ironic." Granowski stared into space. Then, quickly, "But, of course you aren't interested in Rachel's conduct. You can clearly rule her out as a suspect."

Tarkov resisted the urge to say that they were ruling out no one just yet; he asked, "Who else did you show the weapon to?"

There was no way around it. Granowski would have to name them all. Even though none of them could have shot Rachel. Could they? "Trevor Watson."

Petersen and Tarkov looked at Olson as if expecting him to tell them who Trevor Watson was.

Olson complied. "He is one of my appellate attorneys. He's been here for seven years, and is quite good. Before that, he was in private practice in Alameda for two years. He's one of the stars of the office softball team. He can't possibly have shot Rachel. He had no reason to."

The inspectors had heard that before. Once they had established means and opportunity, they would investigate motive. "Who else?"

"Anna Heitz."

The inspectors turned to Olson.

"One of my veterans. She's been in the office for over twenty years. Knows criminal law better than anyone. She has argued four cases in the United States Supreme Court. She can't possibly have shot Rachel. She was almost a mother to her. In fact, she was almost a mother to the entire office. A link to the past, when we could work on every case with loving care, before we became a brief factory. She's one of the nicest, gentlest people around."

The inspectors turned back to Granowski. They did not have to say anything. "Oh, and Fred Olson." The statement was inevitable, but Olson cringed when he heard it. How would they react in Sacramento when they heard that he was himself a suspect? The inspectors turned in his direction.

"Yes, I was curious, too." He felt an explanation was needed. "After years of reading transcripts, I couldn't resist actually seeing the murder weapon. You do understand, don't you? We appellate attorneys live in an ivory tower. Everything is theoretical. When I had the chance to see and touch the real thing, I had to do it. It doesn't mean a thing. Surely you see that."

Did the man protest too much? Petersen wondered. Tarkov reassured Olson. "A little curiosity is normal. It certainly doesn't prove murder." *Nor does it disprove it,* he thought to himself. They turned again to Granowski.

"Bill Kelly." They turned again to Olson.

"Kelly just joined us a couple of months ago. He took a long trip to Europe after law school, and then came to us. He couldn't possibly have shot Rachel. He barely knew her."

"Ramon Aguilar."

"He's a supervising attorney. Been with us about ten years." Olson spoke without the inspectors even turning in his direction. "He's quiet, but an effective supervisor. His office is next door to Rachel's. To my recollection, he has never worked directly with her. Nobody knows him very well. He can't possibly have shot Rachel."

"Brian Howarth."

"He's not on my staff." Olson brightened as he said this. Maybe, somehow, Brian could turn out to be the killer, not a person on his own staff. "He's a member of the prison litigation unit. That's an entirely separate group within the attorney general's office. Most of them moved to a different floor a couple of years ago, but Brian has been here so long, he got permission to stay on our floor. He's been in the same office for about fifteen years."

"What does the prison litigation unit do?"

"It handles litigation arising out of the state prison system. Now that there are so many prisoners, a lot of them sue us, both in state and federal courts. Inmates complaining about their treatment, the size of their cells, the food, medical care, discipline, the amount of time off they get for good behavior, that sort of thing. I understand that Brian specializes in San Quentin. He's worked on a lot of major cases involving that prison, and seems to spend much of his time there. Thomas Oldfield, his supervisor, can tell you more about what he does."

"Did you show the gun to anyone else?" Tarkov wanted to conclude this interview, so got it back on track.

"Beret Holmes."

Olson explained that she was a rather recent addition, was a good attorney, and couldn't possibly have shot Rachel.

"Thomas Atkins."

Olson started to stand up, then sat down again. He drummed his fingers on the desk. Atkins was going to sound like a promising suspect. "Tom's a character. He once played football for Ole Miss before he wrecked his knee during his sophomore year. He's the one who ran to the Supreme Court to announce Rachel's death. For the last two years, he's been Rachel's immediate supervisor, and has reviewed all of her work. In fact, I'm probably going to assign him to take over the *Jones* case because he's already acquainted with it. He couldn't possibly have shot Rachel. They became very close friends. She's such a hard worker—*was* such a hard worker—that she is, er, *was,* a real asset to Atkins's team. Why would he kill her?"

"We'll try to find out," responded Tarkov. "Did he go to watch the victim's Supreme Court argument?"

Olson looked up, surprised. "No. I guess he didn't. He was on this floor when we heard about her death."

"As her supervisor and, as you put it, close friend, wouldn't you expect him to watch her argument?"

"Yes. I would. In fact, it's official office policy that the immediate supervisor must attend every Supreme Court argument. It's written in one of our policy manuals somewhere. At least, I think it is. But there's probably a logical explanation for his not being there. In fact, maybe I'm wrong. Maybe he did go, and then left to look for Rachel. I bet that's it."

As Petersen turned once again to Granowski, Olson reluctantly continued speaking. He knew they would find out eventually. He might as well tell them. "One other thing. Atkins is our office weapons expert. That is, he is our expert on weapons laws—you know, what kind of weapons are illegal, restrictions on sales of firearms to juveniles and felons, things like that. He's not necessarily an expert on guns themselves."

The inspectors perked up. "Has he fired handguns very much?" Petersen asked the question.

"Some, I would think, but he strongly believes in gun control. At least some degree of gun control. He would never actually fire a gun at a human being."

"We'll check it out." To Granowski: "Anybody else?"

Granowski pondered for a full twenty seconds. "No. I think that's it. Wait. There was one other. In fact, just yesterday. Michelle Hong was really interested. She wanted to know exactly how the silencer worked, and I showed her."

Olson gave his information. "Michelle has been with us about two years. She's an excellent brief writer, although still a little nervous at oral argument. She's sometimes quiet but very well liked in the office. I'm sure she knows nothing about firearms. She couldn't possibly have shot Rachel."

Tarkov ignored this last comment. A few more questions, and the interview could be terminated. "Is that everyone?"

"Yes, definitely. No one else came by."

"If you should think of anyone else, let us know. But for the record, did you show everyone how the whole thing worked."

"Yes. It was always the same. I showed them everything: how to load the gun, how to attach the silencer, how to shoot it. I have to admit, I kind of enjoyed showing off my exhibits. We don't

normally have this sort of thing in our offices. They're more exciting than transcripts and briefs." Olson put his hands over his head
in despair. *How unprofessional. Please don't let the people in Sacramento hear of this.* A murder was bad enough. One of his own
attorneys enthusiastically showing anyone who cared to learn how
to use the murder weapon was worse.

Petersen asked Olson, "How far is the courtroom from here? Or
rather, how long would it take a person to walk from the victim's
office to the courtroom?"

"It's not far at all. The courtroom is only two flights down.
There are stairs and an elevator. A person could easily walk it
within two minutes."

"What about going to the killer's office first, then to the courtroom?"

"That would obviously take a little longer, but not much. At
most, five minutes, depending on where the office is and how fast
the person walks."

Tarkov made some final notes, and turned to Petersen. The
latter nodded. Tarkov said, "That's it for now. If you think of
anything else we should know about, please call." He gave Olson
and Granowski his card. To Olson, he said, "We will need a floor
diagram telling us which attorney is in which office."

Olson responded, "I'll see to it that you get one. If you need a
center of investigation around here, you can use the conference
room down the hall." He led the inspectors to the room and left
them.

Chapter 4

As soon as they were alone, Tarkov asked Petersen, "What do you think, Sandy?"

"Until we get the results of the criminalistic investigation and check out the alibis, we can't rule out anything. But I bet our killer is one of those who Granowski showed the gun and silencer to."

"Or Granowski himself."

"Or Granowski himself." Petersen was tired. His recent vacation now seemed so long ago. He had spent two weeks visiting his daughter and her family in San Diego, long enough to really relax. How could he get so tired again so quickly? "For right now, let's concentrate on these people. I'll call them the prime suspects. There are what, nine?"

"That's what I count. Watson, Heitz, Olson, Kelly, Aguilar, Howarth, Holmes, Atkins, and Hong. Nine suspects. No, ten counting Granowski. That should keep us busy for a while."

"Busy enough. With any kind of luck, some of them will have confirmed alibis. If we are really lucky, all but one will have an ironclad alibi. Then we will have our killer."

Neither expected they would be that lucky.

They were not that lucky. Tarkov and Petersen interviewed the nine who had been shown the murder weapon. Kelly and Holmes both said they had sat next to each other in the Supreme Court courtroom from eight-thirty on. Rachel had probably still been alive at eight-thirty. They would find out for sure from the autopsy report. Those two thus had pretty good alibis. It was unlikely both were lying. The inspectors were now down to eight prime suspects, on whom they would concentrate. But they made no further progress that day.

Thomas Atkins said he had been in his office from eight o'clock until the time he heard Elizabeth Cronin scream. He ran to the courtroom to tell the news. When asked why he had not gone to observe the argument, Atkins became evasive. He would only say that he was working on an important case and did not want to be disturbed. He worked with his door closed, which was not his usual practice. He thought his secretary could confirm that he was in his office. She could not. Nor could anyone else.

Anna Heitz said she had worked in her office after her arrival around eight-ten until the body was discovered. Her door was open; she was sure lots of people could confirm her alibi. None could. A few had seen her in her office, but could not say she stayed there. As far as anyone could remember, she easily could have slipped out long enough to get the gun and shoot Rachel.

Ramon Aguilar, Brian Howarth, Trevor Watson, and Michelle Hong all said they had gone alone to the courtroom shortly before nine to watch the argument. They could not remember the exact time, but each was confident that someone could supply a full alibi. No one could. One person or other had seen each of the four that morning, but no one could remember the exact time, and no one could preclude the possibility that any of them had stopped to kill Rachel before going to the courtroom.

All of these prime suspects denied any involvement in the shooting. Each liked, respected, and even admired Rachel, and had no possible reason to want her dead. It had to have been an outsider.

Elizabeth Cronin confirmed that she had seen Fred Olson in his office that morning. Twice he had given her case files to deliver to the office of a supervisor—once to Ramon Aguilar's office (when she found the body) and once to Atkins's office. Atkins was not present. She just left the files on his chair, as she usually did. That was around a quarter to nine. Or was it closer to ten to nine? When told that Olson had said he gave her files four times, she said she thought it was only twice, but if he said it was four times, he would know. They could find out for sure by checking with the other supervisors. Tarkov did check. Only Aguilar and Atkins had received new case assignments that day.

Jeff Hines, Rachel's secretary, had little to say that was useful. He liked Rachel, and was "torn up" by her death. He saw her enter her office that morning, and saw various people come and go in the area, but could remember nothing specific. Everybody loved Rachel. Hines couldn't imagine that anyone had any reason to kill her. Surely nobody in the office. It must have been an outsider. The receptionists, he explained, were notorious for letting any riffraff onto the floor. Yes, that was it. Probably some outsider.

After these interviews, the inspectors left for the day. Tarkov was disgusted with the results so far. But, with any kind of luck, he thought, the autopsy report and criminalistic reports would help. Surely the scientific evidence would solve the case. Petersen had expected no more than they had gotten so far. He also held out little hope for science. Legwork would be needed to solve this case. He went home with a headache.

At three o'clock that afternoon, Olson presided over an emergency meeting of the criminal division in the library conference room. Everybody was there. Surrounded by Ansel Adams photographs on the walls, the group sat in subdued silence. The revelation of Rachel's death, the swarming presence of the police, the interviews of almost everyone on the floor, the realization that several people in the room were suspects in the murder, that one probably *was* the murderer, combined to create an atmosphere of exhausted despondency.

Criminal division meetings normally were lively affairs, with vigorous expressions of opinions and hot debate, typical of attorney gatherings everywhere. This one was quiet. Bill Kelly sat next to Beret Holmes. Before that day they had barely known each other, but because they had been sitting next to each other when the terrible news was broadcast, they seemed drawn together by some bond. Perhaps it was the mutual alibi they provided. Each had a pen and a white legal-size pad of paper. Beret was doodling in the margin. The pads were otherwise blank. Neither spoke.

Thomas Atkins sat in his usual chair at one end of the large oblong table that dominated the room. For years, longer than most people could remember, he had been sitting in that same chair. In a mock ceremony a year before, the chair had been facetiously dubbed the "Thomas Atkins Memorial Chair." No one else would even think of taking that spot.

Trevor Watson, usually outspoken, or, as some of his colleagues put it, *obnoxious,* had little to say. He had not even been seen flirting with any of the secretaries all day. As Ramon Aguilar had said to Michelle Hong, that proved how shaken the criminal division was by the day's events.

Olson sat at the end of the table opposite Atkins. He spoke in a voice he tried to make dramatic but which in fact was only a monotone. "We will all have to live with this terrible tragedy that has been visited upon us. Rachel Brandwyn, whom we all loved, will no longer be among us. We will miss her greatly. Her caseload will have to be reassigned, and all of us will have to shoulder the increased burden caused by her no longer being able to be assigned more briefs." He looked directly at Atkins. "Tom, as her supervisor, I'll need a full written report on her assignments by ten o'clock tomorrow morning. Tomorrow afternoon we'll reassign her cases." Atkins duly made a note on his pad of paper, the first thing he had written on it.

Olson continued. "This is a shattering blow to us all, and everyone has permission to attend the funeral, which I understand will be Friday morning at ten o'clock." Olson had considered this carefully. Many attorney hours would be lost, but he did not think he could prohibit people from going to the funeral. He reluctantly concluded that even office business would have to yield to sentiment. Ten o'clock was an inconvenient time, too. It would be hard to expect people to do much work before the funeral, then would come lunch. Almost half a day would be wasted. Olson would definitely include this information in his report to Sacramento regarding the murder's impact on the Backlog. Let's see, he thought, forty attorneys, each spending three hours on the funeral —no, make that four hours—comes out to what . . . about 160 hours of attorney time, or almost one attorney month. That's about three or four cases worth of time lost on the funeral alone. Yes, he would stress that in the report. Anything that would help get authorization to hire more attorneys.

"But once we're over the mourning period, and we'll have to make it as brief as possible, we'll have to really get down to work. As you know, our Backlog is already too extensive. The appellate courts will sympathize with our loss for a time, but when they examine how long it's taking us to file our briefs, they won't remember it. It's up to us to respond professionally. You know I hate to make pep talks, especially at a time like this"—they knew no such thing—"but we are really and truly going to have to buckle down. In fact, I'm going to establish as a goal for the next two months that everyone file one respondent's brief more than usual. After the two months we'll reassess the situation in light of the progress we have made."

Normally a pronouncement of this kind would elicit loud groans, or maybe humorous but resigned repartee, but this time everyone simply made a note on his or her white legal pad and resumed staring at the Ansel Adams photographs. Olson continued. "Rachel would certainly not have wanted her death to cause an increase in the Backlog. Let's be true to her memory and redouble our efforts to maintain the high professional standards of this Office." Olson had the habit of speaking the word "Office" (capital O) the same way a career officer would talk of the Marine Corps. Olson paused to let his words penetrate, and to await a response. When the ensuing silence made it painfully apparent that Olson wanted someone to say something, Brian Howarth came to the rescue, as he often did in such situations.

"I'm not in your section, Fred, but I'm sure I speak for everyone when I say that we won't let Rachel down. We *are* professionals, we *are* dedicated to our jobs, and we *will* continue to perform them well." Was there a hint of mockery in his voice? Even Olson, usually a good judge of such things, could not be sure. The words, however, were welcome.

"Thank you, Brian. We appellate attorneys are no less professional than you people in the prison litigation unit. Everyone here, from the veterans"—looking at Anna Heitz—"to the newcomers"—looking at Bill Kelly—"will come through in style, as you always have. We will put our nose to the grindstone, keep on trucking, and jump through whatever hoops the courts demand of us."

Beret Holmes had a little trouble visualizing this last statement, but agreed wholeheartedly with its spirit. But what about the murder? she thought. She put her thoughts into words. "We should also do everything we can to help the police find out who killed Rachel, shouldn't we? That's paramount." With one notable exception, everyone agreed with this sentiment. With no exceptions, everyone supported it vocally, Anna Heitz and Trevor Watson most enthusiastically.

Olson agreed. "Yes, of course, I want this crime solved as much as anyone. This Office" (read that "Corps") "will suffer adversely as long as the absurd notion continues that one of us is a murderer. The police seem to believe that one of us shot Rachel, but I for one don't believe it." If Olson expected a chorus of "Here! Here!" he was disappointed. There was only silence. "In the next few days I will appoint a committee to look into this matter and report back to me." He paused to write a note to himself on his white legal pad. "In fact, let's take care of it right now. The committee should report back in six weeks. That would be when? . . . The third Monday in June. Yes, you, Ramon, can chair it." Aguilar made a note. "You can choose four others to be on the committee." Aguilar made another note. He knew, however, that he and everyone else would be too busy to actually do anything, and that the committee would soon be forgotten. There would be no report.

"In addition to the committee, it goes without saying that each of you should cooperate with the police to the fullest of your ability. Tell them the truth. Anything you don't want to tell them, tell me. Or the committee. It would be fantastic if we could solve this little mystery ourselves, without the police." Even better, he thought, if the murderer should turn out to be an outsider. Maybe even someone who killed Rachel because of her role as a crime fighter. What great publicity that would be.

"Let's all buckle down and solve this thing. But not, of course, on office time. Office time is for writing briefs." Olson's little attempt at humor elicited only silence. Or, as he might have put it himself, it went over like a lead balloon. He cleared his throat. "Just joking. We must do whatever it takes to solve the crime. Report any and all clues, and let the chips fall where they may. Now we can write briefs for the rest of the day."

That seemed to be the signal that the meeting was over. Slowly, even reluctantly, the attorneys stood up, grabbed their legal pads, and left the room, singly and in small groups. Only after they had gone through the library into the long interior hallway did they start talking among themselves. When they did, it was about the murder, not the Backlog. No briefs would be written that day.

During the meeting, one person had successfully endeavored to appear normal despite a continually pounding heart. The person was relieved, ecstatic even, that no one suspected the truth. After the meeting, that person left the room alone and, before going back to the office, detoured past the wastebasket in which the rag used to remove the fingerprints had been placed earlier that day.

The person noted with quiet satisfaction that the wastebasket had been emptied; tragedy had not stopped the faithful labors of the custodial staff. The person then joined a group discussing the crime, strongly agreed that the killer must be found, and enthusiastically participated in the endless speculation about who that killer might be.

Late that afternoon, as Beret Holmes sat in her office staring at a pile of transcripts that she should have been reading but was not, she heard a knock on her open door. Bill Kelly was standing in the doorway. The softball game scheduled for that evening had been canceled—how could they play softball the same day Rachel was killed?—and Bill, too, was unable to work. "Are you busy?" he asked.

"Of course I'm busy, I'm always busy. But I'm not doing anything right now, if that's what you mean. Come in." Beret motioned toward a chair in front of her desk; Bill sat down.

"Actually . . ." Bill spoke hesitantly, "I was on my way to the BART station to go home. I was wondering if you might be going that way?" Bill lived near Lake Merritt in Oakland, and commuted by BART under the San Francisco Bay between the Lake Merritt station and San Francisco's Civic Center station. "We could talk about . . . well, you know, everything."

"Sure, I can walk with you to the Muni station." The Muni, the San Francisco bus and trolley system, also had a Civic Center station. Beret lived in the Sunset district of the city, and took the Muni regularly. She grabbed her purse, and the two walked down the long linoleum-covered hallway toward the reception area and the elevators. Beret had always hated the pale-yellow paint that dominated the area; it looked especially depressing now.

Michelle Hong got on the elevator with them. As soon as the doors closed, she started talking. She spoke rapidly, far more rapidly than normal. "A terrible business. Who could have wanted to kill such a nice person as Rachel? I didn't know her very well, but I can't imagine anyone having anything against her. She was so nice and so, so . . ."—Michelle was groping for the right word—"so unassuming. And such a cold-blooded affair. They say he applied a coup de grâce bullet between the eyes from inches away." Michelle shuddered. "I've never fired a gun in my life. I can't imagine shooting at someone. And with a silencer. How ghoulish.

Ghastly even." Neither Beret nor Bill had ever heard Michelle say so much at one time. Maybe it was the universal compulsion to speak with acquaintances who are encountered by chance on the elevator. Maybe it was the murder.

Bill and Beret murmured sympathetic sounds, and the elevator reached the ground floor. Michelle left through the Golden Gate Avenue exit. Bill and Beret walked toward the side exit. Beret spoke next. "I understand Martin Granowski showed you how the gun and silencer work." Bill said he had. "Me, too. I have to admit it was fascinating." Bill agreed. "I guess everyone who was shown the gun is a suspect. Along with Martin himself. And among all of us, I'm told, only you and I have a good alibi." It was a strange bond between the two, the fact that they supplied mutual alibis against suspicion of murder. Of murder! "How lucky that we both went to court early and sat next to each other." Was it just luck, or had she wanted to sit next to him? Beret was not sure, but it had worked out well.

"Yes, but I still would like to have seen the Supreme Court argument." As soon as he said it, Bill felt the statement was graceless. Why did he feel so awkward? He decided to state bluntly what he somehow knew both were thinking. He waited a moment as the two passed and tried to ignore an exceptionally aggressive panhandler in front of the main public library. No, they did not have a spare quarter. Nor a spare twenty-dollar bill. "Look, Beret. We've got to work together to try to solve this thing. We both handled the murder weapon. We're involved. Of everybody who's involved, you and I are the only ones we can both trust. We're the only ones we're sure didn't do it."

"Yes. It's obvious, isn't it?" Actually, nothing was obvious to Beret, but that did not matter. The bond forged by the mutual alibi was at work. It was strong. "We've got to work together. I don't think the police are going to solve the murder. Not without some inside help. The killer is smart. But we know him. That is, we don't know who it is, but we probably know him, whoever he is. Or her. Because of that, we have an opportunity to learn things that the police never could."

They walked in silence a short time past the huge statue of Assurbanipal, a seventh-century B.C. Assyrian king, that dominated the side of the library. Neither had ever understood why a statue of that particular king was in that particular spot.

"Who do you think did it?" Bill tried to answer his own question. "I hate to say it, but I think it was one of us who handled the weapon. It's too much of a coincidence otherwise. Anyway, it's something to focus on. That would be Granowski, and everyone he showed it to. Except you and me." They crossed Hyde Street toward United Nations Plaza.

Beret agreed. "Let's confine ourselves to that group. Somewhere there's a clue. Somewhere there's a motive. If we look hard enough we can find that motive." These last words would prove all too true in the days to come.

For a change, the escalator leading to the underground transit stations was working. As they got on, Beret asked, "Where do we start?"

"I don't know. I've never done this sort of thing before. I guess we'll just have to make it up as we go along. Talk to people. Look for motives. Try to learn what the police know. Things like that." Bill took his BART card out of his wallet. When they reached the entrance to the stations, they had to separate, Beret to the Muni level one flight underground, Bill to the BART level one flight below that.

"See you tomorrow," they said. Each went to a home that was devoid of life except for one pet cat apiece.

Chapter 5

By Friday, three days later, the criminalistics reports and the autopsy report were completed. With one exception that the inspectors were keeping quiet for a while, the autopsy report contained no surprises. To Tarkov's intense disappointment, the criminalists found little of importance. The .357 magnum with the attached silencer that were exhibits in the *Morton* case had, in fact, fired the fatal bullets. There was no evidence of a struggle. Also no fingerprints. No bodily fluids except those of the victim. Nothing to run a DNA test on. Or any other scientific test. No physical evidence suggesting who the killer was.

Inspector Petersen, who had expected nothing else, was philosophic. As he explained to Tarkov, when a bunch of prosecutors are the chief suspects, could they really expect the killer to leave behind his calling card? In many cases, the best thing crime investigators have going for them is the stupidity of the average criminal. But Petersen thought this case might be different. The crime was brilliant in its simplicity, the investigation baffling in its complexity. Eight obvious suspects who could easily have committed the crime and who had no confirmed alibi. If he liked a challenge, this was it. But after so many years, Petersen was not sure he still liked a challenge.

Beret Holmes and William Kelly also made no progress, but that was not surprising, since neither had any idea of what they were doing.

The inspectors returned to the crime scene for the first time since the day of the murder. They had asked Fred Olson to call a meeting of the criminal division for ten o'clock that morning. This time, coffee and doughnuts were served. Tarkov helped himself to a glazed doughnut, then to a second. When everyone had gathered, Olson introduced the inspectors, although they needed no introduction. Olson reminded everyone of his promise to help the police in any manner possible to solve the despicable crime, "for Rachel's sake, and that of the office of the attorney general." Again, it sounded like the Marine Corps.

Inspector Petersen spoke first. "Thank you, Mr. Olson. I'm sure everyone is fully prepared to help us." He and Tarkov scrutinized all of the faces intently. Petersen added pointedly, "With one important exception." A silence, but no telltale looks of guilt. The killer, and the inspectors were convinced they were looking at him (or her), would make a good poker player. They did not really expect anyone to give himself away, but it was worth trying. "We thought it would be easiest to tell you all at the same time the results of our investigation to date." Expectant faces all around. Was any of them visibly worried? All were. Any unduly worried? Who could tell? This case would not be that easy. "Inspector Tarkov will give you the details."

"There actually is little to report. There were no fingerprints, and no other physical evidence to help us find out who the killer was. Whoever did it was very careful and wiped away all the fingerprints." With one exception, everyone was disappointed. The one exception smiled inwardly. The efforts at concealment had succeeded. Knowing from professional experience what kind of clues could be left behind had enabled the person to avoid making mistakes. Not having made any mistakes so far, the person was not about to start now. The smile of relief was inward only. There was nothing visible. Not to the inspectors anyway, although they looked closely. The killer gave no hint of undue concern.

"We have reconstructed the crime. There was no struggle, and Rachel was in her chair when she was shot. We think she knew her killer." No visible reaction. "In fact, we think the killer is in this room right now." The collective involuntary shudder was almost audible. Tarkov's words could not have surprised anyone, but to hear them spoken was terrible. The inspectors could discern nothing useful in the reaction. "You all know the facts of life. Or, in this case, of death. One of you is the killer. If anyone has any idea, or knows anything that might help us, please tell us. And be careful. The killer is cold-blooded. We don't want a second murder."

The thought of a second murder had never occurred to anyone. Or maybe to one, but to no other. But once the words were spoken, everyone understood the somber reality. A person had killed for an unknown reason, but for a reason important to that person. Mightn't the person kill again?

Olson sank deeper into depression. How could he expect high productivity under these circumstances? How could the Backlog be kept steady, much less reduced? Most of his attorneys, and many secretaries and other support staff, had gone to Rachel's funeral and missed about half a day's work each. He did not expect otherwise, but it was still a severe blow to the output of briefs. The funeral was touching, even inspiring, but not conducive to writing prosecution briefs. Olson might have to call another division meeting to give another pep talk. What quotas should he announce next time?

Tarkov continued. "Oh. And we also received the autopsy report." A macabre expectation mixed with horror swept over the faces. But no clue. Everyone, with no exception, wanted to hear the full report. "The victim was shot three times with .357 hollow point bullets. The killer used a silencer. He used the exhibits from the case of *People* v. *Morton.*" Involuntarily, everyone looked at Granowski, who faced forward stoically. "It appears the victim was shot first below the left breast, through the heart, and out the back. Next came a shot into the stomach area, also penetrating the back. Finally, about thirty seconds to a minute later, was a shot between the eyes, penetrating the brain. The time of death was about ten, and no more than twenty, minutes before the body was discovered. The first and third bullets alone would have been fatal, the second possibly but probably not. The third would have killed instantly. There were no defensive wounds, meaning no struggle. In short," Tarkov spoke deliberately, "the victim had no chance."

The listeners were beyond reaction. After three days of denial, reality was hitting them again.

Petersen took over the briefing. "One other thing." The audience looked at Petersen intently. Petersen and Tarkov returned the look just as intently. This was the moment they had been planning. Did the killer anticipate what they were about to say? Would the killer do something, anything, to betray his identity when they said it? Was it the reason for the murder? Or would it be a complete surprise? If any hint of an answer were to appear on one of the faces, no matter how briefly, the inspectors were determined to spot it.

"The victim was pregnant."

A deep silence. Prolonged. Despite himself, Inspector Tarkov could not resist the irreverent thought that it was a pregnant silence. Most were stunned. Were they *all* stunned? Did anyone react differently from the others? Despite years of training, despite keen anticipation of this moment, the inspectors could not tell. They continued their scrutiny, seeking a clue, any clue, but not finding it.

Fred Olson, the leader of the office, felt obligated to speak. When he did speak, it was nothing brilliant. "Pregnant?" This broke the spell. Suddenly everyone moved. Rapidly. Each looked to the neighbor. Each felt this was beyond awful. It was, well, very awful. Someone murdered a pregnant woman. Maybe the father? Maybe one of them in that very room!? It couldn't be. Surely this was a joke, a cruel test of some kind, to see how they would react.

"Yes. About eight weeks pregnant. The victim had gone to see her doctor and had it confirmed a week before her death." Petersen was in full control now. "Did anyone know anything about it?"

No one in that room had known anything about it. Quite certainly no one had. With great vehemence, no one had. Everyone in the office was vaguely aware that Rachel had had a painful breakup of a long relationship a few years earlier, but as far as anyone knew, she was not dating, and did not have a boyfriend, in the months before her death. Whoever made her pregnant was most definitely not in that room. Impossible. They all liked and respected, even admired Rachel, but to be her lover? No, absolutely not.

The meeting broke up soon afterward. Everyone left in a buzz of conversation. First murder, now this. Fred Olson, who thought things could not get worse for him, had been wrong. How would this look in Sacramento? To his surprise, he found that he didn't particularly care just now. He decided to just go about trying to reduce the Backlog, and to hell with Sacramento.

The inspectors had learned nothing. That was not surprising, but was still disappointing. Petersen, who thought he could read faces as well as anyone, had read nothing. This killer was smart and careful. Also dangerous? Without a doubt.

The inspectors asked to speak with Olson in his office. Olson had little choice but to agree, although he wanted nothing so much as a brief respite from the horror of this case, and time to absorb the new revelation. The three trudged back to Olson's corner office.

"Our killer left behind no physical clue to his identity." How it pained Tarkov to repeat that. "We're going to need as much help as you can give us. We're convinced the killer is among your people, probably one of those Granowski showed the weapon to, if not Granowski himself." Olson was too tired to protest this statement. Or even to point out that Howarth was *not* one of his "people." "We need inside help."

"Anything you want." Where was this going? Olson wondered. Secret agents? Will this take people away from writing briefs?

"Two of your attorneys are psychologically involved. They were shown the weapon, but apparently have ironclad alibis. William Kelly and Beret Holmes. With your permission, we'd like to talk to them, and solicit their help. By talking to others on the floor, they might be able to get information we never could." When Olson hesitated, the inspector said, "It shouldn't take them away from their work much. Just a little talk and occasional reports on the telephone. They can still carry a full workload."

"In that case, please use them, and good luck. When would you like them to start?"

"As soon as possible."

Olson called his secretary on the telephone. "Elizabeth, get Holmes and Kelly down here."

Bill Kelly had never been summoned to the corner office before, Beret Holmes only once, to receive an administrative assignment involving a state legislator's request for information on child-abuse laws. When the two entered the office, they were surprised to see the inspectors. Petersen and Tarkov looked at Olson, who reluctantly left the office. The inspectors closed the door behind him.

Kelly and Holmes were astonished to hear what the inspectors had in mind for them, but they were willing to do anything possible to help solve Rachel's murder. She was so nice; nobody could possibly have had any reason to kill her. The two explained that they had already joined forces to see what they could do—which to that point was nothing. What did the police want of them?

"Just talk to people and listen to what they say," Tarkov explained. "Report to us anything you think might be relevant. Leave the rest to us professionals." Tarkov had not wanted to bring in amateurs, and emphasized this last point. "In an unguarded moment, someone might say something they shouldn't. When they do, we want you to note it. A motive, a hint of violence, fascination with weapons, animosity toward the victim, anything. If you have any doubt whether we would be interested, assume we would be, and tell us."

"But," cautioned Petersen, "don't try to solve the case yourself, or do anything foolish. Our killer is smart and dangerous. If he learns that you are working with us, and thinks you are getting close, no telling what he might do. He has killed in cold blood once, and can do it again." Petersen, too, was concerned about asking novices for help, but thought it necessary. "Call us at this number any time of day or night." He gave both of them their business cards. "In an emergency, one or the other of us can be reached through this number even if we are not in."

Bill Kelly and Beret Holmes accepted their instructions with a blend of eagerness and apprehension. They wanted to help, they felt the thrill of the hunt, and they were flattered to be consulted. But a bit of fear was mixed in, together with misgivings about spying on their friends. Bill had not yet been assigned a murder case; Beret had worked on three. But handling a murder case on appeal and being involved in a murder investigation were quite different matters.

"One other thing." Tarkov again. "We didn't tell the others, and are keeping it quiet for the time being, but it might be helpful for you to know one other fact. Four days before her death, the victim discussed her pregnancy with her doctor. Among the options she was considering was abortion."

Both Bill and Beret were surprised by this information, although they should not have been. It did not seem like Rachel to want an abortion. Of course, it was also not like her to get pregnant. She always seemed so much in control. They said nothing, but Petersen sensed their reaction. "She didn't say she wanted an abortion, only that she was considering it," he stressed. "According to the doctor, she questioned him exhaustively. She especially wanted to know how long she had to make up her mind. She was also trying to decide whether to discuss it with the father."

"Did she say who the father was?" Bill felt compelled to ask, although he knew what the answer would be.

"No, we weren't that lucky. The last that the doctor knew, the victim was trying to decide whether to tell the father she was pregnant. The doctor has the impression, but only the *impression,* that the victim was unsure what kind of reception she would get if and when she told him. She was unsure if he would be angry, or accepting, or even happy. She was unsure if it would solidify their relationship, or end it. She was even unsure whether she loved him, let alone whether he loved her." In his many years of investigating crimes of passion, Petersen had often encountered such emotions. As always, he felt inadequate to describe them, just as the doctor had.

"Poor Rachel. Didn't she have a friend she could talk to?" Beret had never been in such a predicament and prayed she never would, but she instinctively sympathized with Rachel's suffering.

"That's one thing we're hoping you can find out." Tarkov brought the conversation back to the investigation. "Did she confide in someone? Did she eventually tell the father? Did the father kill her when he found out? Did she discuss with him whether to have an abortion? If so, did they make a decision? How would that have affected a decision to kill her? Answer these questions, and we might find our killer."

"We'll do what we can." Bill and Beret felt a natural aversion to probing into personal matters, but the image of Rachel sitting in her own chair in her own office blankly staring at the ceiling, her bloody body riddled by three bullet holes, spurred them on. Realizing that the inspectors had concluded the interview, the two got up to leave.

"But be careful" was Petersen's parting advice.

Chapter 6

By the next Wednesday, more than a week after the murder, Beret and Bill had made no progress. They had talked to people. They had listened. No one seemed to know anything. No one said anything he or she shouldn't have, at least not as far as they could tell. No one gave any clue who the father was. Rachel had confided in no one, as far as they could discover. The two discussed the case at length, but to no avail. Then came a lull in their efforts, as they resumed work on their appellate assignments. Their work, and that of everyone else, had naturally suffered for a few days after the killing, but as Fred Olson never tired of pointing out, the work of the office (corps) went on; the Backlog would not disappear even during mourning.

On Wednesday, Bill had oral argument on the 9 A.M. calendar of the Court of Appeal, First Appellate District, the intermediate appellate court that sits in San Francisco. The Court of Appeal used the same courtroom as the Supreme Court. Bill had already argued two cases in that court, but this was the first time he had written the brief himself. The first two cases had been briefed by an attorney who had since joined a private law firm. The one this morning was Bill's responsibility from the beginning.

He found the case interesting. The defendant, a self-styled "environmental positivist," had entered the Palace of the Legion of Honor in San Francisco, and splattered a jar of bright purple paint onto a primarily blue painting by Picasso. He claimed he was protesting air pollution in Alpine County, and had chosen purple because he associated that color with the company he claimed was at fault. He did not explain what Picasso or that particular painting had done to merit such treatment. After his arrest, he tried to give a lengthy political tract to anyone who was interested. None was, until the defendant found a police officer who felt compelled to take the document as possible evidence. Painstaking and loving labor over several months repaired much of the damage to the priceless painting, but it would never be quite the same. The defendant was placed on probation, and had to serve six months in county jail. He appealed.

Issues in the appeal included what crimes, if any, the defendant had committed, whether he should have been allowed to show the political tract to the jury (to his anger, the prosecution refused to introduce it as evidence), and whether the museum guards used excessive force when they prevented him from pouring onto the painting a jar of green paint he had held in reserve. Bill, an art lover, although no great fan of Picasso, took great care on the case. He had prepared fully for oral argument; he had, in fact, over-prepared.

His was the sixth case on the calendar. The first five were civil matters handled by private attorneys. During the first argument, Bill tried to read the briefs of his case one more time, but found that he could not. He had read them too many times. He then tried listening to the arguments. This was not much better.

The second case involved a limited partnership agreement to convert apartments into condominiums and the resulting establishment of a homeowner's association. Somehow the interpretation of the "CCRs"—apparently shorthand for "conditions, covenants and restrictions"—was also involved. It was all very complex. And boring. Very boring. Bill gathered that a lot of money was at stake, hundreds of thousands of dollars. He could not help but wryly think that the way the attorneys were droning on, they must be getting paid by the hour. The three judges who would decide the case asked occasional questions, but generally appeared as bored as Bill.

Eventually, the appellant's attorney got up for his rebuttal. It seemed that everything possible had already been said. The presiding justice pointed this out. Not taking the hint, the attorney proceeded to repeat what he had said before.

When the attorney finished at last and sat down, Bill looked at his watch. He tried to estimate how long he must still wait before his case would be called. Why, he wondered, did the court of appeal so often place the criminal cases after a spate of boring civil cases? Was there something cruel and unusual in that practice?

The attorney in the next case got up, introduced herself, and proceeded to talk about civil discovery, or the lack of it, from the opposing side. It seemed that during three depositions that the attorney had tried to take of the defendants, opposing counsel had repeatedly, maliciously, for no good cause, without provocation, and in bad faith (why do lawyers have to repeat themselves? Bill mused) objected to perfectly proper, appropriate, and acceptable questions, and had instructed the deponent not to answer. The attorney wanted the court to order the questions answered and, possibly more important, wanted opposing counsel ordered to pay substantial and significant monetary sanctions to teach him a lesson. The trial court had inexplicably failed to see the justice in her arguments, so she was forced to turn to the most honorable court of appeal for relief. Surely the court would not fail her.

Bill's mind began to wander. Inevitably, it wandered toward the great mystery that seemed beyond his abilities. Bill had read murder mysteries in the past, although not for a long time. What would Sherlock Holmes do in this situation? Or Lord Peter Wimsey? Or, since there were no physical clues, and psychology might provide the key, what would Hercule Poirot do? Bill had no idea. But now that he had some enforced leisure time, he felt he should do something. He had a vague recollection that sometimes in the novels the hero would prepare a chart of the suspects, containing motive, opportunity, and the like. In the novels the chart was invariably helpful. Yes, Bill would prepare one. Surely a chart would provide valuable insight, or at least narrow the issues.

Bill took his notepad, and drafted a chart. The first column was for suspects. *Let's see,* he told himself, *there are those who were shown the murder weapon, except for Beret and me.* Ramon Aguilar, Fred Olson, Brian Howarth, Trevor Watson, Anna Heitz, Tom Atkins, and Michelle Hong. Plus Martin Granowski. It seemed strange to write down the names of these friends and colleagues as suspects in murder. But it had to be done. They *were* suspects. Next, Bill wondered what went into the other columns. As he pondered, the court called the next case.

The next attorney started discussing the adequacy of the environmental impact report on a proposed residential development in central Contra Costa County. At least, Bill assumed, the environmental and growth-versus-no-growth issues would be interesting. And so they were at first. But as the argument delved ever deeper into the intricacies of the California Environmental Quality Act, talking about the necessity of certain findings by the affected agencies, even this case became dull. Bill lost the thread of the argument, and his mind wandered back to his chart.

Opportunity. There's got to be a column for opportunity. Also means. Everybody talks about means in the murder mysteries. Then obviously motive. Anything else? I can't think of anything. Let's go with this, and see what happens. Opportunity, means, and motive. Bill, being somewhat artistic, drew a very pretty chart, using one of the briefs as a straight edge, and his black ballpoint pen and red marking pen (he always used a red pen to mark in the briefs) for contrasting colors. He placed the suspects in alphabetical order, and wrote "yes," "no," or "unknown" for each column. This was the result:

Suspect	Opportunity?	Means?	Motive?
Ramon Aguilar	yes	yes	unknown
Thomas Atkins	yes	yes	unknown
Martin Granowski	yes	yes	unknown
Anna Heitz	yes	yes	unknown
Michelle Hong	yes	yes	unknown
Brian Howarth	yes	yes	unknown
Fred Olson	yes	yes	unknown
Trevor Watson	yes	yes	unknown

Somehow, Bill found the exercise less useful than he had hoped. It didn't seem to narrow the field much. But motive appeared to be the key to the case. Find who had the motive and you might find the killer. Had he read that somewhere? Whatever, it made sense. They had to find the motive. That's why Tarkov and Petersen had brought him and Beret into the case. They, not the police, could best learn the motive.

While Bill was absorbed by these thoughts, the court called his case. Bill went to his seat by the podium, reorganized the briefs and his notes, and, after opposing counsel had finished her argument, proceeded to discuss with the three judges purple paint, art, the California Penal Code, questions of evidence, and the use of force in making arrests.

That afternoon, Bill was in his office working on a new brief. This case was the armed robbery of a liquor store in Oakland. For Bill, who lived in the heart of Oakland, it came a little too close to home. The reporter's transcript that he had to read was about eight hundred pages long. The defense brief challenged the validity of a search warrant, questioned the fairness of the lineup in which the witnesses identified the defendant, alleged misconduct by the prosecutor, and inevitably claimed that the defense attorney had been incompetent.

Bill's argument in court that morning had gone well. After some initial stammering caused by nerves, Bill had settled down and was reasonably articulate. He had credible answers to all of the judges' questions. The judges had seemed to like him, and also seemed likely to decide the case his way.

Trevor Watson, who had been in the courtroom awaiting argument in a different case, was quite complimentary afterward. Watson had a few specific suggestions (talk more slowly!), but no major criticisms. He especially liked the fact that Bill took only two pages of notes with him to the podium. "It's absurd," he said, "how so many lawyers, especially those who are unsure of themselves, take reams of notes, sometimes even an indexed three-ring binder, to the podium. When they are asked a question, they invariably can't find what they are looking for, and just appear foolish. No, it's best to have it in your head, with only a short outline to remind you where you are going, and maybe a list of the major cases. You did well." Watson's helpful friendliness made Bill feel guilty about listing him in the chart as a murder suspect. But there was no way around it. He had to think of these people as suspects until they could be eliminated or the real killer caught.

While Bill was musing on these matters, Fred Olson entered his office, followed by Tom Atkins. "Have you got a minute?" Fred asked.

"Yes, of course." Translation: for the boss, any time. Atkins, Bill's supervisor, had been in his office many times, but, as far as Bill could remember, Olson only once before.

Olson and Atkins sat down in the two chairs in front of the desk. "How's your workload?" asked Olson.

Warning signals arose in Bill's mind. If Olson, the source of all assignments, asked that question, it did not bode well. "Well, uh, OK, I guess. That is, I've got plenty to do, but I'm on top of things." Translation: I'm more or less on top of things, at least I'm not drowning, and I can't categorically refuse if you dump something else on me now, but I really don't want another big assignment at this time, thank you.

"Good," replied Olson. "As you know, Rachel Brandwyn's caseload has to be reassigned. You were on her team. She was handling a lot of cases, and it's hard to find experienced attorneys to absorb all of them. Tom has assigned himself the *Jones* case, which she was supposed to argue the day she was killed. The argument has been rescheduled for June, so he can't take over much else himself. The rest of the team has to help."

Bill understood Olson to mean that they were so desperate they were turning to a rookie like him. "I'll do what I can."

Atkins took over the conversation. "If possible, we'd like to give you one case she was working on at the time of her death. It's an important case involving the smuggling of drugs into San Quentin. The two defendants were convicted of conspiring with an outsider, code-named 'Unicorn,' to smuggle crack cocaine and methamphetamine into the prison. The defendants used some of the drugs themselves and sold the rest to others, sometimes for money, sometimes for sexual favors. As you can imagine, it was a tough case to put together. Most of the witnesses were 'dirty' themselves; they had also bought, sold, and used drugs. But the defendants were kingpins, and the convictions were major victories. We would normally give the case to someone with more experience, but the appellate issues don't seem to be too complex. Your work has been very good, and I think you are ready for a case like this. Besides, there's no one else. Fred and I agreed that if you have the time, the case is yours."

It sounded intriguing. They must *really* be desperate. Bill would make the time. "I can handle it. What time frame and what size record are we talking about?"

Atkins glanced at Olson. "The reporter's transcript is over three thousand pages long, but some of it is jury selection. You probably only have to read about two thousand pages of it closely. The appellants' briefs are each seventy-five pages long." That just happened to be the page limit under court rules. "There are eight different issues. Rachel got a first extension of time to file our respondent's brief. Because of her death, you can probably get a second extension, but that's about it. You should have about fifty days total to get the brief filed. Rachel has a few notes that might help, but she had barely started when, well, when she was killed."

That didn't seem too bad. Fifty days. Bill had four other briefs he had to write during that period, but he could manage somehow. He would have less time to try to solve the murder, but that couldn't be helped. He would do it. "Sure, I'll take it."

Atkins and Olson looked relieved. "Jeff Hines will bring you the file and the boxes of transcripts as soon as we get the reassignment logged on the computer. It's a big record, so it might be a few days. I imagine you're in no hurry to get started." Having said that, Olson left. Atkins stayed behind.

"Thanks for taking the case so cheerfully," he said to Bill. "Not everyone has been so graceful about the reassignments. I won't forget it. But the case might be more difficult than we have let on. There are some complex issues. On the other hand, it should also be intellectually challenging."

"Intellectually challenging" sounded suspiciously like a euphemism for harder than hell. But Bill was committed by now. He might as well make the best of it. "That's what I went to law school for."

"The defendants were also convicted of some weapons charges —possession, smuggling them into the prison, and the like. Some of the issues involve these counts, such as what is a dirk or dagger. If you need any help, come see me. I'm the expert on weapons. Besides, I discussed the case in detail with Rachel." Bill agreed to come to him if he needed help.

"The exact configuration of San Quentin was important at the trial. I understand the record contains much testimony about the prison. A tour of the prison might be useful to help you understand its layout and the procedures followed in prison, especially those involving visitors. Fred agrees. Tom Oldfield, the head of the prison litigation unit, has arranged for a tour next week. Beret Holmes has never been there, so she will go, too. We want all the attorneys to see San Quentin eventually. I suggest you talk directly with Oldfield or his secretary for the exact arrangements." Having said that, Atkins left.

Beret Holmes entered Bill's office behind Atkins. "So, Olson and Atkins both in your office. I'm impressed. What's going on? Get any clues?" She sat down.

"No clues, just a new assignment. It won't leave me much time to work on the murder." Bill told her about the case.

"This is our day for new assignments." Beret explained that Olson had also visited her office, this time with her supervisor, Ramon Aguilar. Martin Granowski's *Morton* trial was scheduled to begin soon, and he needed help, or at least Olson thought he did. Olson had asked Rachel Brandwyn to get involved. She had spent considerable time working on the case, but of course was now no longer available. Beret had never handled a trial, and this was a good time to start. Office policy called for all new deputies, even those interested only in appellate practice, to get some exposure to trial work. "It helps for an appellate lawyer to understand what really goes on at trial, and to experience the pressures trial attorneys work under," Olson had explained.

With mixed emotions, Beret had accepted the new assignment. It was flattering that they thought enough of her to have her work on it. Granowski would naturally carry the main load. He was experienced, and was said to be a brilliant trial lawyer, if occasionally careless in his preparation. He was also supposed to be flamboyant. Office talk had it that a couple of years earlier, he had made such an impression during a murder trial in one of the smaller counties up North, and had gotten so much publicity in the local press, that he could have been elected district attorney if he had wanted.

After getting her new assignment, Beret had spoken with Granowski. Briefly. "He frankly didn't seem that pleased to have me on the case," she told Bill. Granowski had said that he could handle the case by himself, he always had before, but that he would find something or other for her to do. She could certainly sit through the trial as frequently as she wanted, and maybe he would let her examine one or two of the unimportant witnesses, but she should not expect to do any cross-examination, or to argue the case to the jury. She had told him that she didn't *expect* anything, but merely wanted to help in any way possible. His parting comment before waving her out of his office was that Rachel Brandwyn had said just about the same thing, and she sure mucked things up.

"I don't know what he meant by that," Beret said, "but it probably doesn't matter. It's awkward for me. Olson and Aguilar expect me to contribute substantially; Granowski wants me to do as little as possible." Bill told her to use her abundant charm, and everything would work out just fine. Beret said she would do just that. Both agreed that unfortunately their new assignments would leave little time to work on Rachel's murder.

Chapter 7

The following Friday, Bill was working in the law library of the attorney general's office. He was trying to crank out a short brief before he finished the Oakland robbery case. Before too long he hoped to start work on the new San Quentin case. Fortunately, Bill was able to juggle two or three matters at the same time. The brief he was writing now involved a guilty plea to a burglary of a private home and a related revocation of probation from an earlier robbery conviction. The only issue on appeal was how much credit for his earlier incarceration the defendant was entitled to receive toward his new prison sentence. Not very stimulating stuff. But important to the defendant.

Bill was the designated official office expert on presentence credits, including credits for good behavior. Issues could get quite complex, especially when a person was arrested on more than one charge in different counties, and was in jail on various charges at the same time. Because he was the office expert by designation rather than expertise, Bill did not know much about the subject. This case would give him a chance to learn something. It did not seem to be too difficult, and Bill wanted to finish the brief quickly. In front of him was a thick volume containing recent published decisions by the Court of Appeal. One of the cases in that volume, *People* versus *Karoni,* had a similar issue, but with particularly complex facts. Bill was absorbed in trying to figure out how that decision, with those facts, might apply to his case. Then he heard on the intercom: "William Kelly, you have a call on your line, William Kelly."

Such intercom messages were common in the attorney general's office, but so far had been rarely directed to him. Bill almost jumped upon hearing his own name. He barely listened to the messages anymore because they were virtually always for someone else, usually for one of a select few who seemed to be called all the time. *Who could be calling me?* he wondered. One of the advantages, or disadvantages, of appellate practice over trial practice was that there was less need for telephoning. Whoever it was, Bill did not want to keep the person waiting. He quickly got to his feet, grabbed his papers, and went to his office. He picked up the telephone.

"Hello, Bill Kelly speaking."

"Hello, this is John Rogers from the Contra Costa County district attorney's office. I have a really complicated issue involving presentence credits, and I'm told you're the AG expert. Is that right?"

"Um, yeah, sure." When Olson designated him the expert on presentence credits, he told Bill that it would not entail much work, but that he would get occasional calls from deputy district attorneys seeking advice. He should be as helpful as possible. This was his first such call.

"I need some help. Do you have a minute for me to run the facts by you?"

"Um, yeah, sure, fire away."

The DA did. Bill had noticed in the past that DAs (and police officers) never call a crime by its common name. Instead they use numbers, corresponding to the section of the California Penal Code that defined the crime. A murder, for example, was never a murder, but a one eighty-seven (Penal Code section 187). Rogers proceeded to speak numbers.

"The defendant was charged with two counts of four fifty-nine. . . ." What was a four fifty-nine? As a deputy attorney general, even a rookie deputy attorney general, Bill could never admit to a deputy district attorney that he did not know what a four fifty-nine was. Fortunately, he always kept a copy of the Penal Code on his desk, within arm's reach. He grabbed it and frantically flipped through the pages to section 459. He tried but failed to follow the thrust of Roger's recitation of the facts as he looked for the right part of the code.

Here it is. Section 459, burglary. Why didn't Rogers just say so? ". . . and then San Francisco placed a hold for two two-elevens and a two-oh-seven." Rogers did not slow down long enough for Bill to look up these sections, and Bill could not ask him to without exposing his ignorance. He already knew what a two-eleven was. Robbery. But what about a two-oh-seven? More frantic flipping. Why is the Penal Code so damn thick? Ah, here it is. Kidnapping. OK.

Rogers was finished reciting the facts. "What do you think? Is the defendant entitled to receive credit for the time he spent in jail in Alameda County?" Huh? What about Alameda County? When did Alameda County get mentioned? Probably while Bill was looking for section 207. Bill had no idea what the question was, but at least now he knew the relevant sections. How could he give some credible advice without admitting he hadn't the foggiest idea what Rogers had just told him? Confidence. He had to exude confidence.

"No problem, I just need to ask you a few questions. What were the exact charges in Alameda County?" Bill figured that if he asked specific questions, he wouldn't give everything away.

"That was the two-forty-five (a)." Damn, another number. Bill was getting good at flipping through the code, and quickly found section 245 (a). Assault with a deadly weapon. This defendant was versatile. He didn't specialize in one kind of crime.

"And how much time did he spend in Alameda County?"

"One hundred thirty-seven days in Oakland. Oh, and I forgot to mention the other seventy-two days in Hayward on the four ninety-six."

Four ninety-six? That took a while to find. Receiving stolen property. At least, Bill thought wearily, this number has fewer syllables than the crime. And this defendant was *really* versatile.

After several more judicious questions, and a fair amount of give and take with Rogers, Bill managed to figure out what the important facts were. He was lucky. Rogers didn't catch on to how lost he had been. Even better, the facts were remarkably similar to the *Karoni* case. All published cases have legal citations so that they can be found easily in the many volumes of case reports. Bill had written the name and citation of the *Karoni* case in the notes he had brought with him from the library. He reached for the notes.

"Yes, I understand perfectly." Was there ever any doubt? "I think you can argue to the court that the defendant shouldn't get credit for the Alameda County time, although he might for San Francisco." The time in San Francisco was much shorter than the time in Alameda County. Since Rogers wanted the defendant to get as little credit as possible, this was the answer he wanted to hear. "If memory serves, the case of *People* versus *Karoni*, at two thirty-six cal app. third, page four twenty-seven, should be helpful. In fact, I think it's right on point."

"Great. They told me I could count on the AG to come through. Thanks." As always, Rogers, a trial lawyer, was impressed by the apparently encyclopedic mind possessed by the appellate lawyers of the attorney general's office. "What was that cite again?" Bill told him. Slowly. After writing the cite down, Rogers said, "We were all shocked and saddened to hear what happened to Rachel Brandwyn."

Bill said it was a shock to them, too. "She was a helluva lawyer," Rogers replied. "Several years ago, she spent a few months in our office on an exchange program doing felony trials. She impressed everyone here. She really helped us out on the *Schultz* case."

"The *Schultz* case?"

"Yes. The case out of Contra Costa County that went to the United States Supreme Court. We nailed the defendant for a first degree one eighty-seven." Bill knew that that was murder. "Years later, the Ninth Circuit Court of Appeals threw the conviction out on a federal petition for habeas corpus, finding that we had prosecuted the case vindictively. Rachel took over the case at that point, and got the Supreme Court to grant her petition for a writ of certiorari. The Supreme Court reversed the Ninth Circuit and reinstated the conviction. Good thing, too, because it would have been hard to retry the case after so many years. The Supreme Court opinion completely revamped the law of vindictive prosecution. The court bought Rachel's arguments completely. You can imagine she was a hero over here."

"I'm glad it turned out well."

"Your office sure butchered the case in the Ninth Circuit, though. I'm trying to remember who had it originally. Yes, it was Anna Heitz. She was supposed to be a good lawyer, and had actually argued some cases in the Supreme Court before, but she sure blew the *Schultz* case. It was a complicated matter, and she made no attempt to learn what the facts were."

Bill now vaguely remembered the case, and remembered that it had been reassigned from Anna Heitz to Rachel after Anna had lost it in the Ninth Circuit. The reassignment had occurred about two years before Bill joined the office. He knew little about it, but was aware that taking a case of that importance away from a veteran attorney would be controversial, to say the least. I wonder how Anna reacted? he thought. Might it be important? Was this the sort of listening that Tarkov and Petersen had wanted him to do? He decided to learn what he could from Rogers.

"All this happened before I joined the AG's office. What did you hear about the case being reassigned?"

Rogers appeared willing enough to talk about it. "Heitz was furious. She was convinced that Rachel had long had her eye on the case, and had asked the DA to request it be assigned to her. My boss did complain to Fred Olson that Anna was not doing a good job, and suggested it might be reassigned before it went to the Supreme Court. But we never mentioned Rachel's name. We were very happy that Rachel got the case, but believe me, we don't get involved in AG affairs."

"I'm sure you don't. How did you find out that Anna was upset?"

"She came to our office in Martinez and pleaded with us to try to get the reassignment canceled. When we refused to get involved, she started yelling. We could hear her up and down the hallway. She said that we would be sorry we got Rachel—she actually called her 'that bitch'—on the case. We tried to explain that we had nothing to do with it, but she wouldn't listen."

"Did she say anything about making Rachel herself sorry?" Bill hoped he was not too obvious, but he was inexperienced at questioning witnesses.

"Well, let's see. Yes, now that you mention it, she did say something about that 'bitch' thinking she was so smart in using her connections with the DA, but that she, that is Heitz, would make the 'bitch' pay for it someday if it was the last thing she did." A pause. "Say, you aren't suggesting this has anything to do with the murder, are you?"

Bill said no, he was sure it did not, and the conversation ended. But he had much to think about. All appellate lawyers dream of going to Washington to argue a case before the Supreme Court. It is the ultimate professional high. Anna was deprived of that experience in the *Schultz* case. She blamed Rachel. Was that a motive to kill? Bill would have to report this to Petersen and Tarkov. He reached for their card.

* * *

The next Monday morning, when Beret arrived at her office, a message was waiting on her telephone voice mail. She listened to it even before she got her morning cup of coffee. The voice was indistinct, almost muffled, as if the person was talking through a handkerchief. Beret could not even tell if the speaker was a man or a woman. The voice spoke in a monotone, as if reading a script. Only with difficulty, and after playing the message several times, could Beret make out the content.

"Ramon Aguilar did it," the voice said. "I saw him and Rachel Brandwyn having drinks together at the Palace Hotel the afternoon before she was killed. They were holding hands at first, but then they suddenly started fighting. Finally, Ramon stormed out of the bar. He was livid with rage, and threatened to kill her. He left Rachel behind. She was crying. When I tried to comfort her, she just said there was no problem. I don't want to get involved, but I think Ramon is the one who killed her. I hope this helps you in your investigation."

That was it, nothing more. Who had left the message, and why did he or she think Beret was involved in an investigation? Beret had no idea, nor did she know whether to take the message seriously. Or rather, she obviously had to take it seriously, but what did it mean? Could Ramon have been the killer? Why? Beret reached for the phone, and called Bill.

Bill listened to the message, but had no ideas to contribute. He said he had no time to worry about it today; he had too much work to do. But they should get together sometime soon. On an impulse, she asked him to come to dinner at her place the next night. He accepted. Because they would be able to talk about the case at length (that was surely the only reason she asked him), Beret was glad he accepted. But it did create a problem. She couldn't cook.

Something new also awaited Bill when he entered his office that same Monday morning: three boxes containing the record and briefs in *People* v. *Wakefield* and *Robinson,* the case he was getting from Rachel Brandwyn. Jeff Hines had apparently placed the boxes in the office that morning before Bill arrived.

In his short time in the office, Bill had not yet had a case that important. Or that big. As Atkins had said, the reporter's transcript, a verbatim account of the entire trial, was about three thousand pages long. There were also various short transcripts of court hearings held before trial. After reading through the appellate briefs, it seemed that the defendants had made just about every pretrial motion possible. They claimed the correctional officers had investigated the case illegally, and asked that the evidence be suppressed on that account. They moved to dismiss the charges because their right to a speedy trial had been violated. They claimed the preliminary hearing in the case was improperly conducted. And so on and so forth.

Bill did not intend to start serious work on the case that day, but he wanted to get organized. The boxes contained about three pages of handwritten notes by Rachel Brandwyn. Her writing was atrocious, and she had obviously written the notes only for her own consumption. Bill could not read them, and made little effort to do so. Rachel had not gotten very far into the case, and he assumed that her notes would probably be of little help even if he *could* read them. He would simply have to start work from the beginning.

Bill went through the transcripts carefully, both to discover what was there and to make sure nothing was missing. He found the transcript of the trial itself and eleven short transcripts of pretrial hearings. But according to the records, there should have been twelve short transcripts. He looked more closely. Yes, one was missing—a hearing held about two weeks before the trial started. That was odd. As far as Bill could tell, the missing transcript had nothing to do with the issues the defendants raised in the appeal, but he wanted to start with a complete record.

It was not a serious problem. Bill could always borrow the original transcript from the Court of Appeal and make another copy. He called his secretary on the telephone, and asked her to do that. While he was talking to her, he also asked if she remembered anything about the Supreme Court case that had been reassigned from Anna Heitz to Rachel Brandwyn a couple of years ago. She remembered that the reassignment had happened, but she had been told very little about it. "It was all kept very quiet," she explained.

Later, when Bill received his copy of the missing transcript, he realized it was not significant to any of the issues in the case. It was just a short hearing on the identity of the outside conspirator.

The district attorney had to convince the defendant—and the court—that he did not know his or her identity. But Bill was glad he had made the record complete. He was always fastidious in that regard. As Tom Atkins had once told him, "A complete record, always make sure your record is complete."

Chapter 8

That same Monday evening, the office softball team in the San Francisco lawyers' league—the Fog City Sluggers— played their first slow pitch softball game since Rachel's murder. They were playing one of the big private law firms from the financial district. The game started at 6:15 P.M. at Ocean View Park, a park without an ocean view. The lawyers' league generally did not get the best fields the city had to offer, and often no umpire showed up. This was one of those games. When there was no umpire, the team at bat supplied one—a scary situation for a bunch of attorneys, but it usually worked out reasonably well.

Bill was the coach and regular first baseman. Beret, he found out, did play softball, and quite well. She played second base. The team had some good players and several who were, to put it charitably, not quite so good. The star was the shortstop, Trevor Watson. At short, Watson had good range and a strong arm, and he made few mistakes. He also had little patience when others made mistakes, a common occurrence on the team. He was especially hard on the women players. Watson hit with consistent power, but was strictly a pull hitter. Or, as Ramon Aguilar put it, he was a spray hitter who used all parts of the field within twenty feet of the left field line, on either side. Every once in a while Watson would cross up the opposition by intentionally going to right field. When he did, he invariably hit a routine fly ball to the right fielder.

Before the game, as always, Bill went over the ground rules with the opposing coach, a time-consuming process in a lawyers' league. They meticulously tried to anticipate all eventualities, most of which never occurred. They then flipped a coin for home team. Bill called tails. It was heads. He was now zero for his career in coin flips. This meant the Sluggers would bat first.

The weather that day was warm and sunny in most parts of the

Bay Area, but Ocean View Park, like many parts of San Francisco, had its own weather. Bill thought of it as the Candlestick Park syndrome. When the game started, a strong wind blew directly from center field to home plate, which helped keep the score down, as the outfielders could play very shallow. Since most of the "Sluggers" couldn't hit even under good conditions, Bill figured the weather would hurt the other team worse than his. It was cold and getting colder. The fog started coming in from the west in the third inning. By the fourth inning, the fog was a nuisance, by the fifth, a factor, as the fielders could hardly see. By the sixth inning, a pop-up was a major adventure for the defense, and the best tactic for the offense.

After five innings of the seven-inning game, the Sluggers trailed five to two. Watson had hit a two-run homer in the second inning after Beret had singled to right field. He was able to hit the ball over the left fielder's head even in the teeth of the wind. In his other at bat, Watson had flied out to right field. Beret's single elicited praise even from Watson. As he put it, "She's a lot better than Rachel ever was, and better looking, too." Rachel, he said, "only thought she could play this game, but then, she thought she could do everything." Watson seemed to go out of his way to belittle Rachel. Bill and Beret thought this strange, as it was so different from his behavior right after her death. He even called Rachel an "egotistical fanatic," which made no sense at all.

Throughout the game Watson was riding the other team, as he often did. He quarreled incessantly, and feelings began to run high. Matters came to a head in the bottom of the sixth inning. The batter for the other team, a short, thin player, hit a pop-up that the third baseman lost in the fog. It dropped untouched. The batter, who had started running slowly, sped up when the ball landed untouched and slid hard into second base. Or at least Watson, who was covering, thought it was hard, too hard. He was knocked to the ground, and came up with his fists flying.

"You're not going to get away with that crap!" he shouted. Players on both teams poured onto the field, most intending to break up the fight. Fortunately, Watson was not as talented with his fists as he was with a bat, and nobody was hurt. But Watson was still muttering under his breath when he ran off the field at the end of the inning. He vowed to "get them." When Bill, to whom this behavior was new, wondered aloud what was going on, Brian

Howarth, the center fielder, explained, "Watson has been known to carry a grudge for weeks. He defends his turf to the death."

In the top of the seventh, with the game out of reach at nine to three, Watson batted. There was one out, and nobody on base. Watson hit a hard line drive down the left field, just fair. Extra bases appeared easy, but Watson loped to first base. When the left fielder reached the ball, Watson speeded into second base. He made it a closer play than necessary. The ball reached the second baseman about the same time as Watson. Watson slid. Hard. Very hard. He knocked the second baseman to the ground. The ball got past him. Watson got up, and headed to third base. There was no play at third, but Watson slid in again. Again hard. He knocked the third baseman down, and the play came to an end.

Angry players again raced onto the field, but none was more angry than Watson. It took several people, including Bill, to calm him down and get him off the field. The two coaches agreed to end the game at that point. Everyone left, but without the usual handshaking between the two teams.

Several of the players went out for pizza in Noe Valley after the game, including Bill, Beret, Brian Howarth, and Michelle Hong. Trevor Watson went straight home, still muttering to himself. Despite Michelle's urging, Ramon Aguilar originally declined to join the group, saying he had to get home to his wife and children. He apparently changed his mind, and showed up about ten minutes after the others.

After the group ordered two pitchers of beer and the giant-size special house pizza, Brian said that today was not the first time Watson had ruined a good game with his temper. "He doesn't like to be crossed, even when it's only in his imagination."

"How long does his anger last? Does he hold a grudge?" Bill asked.

"It's hard to say," responded Michelle. "Sometimes he's over it the next day. But I remember one time Trevor thought that a player umpiring for the other team made a bad call at first base. We played the same team several weeks later. Trevor was still talking about getting even when the game started. Nothing happened, however, and I didn't take it seriously."

"I remember once when we were playing poker," said Ramon. "Trevor thought one of the players accused him of cheating. It was really rather innocuous, but Trevor was bitter about it for weeks. He eventually forced the player out of the regular game. That was typical. Trevor doesn't forget."

"Do you play in a regular poker game?" Bill was curious.

"Yes, a monthly game. Trevor and I and a few others. Rachel sometimes played, too, believe it or not. She was our pigeon. She couldn't keep a poker face. You could always tell when she had a good hand, and when she was trying to bluff. Lucky for her we played for small stakes. Are you interested in joining us?"

"No thanks." Bill laughed. "I'm just like Rachel. I've never been able to lie. I can't bluff, even in poker. You'd have all my money, no matter how small the stakes are."

"How did Trevor and Rachel get along at these games?" asked Beret.

"Actually, they got along just fine," answered Ramon. "Trevor even felt bad that she lost so much, and tried to help her improve." He added, "But she was beyond help."

"After what Trevor said about Rachel at the softball game today, I'm surprised he wanted to help her at poker," said Beret.

"Don't go by that. Trevor says things he doesn't really mean when he gets excited," explained Michelle. Then she added, "But he had been upset with Rachel ever since she accused him of sexual harassment."

"Sexual harassment?" Beret had not heard that before.

"Yes, hadn't you heard? It was no big deal. Rachel complained that he made some improper comments, or put his arm around her waist, or something like that. Nobody paid any attention to it. Rachel liked to cause trouble."

"Whatever came of it?" This was also news to Bill.

"Nothing," responded Michelle. "At least, I never heard anything. Nothing went public. Rachel complained to Fred Olson, but that's about it. I guess she lost interest."

Brian Howarth took a big bite of pizza, chewed it a bit, then spoke. "She lost interest because she found another way to cause trouble. She stuck her nose into my San Quentin case." He was not smiling.

Brian had been working for months defending a class action lawsuit challenging conditions in the adjustment center at San Quentin, the most secure portion of the prison, sometimes known as the "hole." The inmates, all of whom had assaulted prison staff in the past, complained that the extreme security measures, and lack of sufficient human contact or exercise, constituted cruel and unusual punishment. Brian's job was to show that the conditions were not as bad as the inmates claimed, and that the security measures were necessary. The case had been filed several years earlier by a single inmate, but recently several big private San Francisco law firms had joined the inmates' side and were turning it into a test case. Six attorneys were working for the plaintiffs. Howarth had been the sole attorney defending the case. Dozens of depositions had been taken, and the case was scheduled for trial in federal court later that year. It was commonly known as the *Rawlings* case, after the inmate who first filed it.

Brian continued. "Rachel talked to my boss, Tom Oldfield, about her worries even though she isn't in our unit. She enjoyed telling me precisely what she told him. She seemed to want to make me worry. Anyway, she told him she thought there was a connection between my case and her *Wakefield* and *Robinson* case. Why, I can't imagine. That was when Oldfield let her start meddling."

"What do you mean by meddling?" Bill had not heard this before, either.

"Oh, nothing significant. Officially, Oldfield thought I needed help because there were so many lawyers on the other side. Unofficially, Rachel convinced him to let her in on the case. She started second-guessing my tactics. She also mentioned her criticisms to Fred Olson, but nothing came of it It didn't give me a motive to kill her, if that's what you're thinking."

"I wasn't thinking anything. I was just curious."

"We all know you're helping the inspectors. I suppose you'll have to report to them what I just said. Go ahead. It has nothing to do with the murder."

"I'm sure it doesn't," Bill reassured him. Why was Brian so defensive? He was the one who referred to Rachel's "meddling" in the first place. He hadn't had to say anything; he could have just kept quiet. But Brian was right that Bill would have to report these conversations to Tarkov and Petersen. Why had none of this been mentioned before? Probably because it was all trivial, and couldn't possibly have anything to do with the murder. Bill and Beret had more to think about, though.

The rest of the evening was unusually subdued. Michelle Hong spoke little, and then only to repeat how terrible Rachel's death was, and to ask what mentality could possibly think of using the exhibits in Martin's case. The gun had "absolutely" terrified her when Martin insisted on showing it to her. Ramon and Brian said almost nothing more the rest of the evening.

The beer and pizza were perfunctorily consumed, and the group broke up for the night. Beret drove Bill in her Saab to a BART station, where he caught a train for Oakland. They spoke little, having implicitly agreed to postpone any discussion about the murder until dinner at Beret's.

Chapter 9

Beret left work early the next day to prepare dinner for her and Bill in her two-bedroom home in the Sunset district, where she lived with her cat, Brambles. Brambles was part calico, part something else. She was fourteen years old, and had been the Holmes's family pet since Beret was a freshman in high school. When Beret started working in the attorney general's office, her parents, who had recently retired and wanted to travel, asked her to take the cat.

Beret had grown up in a small farming community in the Sacramento Valley. Her father was a fourth generation farmer in the area, her mother the daughter of a second generation Norwegian farmer in South Dakota. Her mother had taught her how to count to twenty in Norwegian, but little else of the language. Beret had attended Mills College, a women's college in Oakland founded in the mid-nineteenth century. There she had majored in both biology and chemistry, and for four years was a key member of the nationally ranked Mills crew team.

Beret had dated an engineering student from the University of California in Berkeley. She had met Tony at an "exchange," a party of both Mills and Cal students, when she was a freshman. She and Tony became inseparable, and everyone assumed they would eventually marry. But during her senior year, his second year of graduate school, they drew apart. He won a scholarship for further graduate studies at Northwestern University. She wanted to stay in the Bay Area. During the summer before her senior year, they chose to go their separate ways. They still exchanged Christmas cards every year, but otherwise she had no further contact with him.

As Beret approached the end of her undergraduate days at Mills, the question of what to do next loomed large. She did not want to continue her scientific studies, but she was also not ready to get a job and join the real world. Her grades were good. She began to consider the one sure way to postpone the inevitable— law school. She had never seriously thought of becoming an attorney. No one in her family had ever been one, and her father had always talked disparagingly of the "shysters." But she had to admit that three more years of school, even of law school, before committing to a career sounded good. For want of anything better to do, she applied to four law schools and was accepted at two.

Inertia, rather than any conscious decision that she wanted to be a lawyer, caused her to commit to Santa Clara Law School. She just never got around to doing anything else, so she went to law school. To her surprise, she enjoyed it. She had a knack for brief writing and did well in the intramural appellate moot court program. In her third year, she competed on the Santa Clara national moot court team that reached the state semifinals before being eliminated by the University of California, Davis. She wrote a note for the school law review.

Beret dated some in law school, but nothing serious. She did not particularly like law students, and had little contact with anyone else. She devoted herself mainly to her studies, and to intramural sports, at which she excelled. She graduated in the top third of her class. By this time, she finally, definitely, had to get a real job. Since she had a law degree, she thought she might as well use it.

Criminal law attracted Beret as much as anything, and she felt an affinity for prosecution. She applied to various Bay Area district attorneys, and especially to the attorney general. Appellate practice seemed best for her. Late in her third year, the attorney general offered her a position in the criminal division in San Francisco. She accepted, with trepidation and again more out of inertia than any desire to practice law. She had never *really* thought that she would actually become a lawyer.

Nevertheless, she went to work in the criminal division. She quickly became one of the young, reliable, hardworking deputies the division needed during a period of an increasing workload. Her prowess at oral argument won her the respect of her colleagues, the judges, and even opposing counsel. During this time, as in law school, Beret dated some, but not much. Lawyers as little as possible. Nothing serious yet.

She also became enamored with the magic of appellate work.

Some of her friends in law school had warned her she would find it boring, but that proved far from true. Beret found it intoxicating to be at the cutting edge of the law, not merely developing facts as at trial, but helping to develop the *law*. The law is forged in appellate cases; being involved, being an agent in its tempering, its nurturing, and its maturing, she found intellectually challenging and emotionally stimulating. Beret delighted in honing her writing and speaking skills, learning to think on her feet when challenged by a penetrating question in the courtroom, above all mastering the art of persuading others that her position was correct and her opponent's was wrong. Not merely the art of writing well, or looking nice, but of actually *persuading* someone—an appellate judge who had already heard every glib argument there was. She learned to defend the weaknesses in her case; she thrived on exploiting those of her adversaries. She was adept at getting right to the heart of a case, of exposing the fatal flaw in the opponent's argument. "Go for the jugular," Ramon Aguilar had once told her. She did, whenever possible.

After she joined the attorney general's office, Beret first lived in an apartment near Lake Merritt in Oakland. She survived the La Prieta earthquake of October 17, 1989, in good shape, although not without a touch of adventure. An avid Oakland Athletics fan, she left work early that day to watch the third game of the World Series between the As and the cross-Bay rivals, the San Francisco Giants, on television. She was on a BART train in the tunnel under the San Francisco Bay when the earthquake hit. The train shook, and came to a halt without power under the bay. There were a few tense minutes as the BART officials checked for damage and switched to emergency power. But the tunnel held and the train was soon able to creep out to safety. Beret's home was undamaged, and her nerves were soon restored to normal.

As soon as she had saved enough money, Beret bought a small house in the Rockridge area of Oakland. She was proud of her first home, and worked hard to relandscape it. It was in the hills and surrounded by beautiful trees and lush vegetation. Three months after she bought the house, and two years after the earthquake—almost to the day—the great fire in the Oakland hills broke out. Beret was at Candlestick Park watching the football game between the San Francisco 49'ers and the Detroit Lions when she first heard of the fire. She would later reflect on how odd it was that the two great disasters occurred while she was concentrating on sporting events.

During the third quarter of the football game, when reports began to make clear how serious the fire was, and Beret could see the billowing smoke all the way across the bay, she left to try to go home. By the time she crossed the Bay Bridge and reached her neighborhood, she was not allowed to enter. It was an inferno. The entire area was evacuated. Houses were being consumed by the dozens, even hundreds. For two days she could not get into the disaster area, and she was uncertain about the fate of her new house, or of her cat, who had been somewhere in that inferno. All she possessed was her purse and its contents, the clothes she was wearing, her car, the contents of its glove compartment, and, in the trunk, two tennis racquets, a can of used tennis balls, and two cans of new tennis balls. One dress had been at the cleaners.

Finally, on Tuesday afternoon, Beret was allowed to enter her neighborhood. Where her house had been, her chimney and her mail box were still standing, and nothing else. Brambles was no-where to be seen.

For a full five minutes, Beret stood staring at the ashes. Then she heard from behind the mewing of a cat. Brambles. Beret would never know how it was possible, or where the cat had gone, but Brambles was safe. The cat ran to her and rubbed against her legs purring loudly. Beret dropped to her knees and picked her up.

During this entire period, when she first heard of the catastrophe, while the fate of her house was unknown, and even when she first observed that she had no home, Beret had maintained a quiet stoicism. She was young and strong enough to withstand almost anything. Her emotions were contained. But now that her cat had returned from hell, she lost her self-control. She started crying.

A photographer for the *Oakland Tribune* happened upon the scene. The photograph she took, reprinted across the country and even the world, of Beret on her knees by her mailbox, facing the ashes that had been her home, tightly clutching a cat named Brambles, sobbing uncontrollably, became one of the enduring images of the great Oakland fire.

But that was in the past. Beret did not want to live in the same area again, so she bought a house in the Sunset district of San

Francisco. Now she had to fix dinner for Bill Kelly and solve a murder. A chemistry laboratory partner had once told her that cooking was just like following a formula in the chem lab. She would find out.

She decided to make spaghetti. Anyone could do that, especially any veteran chemist. She just had to buy some ground beef, some tomato sauce, an onion, and a spaghetti sauce mix. With care, she might be able to disguise the fact she was using a mix. Beret had bought some oregano a couple of months ago, so she felt quite Italian. Now she would be able to use it for the first time. She did not care for garlic, so did not keep any around. A lettuce salad, some French bread, and a bottle of red wine would complete the meal. Neapolitan ice cream for dessert.

The sauce was simmering, the spaghetti ready to boil, and the salad prepared. Beret had a few minutes to sit quietly before Bill arrived. Brambles was on her lap, trying to convince her to scratch her under the chin. Beret began reflecting on recent events. She was starting to feel close to Bill, but was not sure if it was because of the murder they were so entwined in or something else. She wanted him to like the dinner, and not just because it was a prelude to discussing the murder. But she did not want to pursue any romance until they solved the case. Rachel Brandwyn's murder was paramount, and Beret could not be comfortable considering Bill as anything other than a colleague in crime detection until it was solved. Beret believed that he felt the same way. Beret decided it must be business as usual until the killer was caught. After that, who knew?

The doorbell rang. Brambles looked at Beret in disgust, and reluctantly jumped to the floor. It was Bill, a bottle of chilled white wine in hand. A good Chardonnay. "I didn't know what you were serving," he said. "If this is appropriate, we can drink it tonight. If not, save it for later." Beret invited him in. He complained about how hard it was to find a parking space. She apologized that that was the price you pay for living in the city.

They decided on dinner first, business later. They could most effectively discuss the case on a full stomach. Whether the wine would help solve the crime was not discussed, but they drank it anyway. The red. Over salad, Bill asked how long Beret had lived in the city. She said only a short time, that before that she lived in

Oakland, for a while in an apartment not far from where Bill now lived. He asked why she had moved to San Francisco.

Beret wound up telling Bill the whole story of the fire. In detail. It was the first time she had discussed it with someone who did not already know. He was affected by the story, and said so. "I was actually one of the lucky ones. Three days after the fire, the charred body of a neighbor of mine, a popular high school science teacher, was found in the ruins. Dental records were required to identify the body. For me it's over, and I can live my life. I have a new home and new property." A pause. "Same cat, though." As if by cue, Brambles wandered in.

"This is the friend who lived through the fire with me." By this time, they had finished the ice cream. Beret petted the cat briefly, then went into the kitchen to make coffee. Bill followed, and told her about his three-year-old cat, an orange tabby he had found abandoned during law school. His cat was named Prince, after the family dog when Bill was young. Beret asked what kind of a name "Prince" was for a cat. "It's a name for a dog, not a cat," she insisted. Bill said, "Maybe so, but it's a far better name than Brambles. Any self-respecting cat would be embarrassed to have a name like Brambles." Beret disagreed, and said so in no uncertain terms. After a strong debate, they eventually agreed to disagree on this important point, and, somewhat reluctantly, decided the time had come to discuss murder.

"We seem to have come up with some motives." Beret started the discussion over coffee after they sat down on her new sofa. Black for Beret. Cream and sugar, lots of sugar, for Bill. Bill reached for his legal notepad. He felt obligated to take notes. And possibly to draw some diagrams, or maybe a flow chart or two. He consulted the chart he had prepared last week in court.

"Let's take the suspects one by one," he suggested. "First, alphabetically, is Ramon Aguilar. The only development regarding him that I can think of is that strange voice mail message you got. What do you make of it?"

"I don't know. It might be the killer trying to throw us off the track. It might be something innocent. Or . . ."

"Or it might be the break we need," Bill concluded the sentence. "Do you suppose Ramon and Rachel were secretly going together? He's married."

"It's intriguing, isn't it?" she responded. "These days, who can be sure whether a marriage is happy or not? If Rachel and Ramon were having an affair, they sure kept it quiet. But *someone* got her pregnant. I suppose it could have been Ramon as much as anyone. After all, no one knows him that well. He's a very private person."

"Maybe their meeting at the Palace started out as a normal date, and then Rachel told him she was pregnant," speculated Bill.

"And he got angry and stormed out of the place," continued Beret. "It's possible."

"Why would he threaten to kill her? Surely he wouldn't threaten to kill the mother of his own child."

Beret thought a moment. "Not unless she threatened him first. Maybe she said she would publicly expose him as the father; maybe she demanded money. After all, Ramon *is* married; in appearance at least, it's a happy marriage. He and his wife have two children. Rachel might have demanded that Ramon divorce his wife. There are lots of possibilities. Maybe Ramon couldn't handle the news that she was pregnant."

" 'Maybe.' 'Might have.' 'Possibilities.' That's all we can say. It's sheer speculation," observed Bill.

"You're right," she replied. "We're making this all up because of an anonymous and ambiguous telephone message."

"Is the message still on your tape?"

"Yes, I didn't erase it. We'll have to turn it over to the inspectors." When Bill nodded his agreement, Beret continued. "The only other thing I can think of at this point is to talk to Ramon and see what he has to say. He's my supervisor. I'll try to broach the subject."

"Okay," Bill made a notation on the legal pad. "Beret to investigate voice mail message."

"Well, I'll talk to Ramon."

"That's what I said." Bill consulted the chart again. "Next we have Tom Atkins. Anything new there?"

Beret pondered. "Not that I can think of. Rachel's death caused him all kinds of grief. He had a tough time reassigning her cases. As Inspector Tarkov would say, we can't eliminate anyone, but I don't see any motive for him to kill her."

"Me neither. Let's put him aside for the time being." Bill made a check mark on the chart. "Martin Granowski."

"A possible development occurs to me here. Let's get back to him after we talk about Howarth."

"We postpone suspect Granowski until after Howarth." Bill made another notation. "That brings us to Anna Heitz. A significant development there. The *Schultz* case was reassigned from Anna to Rachel before it went to the Supreme Court. I can see the headlines now. 'Veteran attorney loses Supreme Court case to young upstart—kills upstart in revenge.' It's strange that no one mentioned this in the investigation earlier."

"Either strange or suspicious." Beret shifted her position, and directly faced Bill. "But the whole matter was apparently suppressed within the office. Fred Olson never likes public displays of disagreement. He always acts behind the scene and makes sure no one ever learns of the problems."

"Would resentment over a case reassignment be a motive for murder? Even a Supreme Court case? It's hard to believe someone would kill over that." Bill put more sugar in his coffee.

"It is hard to believe, isn't it?" Beret agreed. "It's certainly not reasonable. But murder is seldom reasonable. I've seen weaker motives. We have to consider it seriously. Especially since Anna didn't say anything about it."

"I'll work on this one," Bill said. "I need to talk to Anna about an issue in one of my cases that she is supposed to be an expert on. I'll bring up the subject of Rachel and the *Schultz* case to see what she says. Also, we need to talk to others to see what we can learn." When Beret nodded agreement, Bill wrote on his notepad, "Bill to investigate Heitz motive." He looked up. "This brings us to Michelle Hong. I see no possible motive for her. Surely we can exclude her. She wouldn't hurt a fly."

"I agree." Beret paused to pour Bill some more coffee. "At least for the time being. Let's put her aside for now."

Bill put another check mark on the chart. "Now we come to Brian Howarth. An interesting case. Last night over pizza, Brian himself suggested a possible motive. He said Rachel had started 'meddling' in his case, and that she criticized the way he was handling it."

"Yes, he said that she expressed her criticisms to his supervisor, Tom Oldfield, and even might have gone to Fred Olson." This

point was troubling to Beret. "Yet, Brian never mentioned it before. Why last night?"

"Maybe because he knew we would find out anyway, and he
wanted us to hear it from him first. Somehow he knows we are
investigating the crime."

"Apparently everyone knows. I wonder how?"

Bill put down his notepad, and looked at Beret. "Maybe Fred
Olson mentioned it. But why would he? Anyway, Olson would
know whether Rachel complained to him about Howarth's performance. Should we talk to Olson?"

Beret thought for a moment. "I don't think so. The inspectors
should do that. After all, he *is* our boss. We'll tell Tarkov and
Petersen what we learned and they can take it from there."

"I agree. If the opportunity comes up, we might talk with Tom
Oldfield. In fact, I can approach him about my San Quentin drug
case and try to learn something that way." Bill made another
notation. "Re Howarth—Bill talk with Oldfield if excuse comes
up."

Beret spoke. "This is where I wanted to talk about Granowski.
A hint of a motive might exist. Howarth complained that Rachel
had meddled in his case. When I was assigned to work on the
Morton case with Granowski, Fred and Ramon told me that Rachel had preceded me. If she meddled in Howarth's case,
mightn't she have meddled in Granowski's? Maybe she uncov-
ered something in the *Morton* case that caused Granowski to kill
her? After all, he had the easiest access to the murder weapon. It's
odd that he took no security precautions with the weapon. He
kept the gun, the silencer, and the bullets conveniently together
where anyone could get them. He didn't keep it a secret. Why, he
practically advertised the weapon."

"He might have just been careless, as he said."

"It's possible. But he might also have wanted to spread suspicion as widely as he could to mask his easy access to the murder
weapon. He was not happy when I was assigned to work with him
on *Morton*."

Bill stood up and started pacing, the cup of coffee in his left
hand, the pad of paper in his right. "You might be on to something. It's only speculation, but it's good speculation. I think this
one is yours. You are on the *Morton* case. See if you can dig up

something solid." Beret nodded, whereupon Bill put down his coffee and wrote, "Granowski—Beret to investigate further."

"Who's next?"

Bill consulted the chart. "Fred Olson. He may have a motive. Sexual harassment. Other department problems. Everybody knows his position as head of the San Francisco criminal division is shaky. The people in Sacramento are looking for an excuse to remove him. As long as things run smoothly in San Francisco, he's probably safe. But internal discord or clumsy personnel moves could hurt him deeply. He lives for his job."

"But what could be worse for him than murder within the division?" Beret asked the obvious question.

"I don't know. That's what we need to find out. Rachel Brandwyn seems to have rocked the boat more than is generally known. Fred seems to have covered up a lot of things. Was Rachel no longer willing to keep quiet? The sexual harassment complaint is the most troubling."

Beret agreed. "Ever since the Clarence Thomas Senate confirmation hearings, everybody is paranoid about sexual harassment. If such charges are made public, it could tear the office apart."

"And cost Fred his position," Bill added.

"And cost Fred his position. Which he dearly loves. Nothing is more important to him than the San Francisco criminal division. But would he kill to prevent a public airing of sexual harassment charges?"

"It's hard to imagine he would prefer a murder scandal to a sexual harassment scandal."

Beret took a sip of coffee, and considered the point. "Yes, unless he thought that sexual harassment charges would reflect badly on his management of the office and on his handling of the charges. After all, right now no one can blame the murder on Fred. In fact, because of the problems the murder is causing, it might be harder than ever to make a major change. I can conceive of Fred thinking murder was preferable to the alternative."

"So can I. Just barely. Where do we go from here?"

"We have to find out how far the sexual harassment complaint went. If you want to learn this kind of inside information, where do you turn?"

Bill smiled. "A secretary. They would know if anyone does. Jeff Hines was Rachel's secretary. I'll talk to him." Bill made another notation. "Olson—Bill to talk to Hines re sexual harassment (or anything else)." He stopped pacing and sat down next to Beret. "That leaves Trevor Watson. What we said about Fred Olson goes for him. Sexual harassment charges are a strong motive. Watson can be bitter, and he's been known to hold a grudge. He is ambitious, and would not take kindly to public charges that could be a permanent blight on his career. We've got to learn more about the claim."

Beret agreed. "Anything else?"

"No, that's about it. Tomorrow I'll call Tarkov and Petersen and report what we've learned. Then we just talk to people."

Beret stood up and began carrying the coffee mugs into the kitchen. She smiled. "And we might even do some lawyering if we find the time. It's easy to forget that the appellate load keeps piling up. Until we enter our offices."

Bill commented wryly that it was too bad work had to interfere with their detecting. He looked at his watch. "And now it's time for me to go. I have to get up early for my morning run around Lake Merritt. I try to run it three days a week. Tomorrow's one of the days."

This comment initiated a lengthy discussion about running. Beret, it turned out, was also a runner. The two talked about their times, their shoes, the courses they ran, and, above all, their many minor aches and pains. Both elaborated on their feet problems, their muscle strains, their sore joints, indeed, almost every physical and mental ailment possible. Why do they do it, if it was so painful? Bill mused. Beret laughed that true runners are never really content unless they are totally miserable.

"Have you ever run the Bay-to-Breakers?" asked Beret. The Bay-to-Breakers is a twelve-kilometer race run in San Francisco every May. It traverses the width of the city from the bay to the ocean at the west end of Golden Gate Park. Around eighty thousand to one hundred thousand people of all ages run, making it one of the largest participation sporting events in the world. A few serious runners start at the front, the masses behind them. The race is famous for runners wearing costumes of all kinds, and for its "centipedes," chains of thirteen or so runners connected together, some in costume, who compete for the title of fastest centipede.

"No, I've never run it. Have you?"

"Three times," she said. "It's wild, if you don't take it too seriously. I'm running it again in a couple of weeks. Care to join me?"

Bill said he would. The two agreed to run together, and discussed when and where. Bill looked at his watch again, and again said he had to leave. He did, without further ado.

As Bill Kelly was driving home across the Bay Bridge, he did a lot of thinking, both regarding the murder investigation and about Beret. Beret was attractive to him, but, like her, he felt that the investigation had to come first.

Bill had been born in Seattle, Washington, the descendant of Irish farmers who emigrated to the United States in 1851 in the wake of the great potato famine in Ireland. Bill's father had worked for Boeing, then had become a high school teacher. On his mother's side, Bill was of German descent, specifically of Volga German descent. One of his maternal great-grandfathers had come to this country in 1886 at the age of four from a German colony near the Volga River in Russia. His ancestors had been farmers there for over a century, since 1767, when Catherine the Great, herself originally a German princess, had invited western Europeans to come to settle the Volga region.

When Bill was ten years old, the family, including his three sisters, moved to California. After a few years in two different small towns, they eventually moved to Sunnyvale, in Silicon Valley, where Bill graduated from the same high school at which his father taught. Unlike Beret, Bill knew from an early age that he would be an attorney. Once he had gotten past the stage of wanting to be a sheriff or a fireman, around the fifth grade, he settled on the legal profession. He was never clear as to why, only what.

The family finances mandated a public university. Bill's grades allowed him to choose his campus of the University of California. He selected Santa Barbara. His officially stated reason was the excellence of its history department. Unofficially, Bill's love affair with the ocean was the real reason. He selected Santa Barbara once and for all about three point two seconds after being shown a photograph of the campus's beautiful beach, with the university buildings and dormitories in the background.

He majored in history, with an emphasis on medieval European history, not because he thought it had practical value, but because he loved the subject and intended, in any event, to go to law school. His minor was theater arts, and he performed in several school plays, his best part being Major Petkoff in George Bernard Shaw's *Arms and the Man*. Bill also played tennis on the varsity team his first two years, but never quite made first string. He studied hard, got good grades, partied as much as possible, and enjoyed the beach, not necessarily in that order.

He spent his junior year studying at the university in Göttingen, a city in northern Germany, as part of an education abroad program. He learned German quite well, and was able to travel extensively, getting as far as Greece and Bulgaria in one direction, and Ireland in the other. When the local professional repertory theater company expressed an interest in having one of the Americans participate, Bill got an unimportant role in a production of Friedrich Schiller's *Don Carlos*. He was paid a small amount per performance; it was the first, and would be the last, time he was paid for acting. He also played soccer in local pick-up games, finding it a good way to meet Germans. He became interested in the Bundesliga, Germany's major league of soccer. His favorite team was Werder Bremen. A German friend from Bremen was a fanatic about the team.

And Bill fell in love. Irmgard was his age, but in her second year of law school. She came from Karlshafen, a town on the Weser River, also in northern Germany, and was descended from Huguenots, who had been driven out of France during the reign of Louis the Fourteenth. She had a captivating smile, and she shared many of his interests. Between semesters, they traveled together through southern and eastern Europe in her old Volkswagen bug (or, as she called it, her "Kaefer"). In the summer they went to Ireland, where Bill visited the area from which his ancestors had emigrated. They also visited the area in France where her ancestors had lived. It was intoxicating.

Then the year came to an end. Bill had to return to the United States to complete his studies. Irmgard, determined to become an attorney, had to stay in Germany. It was decision time. After considerable agonizing, they chose to part, and did. There was no future for them together.

Bill completed his undergraduate studies, and, as long planned, went to law school. Santa Barbara had no law school, so Bill selected the University of California at Davis. There he continued to get good grades, was on law review, and successfully competed

in moot court. He had roles in a couple of small theater produc-
tions, and played intramural soccer for three years, organizing his
own team. He socialized as much as he could, but had no serious
romance. At the end, he accepted a job in the San Francisco
criminal division of the Attorney General's office.

Bill got permission to visit Europe before he started work. After
he took the bar exam, he got on a plane for Frankfurt, and traveled
around. He was in Toledo, Spain, just after Thanksgiving when he
learned that he had passed the bar. He experienced a traditional
German Christmas with some friends in Hannover. He toured
what used to be East Germany, then returned to Greece for three
weeks, mostly visiting his favorite region, the Peloponnesus. Once
again, he was charmed by Sparta, a sleepy little town nestled in
the mountains. He spent five days in Göttingen, staying with old
friends. He traveled along the Weser and passed through Karlshafen. He did not visit Irmgard. There was no point in it.

Bill returned to California in late February, and began his legal
career the next week. Like Beret, he discovered that he loved
appellate work. And now, to his amazement, he was enmeshed in
a murder mystery.

Chapter 10

B ill called Inspector Petersen the next day, using the telephone number on the card the inspectors had given him.
Neither Petersen nor Tarkov was immediately available,
but Tarkov called Bill back about ten minutes later. The inspector
agreed to come to the office to discuss the case. Petersen was
investigating a new murder in San Francisco's Richmond District
and could not come. Tarkov arrived around 10:30 A.M. He met
with Bill and Beret in Olson's office. Olson tactfully managed to
find something to do in the other end of the building. The two
attorneys then gave a full report on recent developments. Tarkov
took copious notes, and interrupted frequently with questions.

When Beret told about the telephone message talking about
Ramon Aguilar, Tarkov perked up. He eagerly asked if Beret had
erased the tape. She assured him she had not. "Good," he exclaimed. "We'll record the message and get the voice people on it
right away. There's a new scientific voice-analysis technique that
never fails to identify the speaker. That is, I don't think it ever
fails. At least, I think I remember hearing something once about
voice analysis." His voice trailed off rather vaguely, but his eyes
gleamed at this renewed hope of obtaining useful scientific evidence.

At Tarkov's insistence, the three immediately trooped together
to Beret's office, and shut the door behind them. Their long walk
down the hallway was noticed by virtually everyone, and elicited
more than a few comments. It was an open secret that Bill and
Beret had been recruited to help the investigators, although *why*
was not generally understood. One person in particular observed
the three with great interest. When they walked by, that person
sat behind a desk and stared into space for several seconds. What
exactly were they doing, and how close were they coming? the

person wondered. The person, however, did nothing overt to betray such thoughts to the public.

Beret replayed the message. Inspector Tarkov listened carefully while simultaneously taking detailed notes, a skill he had honed over the last few months. He listened to the message a second time, then a third. The more he listened, the less eager he became. The voice was indeed muffled. Tarkov began to doubt that analysis would reveal any of the message's secrets. But it was worth trying. If anyone could learn anything useful, his voice experts certainly could. Or at least they could try. Tarkov made a note to have someone do the necessary work.

The three then trooped back to Olson's office, a trek again noticed by all. Inspector Tarkov seemed to want to conduct business in the biggest office available. He generally approved the plan of action Beret and Bill had worked out the night before. He even complimented them on their good work, a significant development given his initial reluctance to elicit their aid. The three agreed to continue exchanging information as needed, and the two attorneys left the office. At Tarkov's request, Elizabeth Cronin asked Olson to return to the office.

When Olson appeared, Tarkov was sitting in the chair behind the desk looking out the window, obviously in deep thought. Olson hesitated over whether to remain standing or to sit in one of the other chairs. He cleared his throat. Tarkov started, looked down at the chair he was in, and hastily stood up.

"Sorry, you can have your chair back. I was just trying to think." Olson sat down in his chair. Tarkov sat in another chair in front of the desk. He stared at Olson as if again deep in thought.

After a few moments of awkward silence, Olson asked how the investigation was going. "Not well" was the reply. "Our killer is smart. He is a cool customer who either knows what he is doing or is a quick learner. He did not leave a calling card behind. He is either masking his motive well or he killed for insignificant reasons. Of course, the reasons for killing usually seem insignificant." Tarkov looked at the floor and muttered this last comment almost as if it were directed solely at himself. Then he looked intently at Olson. "But nobody escapes Inspector Tarkov permanently. We'll get him yet." If Tarkov had expected a reaction from Olson, he was disappointed. He decided to get to the point of the interview. "I understand the victim came to talk to you about Brian Howarth's San Quentin case before her death." He took out a notepad and pen, and poised himself to write.

Olson tensed visibly. "Yes. That is, well, how did you know?" When Tarkov did not answer, Olson continued. "I mean to say, she didn't really talk to me about the case, only that she wanted to. What do you know about it?"

"What I know doesn't matter. What matters is what *you* know. When did she first approach you?"

Olson fidgeted with a pen on his desk. "She only—only came to me, or approached me, as you put it, once. A couple of weeks before she was—before she died. No, it was only a few days before." He stopped, and placed his right hand on his forehead as if trying to concentrate. "That's right, it was three days before she died. She said she had learned something interesting about Howarth's case."

"The *Rawlings* case, I believe it is called?"

Olson looked up dumbly as if the interruption had broken his concentration. "That's right, the *Rawlings* case. It's a class action challenging conditions in the adjustment center—that's the maximum security area—at San Quentin. Everybody knows about the case; it's a big one, although my division is not handling it. The case comes within the jurisdiction of the prison litigation unit. I don't know much about it. We don't interfere in their business, and they don't interfere in ours. Thomas Oldfield is the San Francisco head of the prison unit. You can talk to him if you want to know more."

Tarkov gazed at Olson coolly. "We might do that. Did the victim come to your office here?"

"Yes." Olson met Tarkov's gaze briefly, then looked down. "That morning she said she wanted to talk about Howarth. I had a meeting with some district attorneys in a few minutes, so I asked if we could talk that afternoon. She agreed, and came back around three. Elizabeth was in my office. Yes, I remember, Elizabeth and I were going over some administrative assignments. Anyway, we were almost finished, so Rachel waited until Elizabeth left."

"Did she seem nervous?"

Olson considered the question. "Not particularly. No more than usual. She always seemed nervous talking to me." He sat taller in his seat and straightened his shoulders. "Must have been my position as head of the office."

Tarkov glanced up from his notepad, and smiled to himself. "What did she say?"

Another pause. "Well, I, uh, I don't remember exactly, I mean, well, uh, it had to do, at least I think it had to do with the uh—"

"With the *Rawlings* case?"

"Yes, that's it. Rachel had some expertise, or at least some interest, in San Quentin. I think she knew an inmate there, or something. Even though she was not in the prison litigation unit, she kept herself informed about their cases. She was always talking to the attorneys over there. Why, I can't imagine. I try to stay as far away from prison litigation as I can. Of course, Rachel liked to get involved in almost everything around here. Her interests were always expanding. Why, I remember one time—"

"Can we get back to this case?" Tarkov had been furiously writing notes, but stopped when he realized that Olson had begun to wander. "What did the victim say on this occasion?"

"Well, I don't remember exactly."

"I know. You just said that. Tell me what you *do* remember."

Olson again fiddled with the pen. He absently flipped it in the air. "Just that she was concerned about Howarth's performance in *Rawlings.* It sometimes seemed that she was always concerned about the attorneys' performances. I'm sure Howarth is a good attorney, and was doing a good job."

Tarkov waited a few seconds. When he realized Olson was not going to volunteer anything more, he spoke. "Did she say anything specific?"

Olson examined the tip of the pen in minute detail. Finally, "She said—no, she didn't say anything specific. I didn't pay much attention. Rachel was always coming to my office with problems like this. Look, I'm sure it has nothing to do with the murder. I've told you everything I can remember."

"That's it? She made an appointment to talk to you about this matter, then just made some vague comment that she was 'concerned?' "

"Well, she didn't exactly make an appointment. I was busy the first time she came, so she agreed to come in the afternoon. It happens all the time. Actually, I remember now. I didn't have much time even in the afternoon, either. It's the nature of my position. I was expecting an important telephone call from the people in Sacramento. Rachel could be a real nuisance sometimes. I frankly just wanted her to go away. Yes, that's right. I just wanted her to go away. She never got specific. In fact, I said that if she had a problem, she should put it in writing in a memo to me."

Tarkov looked up from his notetaking. "Ah, I see. And did she?"

"Did she what?"

"Put it in writing?"

Olson gave the inspector a puzzled look. "No. That is, not that I know of. No, I'm sure of it. If she had, I would know."

Tarkov elicited no further information from Olson, and soon terminated the conversation. He left the building pondering the significance of what he had learned.

When the technicians reported back, they said, to Tarkov's disappointment, that they could learn nothing from the recorded message. The voice was so muffled they could not even determine whether it was male or female. Tarkov resigned himself to the likelihood that science was not going to solve the mystery. He hoped something would.

After he left Tarkov, Bill spent the rest of the week concentrating on his caseload. More than two weeks had passed since Rachel's murder, and his assignments were not going away on their own. No convenient occasion arose to talk to anyone about the murder. In truth, Bill felt relieved to be able to do something familiar for a while rather than continually being a detective. He completed one brief that week, and got a good start on another. On Friday, however, Bill had occasion to talk with Jeff Hines, Rachel Brandwyn's former secretary, about the *Wakefield* and *Robinson* case he had inherited from Rachel.

Hines repeated that Rachel's death was really tragic, really sad. He said that he had always liked and respected her "even though she could sometimes be a gadfly."

The comment alerted even Bill's undeveloped detecting instincts. "What do you mean by that?" he asked.

"Oh, nothing. You know what I mean."

"No, I don't."

Hines shrugged his shoulders. "I didn't mean anything, just that, you know, sometimes she could bother people."

"Did you have anything specific in mind?"

"No, not really. Just in general."

Bill decided he would get nothing further from Hines without a specific question. He went right to the point. "Did Rachel ever make any comments to you about sexual harassment?"

Hines suddenly became defensive. "I have always behaved in the most proper manner with her. I have never come remotely close to harassing her. In fact, I was very careful not even to give her the opportunity to get the wrong impression. She never accused me of sexual harassment." A pause. "Did she?"

"No, you misunderstood me. I didn't mean comments *about* you, but *to* you about someone else."

Hines relaxed visibly. "Oh, well, in that case, let me think." He looked at Bill for a moment, shrugged his shoulders again, then replied, "Funny you should ask."

When Hines did not continue, Bill prodded him. "Did she make any comments to you?"

"No. Not to me directly. You couldn't expect her to, me being a male secretary and all that. But she did have some complaints. That I know."

Again silence. Bill asked, "What do you know?"

"That Rachel thought she was the victim of sexual harassment. At least she complained about it. I think she complained to Tom Atkins and then to Fred Olson."

"What about?"

"Sexual harassment."

"By anyone in particular?"

Hines looked at Bill in surprise. "Why, yes, of course. I assumed you knew. Trevor Watson."

Now we're getting somewhere, Bill thought. "What did Trevor Watson do?"

"I have no idea."

Cross-examination of a hostile witness is harder than this, thought Bill. "OK, let's try it this way. What did Rachel claim Trevor did?"

"I don't know for sure. That is, I don't remember exactly. He put his arm around her, made inappropriate comments, pressed her for a date, that sort of thing. He wasn't her type, and I'm sure she let him know it. Trevor found it hard to believe that any unmarried woman, or any other woman for that matter, could resist his charms."

The statement fit with Bill's knowledge of Watson. "Try to think what she said," he urged. "It could be important."

"To what? Oh, I see. The murder investigation. You're on it, aren't you?" Hines's eyes opened wider. "You think Watson murdered Rachel because she accused him of sexual harassment? That's impossible. Watson's not a murderer. He may flirt, but it's all in fun. He wouldn't kill, and certainly not a good-looking woman."

"It's probably irrelevant, but please tell me everything you can remember."

Hines clenched his fists and tried to concentrate. "I really can't remember the details. When I type something, I generally don't pay attention to what I'm typing."

"What do you mean, when you type something?"

"I mean her formal complaint for sexual harassment. After she complained to Olson, she didn't think she was getting satisfaction. So she wrote out a complaint to the people in Sacramento and had me type it."

"Did she send it?"

"No, I don't think so. No, I would have been the one to send it, and I didn't. She said she wanted to think about it some more before she actually sent it. She knew that going over Olson's head with a formal complaint was a big deal. After the Thomas hearings, any claims of sexual harassment could tear the office apart. The issue would divide the office into two camps, his and hers. Rachel wanted to think about it carefully. And then, I guess, she was killed before she could make up her mind."

Bill was amazed at these revelations. Why had none of this come out before? Was there a conspiracy of silence? "Does this memo still exist?"

"Not a final draft, no. One was never prepared."

"Of *any* draft?" Bill found it difficult to keep from shouting. Was Hines being intentionally obstinate?

"Yes, I suppose so. I mean, she kept the draft to decide if she wanted to send it. It wouldn't do any good not to keep at least one draft now, would it?"

"Do you know where the draft is now?" Bill tried to remain patient.

"I might." A pause. Then Hines smiled and shrugged his shoulders again. "I bet you would like me to tell you where it is." Bill nodded. "I guess there's no harm in it. I think it's still in Rachel's file cabinet."

"Can you show me?"

"I suppose. Come on." Hines led Bill to Rachel's office. Because of the hiring freeze, a replacement for Rachel had not yet been hired. Although her window office was highly desired by those who had interior offices, no decision had yet been made as to who would receive it. Attorney general office shifts were always complicated affairs, as more senior attorneys with window offices wanted bigger window offices, and those without a window wanted one, in as big and prestigious an office as possible. The politics of the matter were sensitive, to say the least. The easiest approach was to do nothing until someone was hired. Even then, action could sometimes be postponed, as in the case of Bill Kelly, the last new addition before the hiring freeze. Bill was temporarily occupying a window office that had belonged to an attorney who had left the office the same time Bill was hired. After Rachel's case files had been removed, her office was kept the way it was.

Hines stepped to the file cabinet in the corner, and opened the second drawer from the top. He flipped through the manila folders casually, then more intently. After searching the drawer at length, he suddenly closed it, and looked at Bill. "Oh, yes," he said. "I forgot. A couple of days before she died, Rachel rearranged her entire file cabinet. She said it was getting too disorganized. Or maybe she was worried that people were removing things from it. I don't remember." Hines opened the third drawer and fingered through it, then the fourth. Finally, he took out a manila folder. He glanced at the papers inside, and removed a three-page document.

"Here it is. I typed this for Rachel." Hines handed it to Bill. Labeled "draft," it was a memorandum from Rachel Brandwyn to the chief of the criminal division in Sacramento regarding "sexual harassment." This is what it said:

"I write to place before you a formal complaint for sexual harassment. I take this step gravely, as I fully understand the serious nature of what I do. But I have no choice. My efforts to resolve the matter informally at the local level have been rebuffed, so I must now take this route. It is unfortunate that I have to do this, but the situation must stop, and I have gotten no satisfaction so far."

(This is a devastating indictment of Olson and Atkins, Bill thought, although at least she did not name them personally.)

"Over the last three months, I have been the target of repeated acts of sexual harassment on the part of one Trevor Watson, a deputy attorney general in the San Francisco criminal division. My repeated complaints to him and requests that he cease and desist his offensive behavior at once proved to be of no avail, so I was forced to make informal oral complaints to Fred Olson. No action has been taken, and the situation has not improved, so I now turn to you."

(So she did name Olson personally, but not Atkins. Interesting. It really makes Olson look bad.)

"The following is a partial but incomplete list of offensive and improper actions Watson has committed over the months.

"(1) Watson has on more than one occasion asked me for a date. I had no complaint the first time. One request was reasonable. But I made it clear at that time that I was not interested in dating him. Subsequent requests are offensive. He has been pressuring me to go out with him.

"(2) Watson puts his arms around me in an improper fashion whenever we are alone. He never does this in front of others, only when we are alone.

"(3) Watson continually tries to talk to me about his sexual life and especially his many and varied sexual exploits. When I state clearly to him that I am not interested, and do not want to hear more, he insists on getting graphic. I will not repeat the details, but it has become extremely offensive.

"(4) One time, after I had repeatedly complained to him of this behavior, Watson placed his right hand on my knee in my office, and said he did not believe I really was not turned on by him. I slapped him, but he just laughed.

"(5) Twice Watson started to talk to me about some pornographic movie he had seen. Only when I emphatically forbade him from continuing did he stop. I fear he will try it again.

"(6) Watson hugged me one time in front of others after I had won a big case.

"I hereby request a formal investigation resulting in appropriate discipline and guarantees that such harassment will cease and desist. If I do not receive satisfaction from this memorandum I will have no choice but to seek relief in some other forum."

The memorandum was unsigned and indicated copies were to go to the attorney general himself and to his press secretary.

After Bill finished reading it, he told Hines he wanted a copy. Hines agreed to make one.

"Did Olson know she wrote this?" Bill asked.

"I think so. I showed the memo to Elizabeth Cronin, and I'm sure she told Olson. It was no secret. I told Elizabeth I hadn't sent it yet and promised her I wouldn't without telling her first."

"Did Watson know?"

"I'm not sure. I assume he did. Rachel never hid what she was doing. It was no secret."

Chapter 11

The next Monday morning, Bill and Beret arranged to have lunch together; whether to discuss the murder or for some other reason was not mentioned. They chose a nearby Cambodian restaurant, a favorite lunch spot for members of the Attorney General's office. It was one of the many and varied Asian restaurants opened during the previous decade in the Civic Center area by recent immigrants—Vietnamese, Chinese, Thai, Cambodian. Beret and Bill arrived shortly before noon; already the small restaurant was crowded.

Thomas Atkins and Michelle Hong were having lunch together at a small table near the front. They appeared engrossed in conversation and did not notice their colleagues. Michelle's left hand was placed over Tom's right hand. "That's cozy," whispered Beret to Bill. "I've never seen the two of them out alone before. Is something going on we don't know about?"

"Don't be catty," responded Bill as he peered closely at Tom and Michelle trying to decide whether something *might* be going on. He and Beret then simultaneously observed Elizabeth Cronin eating alone at a table in the back that was large enough to accommodate four. Forgetting about Tom and Michelle, he whispered to Beret that seeing Elizabeth was convenient. "We've been meaning to talk to her; now's our chance."

They approached, and asked if they could join her since there were no empty tables. "Of course you may," she responded. "I welcome the company." Bill and Beret sat on each side of Elizabeth. This was the first time either had been alone with her. They did not know her well. Elizabeth had been a secretary in the criminal division more years than she was willing to admit, and had little contact with the younger deputies. The three talked about how much they liked the restaurant, about the nice weather —"typical of San Francisco in May," commented Beret—and

about how unfortunate it was that the Backlog seemed to be growing ever since Rachel's murder.

During the small talk, Bill had been trying to figure out how he
and Beret could subtly question Elizabeth regarding the murder
and possible motives of some of the suspects. He was sure that
real detectives would not be obvious in their questioning. A
smooth transition was needed. The reference to the Backlog
seemed to him an excuse to talk about the murder.

"Tell me," he asked Elizabeth, "is it true that before she died,
Rachel complained that Trevor Watson had been sexually harassing her?" As soon as he asked the question, Bill felt that it was not
quite the smooth transition he had wanted. Columbo would definitely have done better.

Beret smiled, and said they were just curious, that they had
heard rumors and thought Elizabeth might know something.

Elizabeth looked from one to the other, and said, "So it's true
what they say. You *are* investigating the murder."

Bill squirmed in his chair, and coughed quietly. Beret laughed,
and asked, "Are we as obvious as all that? As I said, we're just
curious. This is hot gossip." She leaned forward. Elizabeth sat
motionless, and said nothing. Beret turned serious. "But we
would like to know. It might be important."

Elizabeth looked at the tables around her, then spoke in a low
voice. "I suppose there's no reason to keep quiet. Better to tell
you than those awful homicide detectives. Besides, none of it was
secret."

The waiter came to their table. Elizabeth had already ordered.
Beret ordered a beef and mushroom dish, Bill, pork and rice. The
soup course came right away. When the waiter left, Bill and Beret
waited expectantly for Elizabeth to continue.

She took a deep breath. "All I know is that one afternoon, a few
days before she died, Rachel complained to Fred that someone
was harassing her. I didn't hear who, and couldn't catch the details. After a while, Rachel started shouting, and Fred closed the
door. I don't know what else was said, but a little later, Rachel
stormed out of the office. A few hours after that, Fred called
Trevor to his office, and they talked privately for almost an hour.
That's all I know."

A few moments of silence ensued. Elizabeth finished her soup
and then examined her napkin in detail. Bill and Beret looked at

each other. "Tell me," Beret asked innocently. "Was anything ever put in writing?"

Elizabeth again glanced around, then continued her examination of the napkin. "Well, now that you mention it, Jeff Hines did say something about a memo Rachel had written."

When Elizabeth did not continue, Bill prodded her. "What exactly did Jeff tell you?"

"Only that Rachel had written a memo but had not yet sent it."

"Did he say anything specific?" Beret asked.

"No." Elizabeth began folding and unfolding the napkin. "Well, he did say something like the memo was a time bomb waiting to be detonated. I don't remember exactly. It wasn't important."

"What did you say?" Bill asked the question.

"Nothing. Well, only that as a courtesy to Fred, Jeff shouldn't send the memo to Sacramento without telling me first." She stopped fidgeting and looked directly at Bill. "There was nothing wrong in that. I thought it might be important for Fred to know before the memo was actually sent. That's all. I didn't try to pressure Jeff into not sending it. I don't care what he says. All I wanted was to be told before it was sent. Nothing else."

The conversation was progressing so fast that Bill was sorry he did not have his notepad. The urge to take notes was almost irresistible. He hoped, however, that between the two of them, he and Beret would be able to remember everything that was important. "Did you ever read Rachel's memo?" he asked.

"Of course not," she replied immediately. "Jeff never showed it to me, and I never asked to see it. All I know is that Rachel was complaining of sexual harassment. Which was ludicrous. Rachel was always imagining things. Trevor will have his fun, but underneath it all he's harmless."

"Did you talk to Fred about the memo?" Beret asked.

Elizabeth paused while the waiter removed the empty soup bowls and served the main course. When he was gone, she said, "Yes, naturally. Well, why shouldn't I?" Beret assured her there was no reason not to. "Fred always wants to know everything that's going on in the office. The office is his life, and has been ever since he's been in charge. I always tell him whenever I hear of any problem. This was nothing out of the ordinary, and you shouldn't make so much out of it. I'm sure it has nothing to do with Rachel's death. Why should it?" Elizabeth paused to take a breath, then added, "I suppose you're going to think Fred killed Rachel to prevent the complaint from being sent. That's ridiculous. It's just as possible that Trevor killed her for the same reason. Although that's also ridiculous. Rachel was paranoid. Nobody was *really* out to get her." Elizabeth began intently to eat her chicken and rice dish.

"What did Fred say when you told him about the memo?" Beret probed further.

"Well, um, he was, um, angry. He shouted that he and Watson were taking care of the problem informally, what more did she want, blood?" She added hastily, "But he wasn't that angry. It was just typical of things that happen all the time in a busy office full of lawyers. He asked me to tell him if I heard anything new about the memo."

"Did he say anything else?"

"Only that—no, nothing else, nothing at all" was the response. The three ate in silence for a while. Beret and Bill each concluded nothing more was to be learned on this subject.

A few moments later, Elizabeth spoke again. She was suddenly more lighthearted, and she smiled. "I'm ready to continue the interrogation. Anything else you want to grill me about?"

Beret laughed. "Now that you mention it, yes, there is something else. Did Rachel ever say anything to you or Fred about Brian Howarth and his San Quentin case?"

Elizabeth thought a moment. "No, not that I know of. Why should she? Howarth is not in this section. He's in prison litigation under Tom Oldfield. Fred has no interest in prison litigation, none at all. You'd have to talk to Oldfield about that." Bill made a mental note of the suggestion.

He spoke next. "I understand there was quite a row a while ago when a federal case assigned to Anna Heitz was reassigned to Rachel before it went to the United States Supreme Court. Did you hear anything about that."

Elizabeth laughed. Bill thought it was a forced, nervous laugh, although that might have been his imagination. "Right, the *Schultz* case. It was no big deal. As I said, one of those things that happens in an office full of ambitious lawyers. Anna is a great lawyer, but sometimes not very tactful. She lost a murder case in the Ninth Circuit. The DA, I think it was in Contra Costa, was naturally not too happy about it. He complained to Anna. Anna said some things she probably shouldn't have, and the DA asked Fred to give the case to someone else, someone who, as the DA put it, had "the best interests of the case and not herself at heart."

"Why did Fred give the case to Rachel?" Bill asked.

"I don't know. To keep the DA happy, I guess. Rachel had been following the *Schultz* case from the beginning. In fact, she discussed it many times with Anna and had helped her on occasion. Or, depending on one's perspective, had interfered on occasion. Anna considered it interference. Anyway, if it was going to be taken away from Anna, it seemed natural to give it to Rachel. I think Rachel had spent some time with the Contra Costa DA. As I recall, everyone knew from the beginning that the case had Supreme Court potential. I know Rachel wanted the case if Anna ever lost it."

"What was Anna's reaction when the case was reassigned?" asked Beret.

Elizabeth laughed again. Was her laugh even more forced than before? Bill wondered. She said, "As always, Anna expressed her opinion in no uncertain terms. But it was no big deal. She always expresses her opinion. I guess she's entitled to since she's been in the office so long. Eleven years longer than Fred himself. She fears no one. She doesn't always stop to consider the consequences of her actions."

"What did she say?"

"Well, she was angry. Naturally she would be. Wouldn't you be if a younger attorney was given your big case before it reached the Supreme Court?"

"But what did she say?" Was Elizabeth trying to avoid the question? "That is, if you remember."

"Oh, I remember all right. Anna is hard to forget. OK, I'll tell you, although you must believe me that she didn't really mean it. You may as well hear it from me as from someone else. She said, 'I'll get even with that bitch if it's the last thing I ever do. She won't get away with her conniving.' "

Silence ensued. Eventually, Bill said, "I bet Fred didn't like that."

"Of course not. He always wants everything to go smoothly. This office is his domain. That's why he simply reassigned the case and tried to keep everything quiet. He gave Anna a couple of other important cases to try to mollify her. I think it worked. I haven't heard Anna say anything about the matter since."

The three had finished eating. They paid their bill, and left.

That afternoon, Bill visited Anna Heitz in her office. He had been meaning to anyway. One of his cases had an issue about whether two police officers had broken the law when they entered a house with a search warrant without first knocking on the door and announcing that they were about to search the house. Anna was supposed to be the AG expert on such "knock-notice" issues.

Anna invited him into her office, and they talked about Bill's problem at length. Anna was helpful. She knew the subject matter, and was able to analyze the issue on the spot and give Bill some useful cases. She seemed almost ebullient, as if she delighted in displaying her legal acumen. When they finished discussing the problem, Bill commented that it was really terrible what had happened to Rachel.

"I can't get over it, either," responded Anna. "She was such a sweet young thing. I can't imagine who would want to hurt her."

Bill did not know what he had expected her to say, but certainly not that. "How well did you know her?" he asked.

"I was practically her mentor. I reviewed most of her early briefs." Anna leaned forward and confided in Bill as if to a fellow conspirator. "Frankly, they weren't all that good. Artificial. Boring. More or less right on the law and the facts, but without pizazz. I worked with her closely and she improved dramatically. When I got done with her, she was ready for the big time."

"I understand it wasn't too long after she joined the office that she won her first Supreme Court case. I think it was the *Schultz* case?" Bill thought he had worked this into the conversation rather nicely. He looked at Anna closely, but, he hoped, without being too obvious. Did she suddenly become nervous?

"That's right, the *Schultz* case. She was quite young when she got it. Quite a plum for her. She did OK, but anyone could have won that case in that court. Still, I was happy for her." There was a short silence; Bill was trying to figure out how to probe further without appearing to. Fortunately, Anna came to his rescue. She spoke dispassionately. "I suppose you heard the case was originally mine." Bill replied that he had heard something like that. Anna stood up, walked toward the window overlooking Golden

Gate Avenue, and peered out. "I can talk about it now without anger. I had set the case up beautifully, and was all ready to take it from the Ninth Circuit to the Supreme Court. I was going to remake the law in a very favorable way. Then it was stolen from me."

Bill made some sympathetic comment, and Anna continued. "I would have won it in the Supreme Court myself if that damn DA hadn't screwed everything up. They just didn't understand what I was doing." She turned around to face Bill. "Rachel and I talked about the case many times while I still had it. She wound up doing exactly what I had told her I was going to do. She used my own arguments and claimed they were hers." This last comment was almost a shout. Then Anna calmed, and said in a subdued voice, "But I was happy for Rachel. You must believe that. If it had to go to someone else, I was glad it was her. She learned everything from me, and put it to good use in the Supreme Court. She deserved a big win, although it shouldn't have been at my expense. When you reach my age you start to wonder how many more victories you have left. The *Schultz* case may have been my last chance." She sat down again. Silence ensued.

Bill could not think of a subtle way to ask his next question, so he simply asked it. "Were you angry with Rachel when she got your case?"

Anna chuckled grimly. "Is that what you think? That maybe I killed her out of revenge?" Her demeanor became sad. Was it artificial, Bill wondered. "No, I was upset at the system, maybe at Fred and the DA, but I was not angry with Rachel. She was a sweet kid, and I always wished her only the best. I helped her in the Supreme Court more than anyone will ever know." Another silence. Then Anna added one more comment. "But I do know that Rachel directly criticized my work to Fred Olson. She told me exactly what she told him. Everything. She seemed to enjoy it." With that, it became apparent that Anna had said all she had to say.

Bill stood up and thanked Anna for her assistance with the knock-notice problem. She replied "anytime," and then said, "Take advantage of your opportunities when you have them. I didn't, and now look at me." Bill hesitated, could think of nothing to say, and left.

* * *

Beret also attended to her sleuthing duties that afternoon. She went to talk to her supervisor, Ramon Aguilar, about a Court of Appeal opinion she had received in one of her cases the day before. The court had reversed a rape conviction because the trial court had incorrectly instructed the jury on the defense that the victim had consented to sexual intercourse. The opinion was published, which meant that it could be cited as precedent in other cases.

Beret was appalled by the reversal, because the victim, in her early twenties, had been brutally beaten by the defendant and had to be hospitalized for two days. The girl was not a virgin, but Beret found it hard to believe any jury would have taken seriously the defendant's story that she had consented to what he did to her. A new trial eighteen months after the first would thoroughly traumatize the girl. At the first trial, the defense attorney cross-examined her aggressively in front of the jury for a day and a half, trying to imply that the whole incident was her fault. The defendant had sat smirking at the girl during the entire cross-examination, although he carefully positioned himself so that the jury could not see. When the trial was over, the girl swore that if she were ever raped again, she would not report it. And now a new trial would be necessary. Either that or the defendant, who had committed three prior rapes (information the jury never learned), would go free.

Beret needed to talk to Ramon about possibly petitioning the Court of Appeal for rehearing in the faint hope it might reconsider its decision, or, if necessary, petitioning the California Supreme Court for review. The Court receives so many petitions for review that it can only grant a comparative few. Only cases with important legal issues receive Supreme Court attention. Although this case was obviously important to the victim, Beret had to find a legal issue of statewide importance that she could credibly present to the Supreme Court. Ramon had extensive experience in this area. Beret hoped he might be able to help. Beret also, of course, hoped to talk to him about something else, about a certain telephone message she had received.

Ramon was in his office. As always, he had time to talk with her about her problem. Beret showed him the opinion. He, too, was disturbed by its implications, both for the case itself and as precedent in other cases. Ramon focused on the case as precedent in analyzing ways to present it to the Supreme Court. If they could show that the Court of Appeal opinion would set a dangerous precedent for other rape trials then maybe, just maybe, they could convince the Supreme Court to grant review. Beret had not yet argued a case in that court. That was her dream. The more she talked to Ramon, the more excited she became over her prospects.

After they had worked out a battle plan for her case, they started talking of other matters. With some guidance by Beret, the conversation turned to the topic of Rachel Brandwyn. She casually told Ramon, "I understand you had lunch with Rachel at the Palace Hotel the afternoon before she was killed."

He looked surprised. Or did he look frightened? Beret could not be sure. "Yes, that's, uh, right. How did you know?"

"A friend of mine mentioned that he happened to see the two of you there. It's a great place for lunch."

Ramon pondered a moment before he spoke again. When he did, he was visibly nervous. He unconsciously drummed his desk with his left hand. "Actually," he said, "we didn't have lunch, just drinks. Rachel ate a bag lunch in her office that day, as she often did. We've been good friends for a long time. That afternoon, I think it was about three o'clock, she told me she wanted to talk about a case, or maybe something else. I wanted to get out of the office, and suggested drinks at the Palace. We met there around five o'clock. She was late, so I had to wait for her."

This seemed odd to Beret. Go to the Palace to talk about a case? "What exactly did she want to talk about?" she asked.

Ramon pondered again. The drumming became quicker, then stopped. "I don't know. She never said."

"What do you mean, she never said?"

"Just that. I met her at the Palace, but she had apparently decided not to talk about it after all. The whole thing seemed strange to me." (*And to me, too,* thought Beret.) "I just assumed she was nervous about her Supreme Court argument the next day. You know how bizarre Rachel acted whenever she had an important court appearance." Beret did *not* know, but she nodded her head encouragingly. "We had a nice conversation, but not about her original concern. I had assumed it was one of her own cases. But later I got the impression it might have been something else. Other people's cases and problems interested her greatly. She told me once that she liked to keep her finger on the pulse of the office. She used to talk to me about all kinds of office matters and even her personal problems. But whatever was bothering her, we didn't talk about it."

"What *did* you talk about?"

"Mostly her argument the next day. I was once her supervisor. Rachel wanted to try out some of her ideas. They were generally excellent, and I said so. She often liked to use me as a sounding board." (Perhaps, thought Beret, but at the Palace?) "Anyway, as I said, we had a good time. Even when we talked business, I enjoyed her company."

"Were you and Rachel dating?"

Ramon looked at her warily. "No, of course not. I'm a happily married man with two kids. No way would I want to endanger that with an affair. It couldn't possibly be kept secret. Rachel and I were friends and colleagues, nothing more. I admired her mind. She often sought my advice. Like you did just now. I didn't get her pregnant if that's what you think."

Beret ignored this last comment. "Did you and Rachel leave the Palace together?"

What was the meaning of the sudden look Ramon gave her? Beret could not tell, but it was not just curiosity. "Why do you ask?" Why indeed? Before Beret could decide how to respond, Ramon continued. "Never mind. We all know you're investigating the murder. And, I might add, you're getting good at it. No, we did not leave together. Rachel wanted to stay behind to go over her opening comments. I had to leave. She had just started her second gin and tonic." He paused to think. Then he added, "Or was it a Vodka Collins? I don't remember for sure."

"Did you see any one else when you left?"

"Well, there were lots of people there. I didn't see anyone I know, if that's what you mean. I was in a hurry to get home by that time."

"I assume you left on friendly terms with Rachel?"

Ramon started drumming the desk again. He stared at Beret. "What did your friend tell you?" Again, before Beret could respond, he continued. "Yes, we parted on friendly terms. Well, not entirely friendly. When I told you I found her ideas about her oral argument generally excellent, I did not mean all of them. Some of her ideas were, frankly, lousy. She had learned too much nonsense from Anna Heitz to be completely sound. She wanted honest advice. I gave it to her. Some of her arguments would have been ridiculous in the Supreme Court. I said so. No in so many words, I was more gentle than that, but I said so."

Ramon started to stand up, decided not to, and sat again awkwardly. When Beret said nothing, he continued to talk. His voice was firm. "Rachel never could take criticism. I tried to be as diplomatic as possible, but she got a little upset with me for a while. She got over it, and everything was calm again before I had to leave. In fact, she asked me to stay longer so we could talk some more. She really seemed worried about something. Her Supreme Court argument, I guess."

"Was Rachel crying?"

Ramon sat quietly for several seconds as if trying to decide how to answer. Finally he spoke in a quiet voice. "No, of course not. She's a professional. We had some disagreements, but that was all. No big deal. As I said, we left on pretty good terms. As I was leaving, she said she would talk to me about that other matter after her Supreme Court argument."

"Did she say anything else about it?"

"No, nothing. As I said, we never got into it."

"Could it have concerned one of your own cases?"

Ramon thought for a moment. "I don't think so. No, I'm sure it didn't. Why should it? I usually don't discuss my own cases with others, and certainly not with Rachel." When Beret said nothing, he added, "I had the impression that she didn't want to talk about the problem until she could discuss it fully and in confidence. She didn't want to say anything she would regret later, so she chose to get her Supreme Court argument over with first." Ramon glanced nervously down. His voice was strangely subdued. "Then it was too late. So, no, I don't know anything about it. I can't help you at all." Ramon looked up, and added in a louder voice, "Except to assure you I did not shoot Rachel. I respected her too much."

With that, Ramon picked up a brief and started to read. Beret left his office pondering what, if any, significance this conversation had.

After he spoke with Anna Heitz, Bill met Trevor Watson by chance in the men's room. Out of the blue, Trevor asked, "When are you going to interrogate me about Rachel's sexual harassment claims?"

"Interrogate you?"

"Yes, you are obviously hot on the trail. Go ahead, if you want. We can talk about it now. I did nothing improper, although Rachel would never believe it. I asked her for a date a couple of times. I put a friendly arm around her shoulder to console her when she needed it. I hugged her when she won a case. I might have kidded her a few times. It was all innocent. She didn't have to make a federal case out of it."

Bill did not know quite what to say. He said the obvious. "I take it she told you about her complaints?"

Trevor laughed bitterly. "Oh, she told me all right. In detail. She told me everything that she told Fred Olson, and what she was going to tell the people in Sacramento if she didn't get her pound of flesh here. She enjoyed it. It was one of her favorite things in life—telling a person's supervisor how bad he was, then telling him exactly what she said."

Bill thought about this remark. "What did you say to her?"

"That was easy. I told her to go ahead and do whatever she wanted. Let's get it out in the open, I said. I was ready to do battle. I knew the truth would prevail." After a moment Trevor added sadly, "But it's too late now. Now it can never be resolved. I can never be vindicated."

Bill and Trevor left the men's room and walked in different directions down the long hallway. Bill had to agree that now Trevor could never be vindicated. But, he thought to himself, the charges could also never be proven true.

Chapter 12

The next night was sleepless for a certain individual. The person lay in bed for a long time, staring at the ceiling that could not be seen in the dark. The person had much to contemplate, all the events of recent days. During the day, the person was confident, and could put on a good public face, but during the night doubts were felt, and fears, sometimes even terror. Even though the person knew there was no reason, absolutely no reason, for these doubts and fears and terrors. Knowing and feeling can be quite different.

Shooting Rachel Brandwyn had, unfortunately, been necessary. The person did not regret doing what was necessary, but did regret the necessity. If only . . . if only . . . *But it couldn't be helped, it wasn't my fault.* The thought was consoling. *She didn't have to . . .* The person tried to stop thinking of the killing, but could not. A full hour passed with the person staring at the unseen ceiling. If only . . .

And now came the gradual but great fear that further action might be necessary. *I thought that killing Rachel would solve everything. What else will I have to do before everything is fine?* The person did not shrink from the idea of again doing what was necessary, but hoped that nothing more would be necessary. Just as the person had hoped—in vain, as it turned out—that the first killing would not be necessary.

At least, thought the person, the first killing was easy. The weapon was at hand, and many people were connected to that weapon. Shooting her was quick and effective. The person regretted the necessity, truly regretted the necessity, but had to admit to some pride at how well the challenge was met. To do what is necessary, to do it with clinical dispatch, to leave behind no clue, that was the mark of an efficient person. *And, after all, was it my fault that the necessity arose? No! Not at all. I was not to blame. I tried to avoid having to kill, and will always try to avoid having to kill. Killing was never my intention. It was Rachel's fault. All her fault. If only . . . But stop! These thoughts do no good. They are debilitating. I must always try to avoid the necessity,* the person thought, *but if it comes—through no fault of my own—I must calmly and without regret again do what is necessary. The act was not my fault, and I am not responsible.*

If that is the case, why can't I sleep? I can. It's only tonight that I can't. It will pass. Won't it? Of course it will. I'm just worried because now I know it might be necessary again. Too much is happening. What does it mean? If it's necessary again, I will again do what is necessary. They say it's easier the second time. I must admit it was surprisingly easy the first time. But how would I do it next time? I can't use the same weapon. I wouldn't want to even if I could. I have too much pride to repeat myself. I want to be versatile. If it's necessary. Will it be necessary? I don't know. I hope not. I don't want to kill again. Do I?

The ceiling. Would the person be staring at the ceiling by the hour if the killing had not been necessary? No, sleepless nights had never come before. Would they come again? *I mustn't think about that. Too much thought might prevent efficiently doing what is necessary if it should again become necessary. Thought mustn't paralyze me. If necessary, I must do it again.* But how to do it as efficiently and effectively as before? It will be more difficult; everyone will be on guard. On the other hand, I now have experience. *Yes,* thought the person. *If it's necessary, I can do it again. But only if it's necessary. It might never again be necessary.*

This last thought was comforting. After staring at the ceiling until nearly the break of day, the person finally fell asleep. The next day, and the days after that, would be business as usual.

Chapter 13

Trial in the *Morton* case, whose exhibits were used to murder Rachel Brandwyn, was postponed for the third time, and was now scheduled to start in four weeks. Beret Holmes had been assigned to assist Martin Granowski, but so far had done nothing. Granowski himself did not solicit her help; if anything, he discouraged it. Beret sensed that he resented (or feared?) her involvement.

The day after her conversation with Ramon Aguilar, Beret decided the time had come to get going in *Morton*, if only to become acquainted with its facts and issues. She insisted that Granowski at least show her the files and documentary exhibits, although not the physical exhibits such as the gun and silencer, which were now safely locked away. He showed her the four boxes containing the police reports, the autopsy reports, the criminalistics reports, the expert-witness reports, and the massive amount of other paper that crimes of this magnitude inevitably generate. The boxes were kept in a large office reserved for records in important cases. Beret, inexperienced in trial matters, found the files intimidating in their size, fascinating in their content.

Morton had murdered three persons on three different occasions. Each victim was a male hitchhiker found on the side of the road with a bullet in the back of the head, hands tied behind the back, and with no wallet or other valuables. There was no evidence of a sexual motive. The police received anonymous tips that Morton had bragged about the crimes, and the investigation soon centered on him. Finally, a friend of Morton came forward in person. Morton had told the friend he was the killer; the friend was able to provide information about the killings that the police already knew but had not yet made public. The police obtained a search warrant. The murder weapon was found in Morton's Chevy van. The silencer was attached; the media seized on this to give Morton the nickname, the Silencer Killer. Ballistics analysis proved that the gun had fired the bullet that killed all three victims. Morton had bought the gun about two months before the first killing. How he obtained the silencer was never ascertained. The wallet of one of the victims was found in a drawer of a nightstand next to Morton's bed. Further investigation established that the defendant had driven the van in the area of each killing around the time of the killing.

A battery of psychiatrists and psychologists had examined Morton. As always, the results were wildly conflicting, although each expert agreed that Morton was at least neurotic. One psychiatrist concluded that he was in a dissociative state at the time of the killings, and was therefore not responsible for his actions. Another concluded that Morton had a schizotypal personality disorder which approached a psychosis, and therefore he was not responsible for his actions. A third was of the opinion that when Morton attached the silencer to the .357 magnum and shot the victims in the head, he did not intend to harm them, but merely wanted to get their attention. One psychologist blamed the crimes on a diet that consisted of too much red meat, and not enough poultry, seafood, or broccoli.

Morton had not pleaded insanity, but Granowski anticipated the defense would claim that because of these mental disorders, Morton was only guilty of involuntary manslaughter. Since it would be difficult for Morton to claim he was not the killer, the trial would undoubtedly revolve around expert testimony. Only twice before had Granowski had a case involving psychiatric evidence; never one as complex as this. He had to immerse himself in the subject to prepare for trial. Such matters were, of course, utterly new to Beret.

Before she knew it, Beret had spent an entire afternoon looking through the materials. It was quite an introduction to the wonderful world of forensic psychiatry. The reports were long, detailed, and full of technical jargon. By the time Beret finished perusing them, she had read much about dissociation, paranoid schizophrenia, and other mental diagnoses, although she was not sure she knew any more than when she had started.

Beret also found several pages of handwritten notes in a style different from Granowski's. Probably Rachel Brandwyn's writing. The writing was sloppy, obviously intended only for the writer's own use. Beret could read little of it, but there were a number of references to Granowski. Some appeared to criticize him for his lack of preparation regarding the psychiatric issues. One time, Rachel wrote in big print, "When is he going to prepare properly!?!?" Another time, she wrote, "Granowski is blowing it! When is he going to get started!?" Both comments were underlined, the second with two lines.

At five-thirty that afternoon, while Beret was concentrating on deciphering the handwriting, she was interrupted by a voice from the doorway. "How's it going?"

Startled, Beret looked up at Granowski's towering figure. Why did she suddenly feel as if she had been caught doing something she should not have been doing? Rather guiltily she responded, "Fine, I guess. This psychiatric mumbo-jumbo is all a bit beyond me."

Granowski laughed and entered the office. "Me, too," he said as he sat on a nearby desk.

"What do you mean, 'Me, too?' "

"Just what I said. You don't expect me to understand all that stuff. I'm an attorney, not a doctor."

Beret peered at Granowski. He did not appear to be joking. At least he was not smiling. "But how are you going to try the case if you don't understand it?"

"Oh, I understand it well enough. I know the facts of the case, and can prove exactly what Morton did. What more is necessary?"

Beret was not sure how serious he was. "Well," she said tentatively, "how about working on the psychiatric testimony? It looks like the real trial question will be Morton's state of mind. You've got to be able to cross-examine the defense shrinks and present your own evidence. Don't you?"

"Do I? No juror is going to take that stuff seriously in this case. Morton obviously knew what he was doing when he selected and killed his victims. No shrink is going to convince twelve citizens good and true anything different. You yourself said the so-called expert opinions are all mumbo-jumbo. I'll be able to poke fun at them when the time comes."

"You mean at trial?" Beret had heard it was sometimes hard to tell when Granowski was kidding and when he was serious. She had always been taught that the crucial thing before trial was preparation, more preparation, and then more preparation. This seemed especially true in a case that would be a war of so-called experts. How could Granowski try the case without a massive amount of preparation? Or was he just teasing her? Rachel had certainly seemed concerned about Granowski's performance. Maybe she also didn't know if he was serious.

"Sure, I'll just wing it."

Beret still could not tell if Granowski was teasing, so she simply asked, "Are you serious?"

Granowski laughed. "Not entirely. I'm working harder on this case than people give me credit for. But it's fun teasing you people. It used to make Rachel furious. She took what I said seriously; she always took everything seriously. I liked to yank her chain. Of course, when I did, I had to listen to long lectures on the proper method for a respectable trial attorney to prepare for trial. To her, I was incorrigible. I loved bugging her about it."

Granowski pointed to Rachel's handwritten notes. "Are you trying to decipher her writing? It's great, isn't it?"

Involuntarily, Beret returned the notes to the box. Why did she feel she had to conceal her interest in them? As Rachel's successor on the case, it was natural that she would be interested in what Rachel had done. And yet, Beret instinctively suspected that Granowski disapproved of her examining those notes. "I was just looking at them. I can't read most of them. I'm sure they aren't important."

"I couldn't read them, either, although I certainly tried." Granowski added in a firm voice, "I'm also sure they aren't important. Rachel thought everything she did was important, but she was usually wrong. She took this psychology stuff too seriously; she thought I should, too. She actually wanted me to learn all about these disorders and the rest of the nonsense."

"Well," Beret said tentatively. "It is a thought." *Is he serious, or is he still teasing me?* she wondered. He seemed serious, but there might have been a twinkle in his eye as he spoke. "I guess different people prepare for trial in different ways. Who am I to judge?"

"Who indeed?" said Granowski. "Who, indeed, was Rachel to judge? She was always meddling even when she didn't know what she was doing."

Beret could see that the last sentence was spoken in all seriousness. The word "meddling" again. How significant was it? "I don't think she was meddling. She was just trying to help you. After all, she was also assigned to the case."

"You mean, she assigned herself. She could always manipulate Fred Olson to get whatever she wanted. She complained to Fred that I wasn't doing the job properly, and got him to assign her to work with me. Her ultimate goal was to take over this case completely and to get me off it. That's why she wrote the memo."

"What memo?"

"You don't know yet? Maybe it's not in the file." He sat quietly for a moment, as if debating whether to continue. "I may as well tell you myself, because I'm sure you'll learn about it eventually in your investigation."

"What investigation?"

Granowski looked at her without a trace of a smile. "Your murder investigation. Don't worry, I know you and Bill Kelly are trying to solve it. That's the reason you asked to work on this case. You don't know the first thing about either trial work or the world of shrinks. How could you possibly be of any help?"

"Well, I . . . well, I could learn. How else am I supposed to get my start? Believe me, I didn't ask for this assignment, although I wasn't sorry to get it. I thought you could teach me something, and I could at least help you with the legal issues."

"Everyone thinks I can't handle this case alone," said Granowski bitterly. "Well, I can. And I will." A pause. Beret could not think of anything to say. Granowski continued. "But to get back to your earlier question, Rachel told me she wrote a memo to Olson, or maybe to the people in Sacramento, I don't know. And I don't care. I never saw it, but I know she criticized me. She told me all about it; she enjoyed tormenting me with all the vicious things she was saying about me. She said I couldn't handle the case and that if I were kept on it, we would lose it. It was all nonsense."

"Where is the memo now?"

Granowski got off the desk, and looked into one of the boxes. "I don't know. I assume it's in there with the rest of her notes. She used it to threaten me. She said she wouldn't send it if she didn't have to, if I did what she wanted me to do to get ready for trial. I considered it simple blackmail, and told her so. I said it was my case, that I knew what I was doing, and that she couldn't force me to do what she wanted." Granowski chuckled. "It didn't sit well with her, let me tell you. She was used to getting her way. She stormed out of my office, but not before repeating that she would send the memo if I didn't 'shape up.' "

"When did this happen?"

"A couple of days before Rachel died—before she was murdered. That's bad timing for me, isn't it? It gives me a motive. You think I killed her to keep her quiet, don't you?" Silence. "Well, rest assured I didn't. Her silly threats weren't worth it. Everyone knows I'm a first-rate trial lawyer; no one would take Rachel's silly blabbering seriously. She always had a vendetta against me; I can't imagine why. I never had any reason to dislike her personally, nor she me. Besides, it would be pretty silly for me to use the same weapon Morton used, wouldn't it?" Granowski looked at his watch. "And now, I have to go home. I have to get ready for a hot date tonight. Unlike Trevor Watson, I'm not just a lot of talk. Much as I am enjoying this pleasant conversation, I don't want to be late." Granowski stepped out of the office. Then he turned around and commented over his shoulder, "I hope I have given you plenty to report to your police inspectors."

Before Beret could respond, Granowski began walking down the hall. He did not turn around again. Beret spent the next half hour looking through the boxes for Rachel's memorandum. It was not there. Beret gave up the search, and left for the night. She knew another source to check for the memorandum. Jeff Hines would know where it was if anyone did.

The next morning, Beret and Bill spoke with Hines. Hines said that he had typed a memorandum for Rachel about the *Morton* case, although he did not remember its contents. He did not think it had ever been sent. "She told me she would send it only if it became necessary," he explained. He typed the memorandum a few days before she died; he could not remember the exact date. When asked whether a copy of the memorandum existed, he said there was one in Rachel's file cabinet.

Hines led the other two into Rachel's office and, after some searching, removed a manila folder. He handed Bill a two-page document labeled "draft." Like the sexual harassment memorandum, this was directed to the chief of the criminal division in Sacramento. The subject was *"People v. Morton."* This is what it said:

"I have been assigned to assist Deputy Attorney General Martin Granowski in the prosecution of the above-referenced case. It is a triple murder, and the trial promises to concentrate on expert testimony concerning the defendant's state of mind during the homicides. The defense has gathered a battery of psychiatrists, psychologists, and other experts to support its claim that the defendant was not responsible for any of his actions.

"I write to express my serious, and ever-growing concerns over the actions, or I might more precisely say *in*actions, of Mr. Granowski in preparing for trial.

"Mr. Granowski has had very little experience with expert mental evidence of this nature. One would expect a person with so little experience in such a complex field to spend considerable time studying, and otherwise preparing himself for the awesome task of presenting the evidence and cross-examining the defense witnesses. But no. As far as I can determine, Mr. Granowski has done little to prepare, and intends to do even less in the future.

"Mr. Granowski has not hired any experts of his own, nor has he personally spoken with any of the court-appointed experts or possible defense experts. I find this appalling. This is a triple murder with horrifying details. Nevertheless, without care, we could lose this case. I do not mean the jury might actually find the defendant not guilty, but it might find him guilty only of manslaughter. We have got to prepare to confront the defense evidence, and we have not done so.

"I have spoken with Mr. Granowski about my concerns several times, but to no avail. He just laughs, and tells me not to worry, that he will think of something when the time comes. Again, this is appalling. This case requires the most careful attention and the highest caliber attorney the office of the attorney general can provide, not some seat-of-the-pants approach by a hotshot cowboy who does not know what he is doing, and cares even less.

"I have expressed these concerns to Fred Olson, but he only says he is confident that Mr. Granowski does know what he is doing. I therefore am turning to you out of desperation. I urge you to do everything you can to assure that this case is properly prosecuted, including, if need be, removing Mr. Granowski from the case.

"If Mr. Granowski is removed, an attorney with substantial experience and ability should be assigned to replace him. I express no opinion as to who that person should be, but if I should be chosen, I obviously would be proud, willing, and able to step in without any loss in time or effort."

The draft was unsigned, and indicated that copies were to go to Fred Olson and Granowski. After Bill and Beret finished reading it, Hines made a copy.

"Did Olson and Granowski know about this memo?" asked Beret.

"I don't know" was Hines's response. "Rachel didn't say anything about it. I assume they did know. As I said before, Rachel never hid what she was doing. It was no secret. In fact, Michelle Hong asked me about it the day before Rachel died. If *she* knew about it, everyone did. Michelle usually did not know much office gossip."

When Bill and Beret left Hines, they had much to talk about. Later that day, the two, with some reluctance, reported this development to Inspector Tarkov. The inspector was effusive in his praise of their sleuthing abilities. He also warned them to be careful, that they were confronting a dangerous killer.

Chapter 14

Bill and Beret were scheduled to visit San Quentin on Thursday. Beret picked Bill up at his home in Oakland, and they drove over the Richmond-San Rafael Bridge toward Marin County. Beret was struck by how deceptively beautiful the cream-colored prison towers looked from a distance. The prison was situated on what would have been exclusive beachfront property but for the minor fact that it was a maximum security prison housing some of the most violent criminals in the state.

The two checked in at the administration building just outside the actual prison walls at eight-thirty in the morning, and met the warden. The warden commented that members of the prison litigation unit came regularly to the prison on business; less often, the appellate lawyers "who see to it that our tenants stay here. . . . If you people would lose more cases," he joked, "fewer people would be sent to prison, and our overcrowding problem wouldn't be so serious." Bill and Beret laughed, and promised to try to do something about it.

"Because we're overcrowded," the warden added more somberly, "and because we have too many murderers and other prisoners who like to file lawsuits against us, the AG's prison litigation lawyers have a lot of business. We have to put up with their presence here all the time. It seems like your Brian Howarth practically lives here. I think he's here today, in fact. You might see him on your tour." With that, the warden introduced the two to Sergeant Lopez, who would be their guide, and sent them on their way.

Before they passed through the main gate, Sergeant Lopez explained to them the prison's no-hostage policy. If there was a riot or other incident, and they were taken hostage by the inmates, it was prison policy not to make concessions for their release. The correctional officers would do all they could to rescue them unharmed, but they would not yield to any demands. Bill and Beret had been told about the policy in advance, but it was sobering to review it while they were standing in front of the actual prison walls. It was one thing to hear it in the comfort of one's own office; it was quite different to hear it in the shadow of the tall watch towers. Bill and Beret said they understood the policy and they agreed to it, but with a little less assurance than before. "Don't worry about it," Sergeant Lopez reassured them with a grin. "This is a very secure prison. Why, we haven't lost a deputy attorney general in years." They laughed. She added, "Well, at least not in several months."

On that note, the three entered the main gate. Bill and Beret showed their attorney general identification, signed in, had their hands stamped, and passed through the self-locking doors. Inside, they were met by an incongruous sight: a courtyard with a well-maintained garden. An inmate, obviously one of the gardeners, approached Sergeant Lopez and conversed with her about the garden. He wanted her opinion about what kind of flowers he should plant in one corner of the courtyard. They decided on golden yellow marigolds with blue salvia. She complimented the inmate on the job he was doing in the courtyard, and the three continued the tour.

Sergeant Lopez commented that the inmate—Joe—always liked to plant blue-and-gold flowers, the colors of the University of California Golden Bears. "He claims to be an alumnus of the school," she laughed, "but I suspect the real reason is that the warden here graduated from Cal. Joe thinks that if he plants blue-and-gold flowers, he'll receive more time off for good behavior."

Bill asked what the inmate did to be in San Quentin. "I don't know," she replied, "and I don't care. I try not to find out why they're here. I'm only interested in how they behave inside these walls. Joe is a model prisoner, and a fine gardener. He takes pride in the courtyard. That's all I want to know. I want to relate to him on that basis, and on that basis alone."

When they left the courtyard and entered the buildings, it became obvious that they were inside a prison. The living units consisted of five tiers of cells, one on top of the other. Each tier contained a long row of cells, each cell about forty-eight square feet. Many of the cells housed two inmates, although most were empty during the day. The cell blocks were noisy, dirty, and cluttered with litter. Sergeant Lopez explained that they tried to clean the blocks regularly, but they seemed to get dirty again instantly. The occupants were not always fastidiously neat. Correctional officers with rifles were visible on high platforms overlooking the blocks. Bill once referred to them as prison guards. Sergeant Lopez explained gently but firmly that they were correctional officers, not guards.

They got the full tour. Inmates were milling about in various places. Some were working at their assigned jobs. Others were playing basketball or other sports. Many were working out with weights. Some were playing chess or bridge or other card games. Many more were simply hanging out passing the time. Bill and Beret saw the exercise yards, the kitchens, the mess halls, even the large room where the laundry was done by inmate labor. They found particularly interesting the prison furniture factory, where much of the state's office furniture was built, also with inmate labor. Both Bill and Beret recognized at a glance where their office desk and chairs had come from. The chief medical officer gave them a tour of the hospital. Routine medical care was provided and some kinds of minor surgical procedures were performed inside the walls. The psychiatric unit was nearby.

They had lunch at a cafeteria operated by inmates. The food was surprisingly good, although neither Bill nor Beret had much of an appetite. Walking through a crowded, noisy prison filled with convicted felons, mostly violent, was stressful for Bill and Beret. Both tried to conceal their unease, but could not shake it. After lunch, they continued the tour.

So far, they had only seen the portions of the prison occupied by the general population of inmates—those who were not special security risks. Now they were going to be shown some of the higher security, or "lockup," units containing the most violent of the violent inmates. They saw, but did not actually enter, death row, where condemned inmates were housed. Then they visited the "adjustment center," which housed the most dangerous inmates, those who had assaulted inmates and staff in the past, often fatally. This was the most maximum security portion of the maximum security part of the maximum security prison. Sergeant Lopez explained that the inmates here would seize any opportunity to assault anybody within reach with any weapon available. Security had to be correspondingly tight. It was. The inmates could do

virtually nothing without intense scrutiny and maximum re-
straints. Their mealtimes, showers, and exercise periods were
closely monitored.

Near the adjustment center was a general purpose cell, slightly
larger than the others, where the inmates could receive counsel-
ing by the psychiatric staff or by a chaplain. The cell was sometimes used for interviews. Bill and Beret saw Brian Howarth inside the cell talking with two inmates. Howarth saw them, waved,
and indicated they should wait for him. "I'm almost done in
here," he said. Sergeant Lopez said she had business in the adjustment center, and left them to wait for Howarth.

A few minutes later, Howarth emerged from the cell. The two
inmates were returned to their cells under close guard. Howarth
approached Bill and Beret and shook their hands, saying, "Welcome to San Quentin-by-the-Bay. What brings you here? Hoping
to buy a home with an ocean view overlooking San Francisco?"

"No, just a simple tour," replied Bill. "I'm working on the
Wakefield and *Robinson* case—you know, the one about smuggling crack into the prison. Tom Atkins and Fred Olson thought
that since I have it, I should tour San Quentin to get a better feel
for what it's about. Beret came along for the ride."

"I remember that case. Rachel Brandwyn had it first, didn't
she? It's pretty complicated for a beginner like you, isn't it?"
Howarth was laughing.

"Atkins was desperate. I didn't run away fast enough when he
suggested giving it to me. But it's not too bad. Atkins has been
helpful. He sure knows everything there is to know about what is
a dirk or dagger. I enjoy the challenge."

The three entered the interview cell. There was more room
inside to talk, although not much more. It was also a bit quieter,
but again not much. Bill and Beret laughed uneasily, and commented that although San Quentin was fine to visit, they certainly
would not want to live there. Howarth agreed.

"Of course," he added, "we in the prison litigation unit visit so
often that we actually begin to feel at ease inside the walls. It can
be intimidating the first time, but after a while you get used to it.
You even get used to the noise. I like coming here. It gets me out
of the office."

"What are you doing today?" asked Beret.

"Oh, just the usual. Interviewing possible witnesses in the *Rawlings* case."

"That's the case involving conditions in the adjustment center?" Bill asked.

"Yes. Murderers who have attacked other inmates and prison guards don't like the tight security. They want to be able to kill more people. So they sue in federal court. It's ridiculous. But the judge takes it seriously, so I have to."

"You're talking to the witnesses for the plaintiffs?"

"Oh, no, that's what depositions are for. Today I'm lining up witnesses for our side. Inmates who say it's not all that bad. Inmates on our side can be very effective."

Beret looked skeptically at the cells about her. "I bet they are effective," she said. "Do you actually find prisoners willing to help your side? It's hard to imagine an inmate not wanting Rawlings to win his case."

Howarth smiled enigmatically. "Normally, it is hard to find inmates to testify for us. But I'm a genius. You have to realize the inmates don't all see it as a 'them' versus 'us' situation. Plenty of them hate Rawlings, who goes out of his way to make enemies. He was a child molester; even murderers despise child molesters. So there are prisoners who will do anything to hurt him, even if it hurts themselves. I find those people. That's how I win cases when others in the prison litigation unit lose them." He laughed. "That's why my good buddy, Tom Oldfield, puts up with me, and lets me come and go as often as I want. San Quentin is practically my second home."

Almost simultaneously, Bill and Beret said that he could have it, that they preferred their nice, safe offices in San Francisco. "Although," Bill added, "it was interesting to see that so much of the work is done by inmates. I thought the gardens by the main entrance were beautiful."

"Yes, Joe does good work. Did you know that he's a nephew of Anna Heitz?" They did not. "He majored in agricultural horticulture, or something like that, at Cal. Then went to law school. Was in his second year when he killed his roommate. Shot him. Apparently out of jealousy because the roommate got better grades. He later claimed the roommate stole one of his papers on the law of consumer protection and used it as his own."

Bill and Beret looked at each other in surprise. The similarity between that crime and Anna Heitz's feelings toward Rachel was striking. Bill asked, "Was Anna involved in the case at all?"

"Not in the crime, certainly. But I think she did testify as a defense witness. I don't remember why." Howarth stood, and placed his hands on the cell bars. "Now I remember. She testified in support of Joe's claim that the victim had stolen the paper. She said she had been helping Joe write it, and so she could identify it. I could never figure out how that was supposed to be a defense to murder. Apparently the jury couldn't, either. It convicted him of second-degree murder. The whole affair was obviously very embarrassing to Anna. She has never talked about it. She was very close to Joe."

The three talked some more, then Howarth said he had to interview four more inmates, and he had to get going. Upon being assured that Bill and Beret were being "treated right," he sent them on their way. They located Sergeant Lopez, and their tour continued.

Bill wanted to see the areas involved in the *Wakefield* and *Robinson* case. Accordingly, they toured the visiting area. Many inmates were visiting with wives, parents, friends, children, in one case a uniformed soldier. Sergeant Lopez explained that the drugs were smuggled to Wakefield and Robinson in the visiting room, and probably to others, although that could not be proven. "Those two were the most careless, so they got caught. No one knows the full extent of the conspiracy. We also don't know exactly how it was done, although it must have been through this room. As you can see, security here is tight, but it's often so crowded and hectic that it can't be perfect. We try to prevent smuggling, but it's impossible to keep out all of the drugs. There are legal limits on how closely we can search visitors. Someone who knows what he is doing can slip things past us. Last week, for example, some heroin was stashed inside a diaper."

Robinson and Wakefield had shared a cell on the third tier of West Block, a housing unit for the general population. Sergeant Lopez showed the cell to her visitors. No one was inside at the moment, but it exhibited obvious signs of occupancy, and was cluttered with possessions. The inevitable color television set was in one corner, visible from each of the two bunk beds. The stain-less-steel toilet and tiny washbasin were in the opposite corner. The current occupants were away at their jobs, one in the laundry room, and one as a cook in the main kitchen. Sergeant Lopez said that the drugs had been found inside both mattresses, along with documentation incriminating the occupants. "Some money was also found, although not much."

As the three started to walk down the tier to leave, they noticed the inmate in the next cell. It was Joe, the gardener. He had finished his gardening duties, and was watching a soap opera on television. Joe recognized the visitors. "I couldn't help overhearing your conversation," he told them. "Are you from the attorney general's office?"

Normally, Bill and Beret would be reluctant to reveal to a prisoner inside a maximum security prison that they were criminal prosecutors. But Howarth's information made them more at ease. They admitted their identity. Upon further questioning, Bill said that yes, he was working on the *Wakefield* and *Robinson* case. Joe said that was good, that those two deserved whatever they got. He then changed the subject. "Do you guys know an attorney by the name of Anna Heitz? She's in your office." They said they did know her, and that she was a good lawyer.

"She's my aunt, you know." Not wanting Joe to know that they had heard about him, Bill and Beret feigned surprise. "She was the one who convinced me to go to law school. Biggest mistake I ever made. I couldn't handle the pressure, and now look at me. As Anna said at the time, if I had to kill someone, I should have made sure I got away with it." Joe smiled at the memory. "I told her that the advice was a bit late. But she helped me in my defense. I give her credit for that. Obviously, as a prosecutor herself, she couldn't be my defense lawyer. But she had a lot of good ideas which my lawyer used. She also testified on my behalf, although it didn't do much good. I was convicted." Joe looked around his cell, and said wryly, "I guess that's what happens when you shoot someone six times. At least I only got second-degree murder, not first degree. I think I have Anna to thank for that."

"We'll tell Anna you said that when we see her," Beret told him.

"Do that," Joe responded. "And while you're at it, tell her to visit me more often. She used to come here for visits quite often. I really looked forward to them. They helped keep me on an even keel. But now she hasn't come for several months." After a moment, he added mournfully, "I guess she's just busy. Like every-body else I used to know."

The two said they would talk to Anna. Then they walked on. The grand tour was over. Sergeant Lopez led Bill and Beret back through the main gate to the administration building. They said farewell to their guide, and returned to Beret's car. After passing through the last checkpoint, where the officer looked into the trunk of the car to make sure no inmate had secreted himself inside, the two were on their way back across the bridge to the East Bay. They could not help but reflect on how easy it was for them to leave San Quentin and return to their homes, and how impossible for most of those they had left behind.

Chapter 15

Friday and Saturday were uneventful. During the week, Bill ran around Lake Merritt a couple of times, once twice around, trying to get ready for Sunday. Sunday was the Bay-to-Breakers race. As Bill trained, he often wondered about Beret. Was she a good runner?

She was. But Bill would not learn for sure until well after the race had officially started.

Early on the morning of the race, Bill drove to Beret's house. From there they took the bus to the foot of Howard Street, where the race was to start. They arrived around 7:15 A.M., a full forty-five minutes before the scheduled 8:00 A.M. start. But the area was already jammed with people. All kinds of people, boys and girls, men and women, the young, the elderly, all imaginable ethnic groups, even handicapped runners in wheelchairs. There was at least one blind woman running with a friend. Many were in bizarre costumes. Bill and Beret could not get near the starting line, but had to wait about two blocks from the front. Within a few minutes of their arrival, they were no longer at the rear of the pack, but somewhere in the middle.

While they waited in cool but not cold weather, Bill had plenty of time to reflect on why in hell he was there. He was not a serious runner, and certainly had never intended to run the width of San Francisco alongside a hundred thousand fanatics. The mass of people was incredible. Would they survive the stampede when the race began? Would *he* survive the infamous San Francisco hills? If he finished the race, would he be in last place? Would he care? Why was he doing this?

Beret was cool about the whole thing. She had run the race before and knew it was not that hard. But she thoroughly enjoyed Bill's feelings of uncertainty, feelings she also had experienced her first time. She said and did nothing to assuage Bill's worries. Indeed, she stressed her agonies of the past.

As 8:00 A.M. approached, the excitement increased. Fathers running with their children were encouraging the children, or, sometimes, the children were encouraging the father. Those in costume were making last-minute inspections hoping that the costume would survive twelve kilometers of running. Those tied together as centipedes discussed strategy one last time. Bill and Beret saw the centipede from the University of California at Davis, his law-school alma mater and the team that usually won the centipede competition.

Beret impulsively gave Bill a kiss for good luck. The press of the crowd, intense and yet, at the same time, gentle, deterred him from returning the kiss as he would have liked. In the distance, a politician, or would-be politician, was exhorting those who would listen to *do* something—exactly what was unclear. The roar of the crowd competed perversely with the hush of anticipation.

The race started promptly at eight o'clock. Given the press of people who had been waiting too long as it was, it could not have started any later. The seeded runners in the front poured down Howard Street at a world-class pace. Bill and Beret never saw them. The winner would cross the finish line before the last of the stragglers crossed the starting line. The mass of ordinary runners surged forward a few feet. But only a few feet. Most then came to a grinding halt, the way cars waiting in line when the light finally turns green move a short distance and then have to stop and wait for those in front of them. As the ones nearest the starting line began to move, those behind followed.

It was almost two minutes before Bill and Beret could move, a full five minutes before they crossed the starting line. They ran under an overpass filled with spectators encouraging the runners on. Actually, they did not exactly run at this point, more like run in place, with sporadic forward movements. It was that crowded. Bill, who had carefully checked his watch to note when he had crossed the starting line, decided there was no point in timing himself. They were going too slow. This was merely a fun run. He might as well enjoy the costumes, he was not going anywhere fast. He gazed at a runner dressed as the Little Mermaid who was making her way past him. How did she manage to run in that outfit?

Gradually, as they moved down Howard Street, they were able to run more and more freely. But they were far from clear of fellow runners. Derelicts drinking wine from a bottle in a paper bag would stare at the passing horde in amazement, not trusting what they thought they saw. Drinking had sometimes made them see strange sights, but never anything like this.

Then the pack turned onto Hayes Street, leading to the infamous hellish Hayes Street Hill that coursed sharply uphill for several blocks. Bill was not tired, for he had yet hardly been able to run above a fast walk. But the sight was sobering. He could see ahead for a few level blocks, and then all the way to the top of the hill. And all he could see in front of him was a mass of churning, undulating humanity. There were so many runners so close together that not a square inch of pavement was visible all the way to the top of the hill. Bill could only see thousands upon thousands of runners, waves of them, almost like one long, vibrating snake. *My God,* thought Bill. *Are we at the very back of the pack?*

Almost as if she had read his thoughts, Beret shouted above the din, "Don't worry. There's that many behind us. When we get to the top of the hill, turn around and look back." By the time they reached the foot of the hill, they were close to being able to run freely.

Finally, they reached the top, just as Bill reached the end of his breath. As Beret had suggested, Bill turned around to look back. He did it for two reasons. First, the reason Beret had suggested, to see if anyone was behind him. Second, and possibly more important, to give him an excuse to slow down and catch his breath. Would it be too obvious if he pretended to trip and fall down?

When he turned around, he saw an equally large mass of churning, undulating humanity behind him. All the way back to the turn onto Howard Street, no square inch of pavement could be seen in this direction, either. Bill might not have been in the front of the pack, but, by God, he was not in the rear, either. The sight inspired him to renewed vigor, and he spurted forward. The fact that the course turned downhill also helped.

Beret had told him that when they reached the top of the hill, the worst would be over. She was right. Running downhill, or even on the level, was a whole lot easier than going uphill. Bill was able to catch his breath and even enjoy glimpses of the sights as the course reached the Panhandle leading to Golden Gate Park.

Beret was running smoothly, confidently, about ten feet in front of Bill. He was determined to keep her there, and not lose contact. He ran on, gamely keeping her within striking distance. Through the Panhandle and into the beautiful park, the course was level or slightly downhill. The cool temperature and thin veneer of clouds made conditions perfect. Beret turned around, saw that Bill was struggling, and slowed slightly. He caught up to her.

A centipede of runners wearing dark business suits, running shoes, and powdered wigs, and carrying briefcases—probably lawyers—passed in front of them. Then they saw two people they knew: Thomas Atkins and Michelle Hong, running hand in hand. "Do you see what I see?" Beret asked Bill. Bill did. Both remembered seeing the same two at the Cambodian restaurant. And now again today. At the office they were never together. Although Beret and Bill told themselves that such thoughts were beneath them neither could resist speculating on what was going on— were Michelle and Tom an item? "What's going on?" Both spoke at the same time, Bill with more difficulty than Beret because of the running. They looked at each other and laughed. Both were curious; why not admit it?

Tom Atkins looked their way. He seemed surprised, and then embarrassed. When he realized that Bill and Beret were looking at them, he suddenly let go of Michelle's hand. "I didn't know you were runners!" he shouted.

"Beret's the runner," Bill gasped. "I thought I was, but now I'm not so sure." He noticed that Michelle tried to take hold of Tom's hand, but Tom deftly pulled it away. The four ran in tandem for a while through the park. Even that late in the race, it was still crowded. Conversation was difficult. None was attempted, as they concentrated on not slowing down as the finish line approached. At least Bill was working hard on not slowing down. Beret, it seemed to him, was only working hard on not moving too far ahead of him. He was less exhausted than at the top of the Hayes Street Hill, but still plenty tired.

Running through the park was a pleasure compared to earlier stages of the race. Bill managed to grab a cup of water at one booth. He drew encouragement from the supportive cheers of the crowds that lined the course through the park. The enthusiasm of everyone was incredible. Most of the spectators, and there were thousands, were there to cheer on one or two runners. But they shouted encouragement to everyone who passed, especially those who, like Bill, appeared to need it.

Eventually, before Bill reached the end of his strength—but not much before—the finish line on the Great Highway at Ocean Beach came into view. Instinctively, Bill and Beret grabbed each other's hand to cross the line together. Tom and Michelle dropped back a bit. They were not holding hands.

Finally, not a moment too soon as far as Bill was concerned, they reached the finish line. At the last moment, Beret sped up to cross about two feet ahead of Bill. She was laughing, apparently not out of breath at all. Bill did not mind. She deserved to finish ahead of him. Just having finished exhilarated him. Almost eight miles! The fact that nearly a hundred thousand others also finished did not diminish his satisfaction. That was the beauty of the Bay-to-Breakers. Except for a precious few, no one was in the race to win. Finishing was enough. Because of the crowd, it was impossible even to be serious about the time. Bill had finished the race on his feet and in good form. That mean, in effect, that he had won.

Bill and Beret, followed by Michelle and Tom, walked through the multitudes catching their breath until they came to a spot on the beach where they could stop and rest. By that time, Beret was breathing almost normally. Bill was still gasping for breath. "Great race!" shouted Michelle above the roar of the ocean and the din of thousands of other runners. She grabbed Tom's arm, and held on tight. Tom seemed uncomfortable. Michelle looked into Tom's eyes and exclaimed, "This was our first Bay-to-Breakers together. I loved it."

Somewhat morosely, Tom agreed. In response to a question, he said that he and Michelle had each run the race before, but never together. He ran it the first time with his ex-wife. Later he ran with Trevor Watson. "But Trevor wanted to go a whole lot faster than I. I just frustrated him with how slow I was. He has no tolerance." Atkins had mentioned the race once to Michelle, and they decided to run it together "just for fun." Michelle put her hand over his, and said that yes, it was "just for fun." Her eyes seemed to sparkle as she said it. Tom seemed less enthused.

Beret suggested that the four have brunch together. They

agreed, and went to a small Italian restaurant not far from Beret's home. The meal was accompanied by animated talk about the race and about running in general. For once, there was no mention of the murder of Rachel Brandwyn.

Chapter 16

The next day was back to normal. Bill dragged his sore muscles to work and settled down to some concentrated work on the *Wakefield* and *Robinson* case. He was finding it fascinating and, because of its complexity, he understood why it had been assigned to an attorney as capable and experienced as Rachel. He would have felt complimented that Fred Olson and Tom Atkins had reassigned it to him if he had not known how desperate they were to find someone, anyone, to take it.

Beret would never admit it to Bill, but her leg muscles were also sore. She had had more strength left than Bill when the race had ended, but not much more. Her confidence and smooth gait at the end were partly a bluff. When two runners run side by side, one who is only slightly stronger and faster than the other can pretend to be *much* stronger and faster. A small reserve of strength can be made to look like a big reserve. So it was with Bill and Beret. They both ran hard, and Beret had come closer to an all-out effort than Bill would ever know.

Beret worked on the petition for review in her rape case, the one in which the Court of Appeal had reversed the conviction because the trial court had incorrectly instructed the jury on the law of consent. The deeper she got into the case, the more she began to feel the Supreme Court might actually take it. This was due in part to the merits of her argument, in part to the natural ability all persons have to convince themselves, and in part to the quiet confidence Ramon Aguilar instilled in the attorneys he worked with. Around noon, when Beret had finished the first draft, she was satisfied with her work. It required polishing, but she would do that another day. She reached for the telephone and called Bill.

"Interested in lunch?" she asked. Bill said he was always interested, but couldn't make it today. He was engrossed in an important issue in the *Wakefield* and *Robinson* case, and wanted to finish without interrupting his train of thought. It was quite complicated, and Bill thought he finally had a handle on it. He would work through the lunch hour.

Beret reminded Bill that someday they wanted to talk with Thomas Oldfield, Brian Howarth's supervisor, about Howarth's San Quentin case. They were hoping to find out whether Rachel had talked to Oldfield about the case, or about Howarth at all. They might uncover a possible motive for her murder. Originally, Bill intended to talk to Oldfield alone, with the *Wakefield* and *Robinson* case as the excuse. They thought that would be less obvious than simply interrogating Oldfield about Howarth and Rachel. But as it became apparent to them that everyone knew they were investigating the murder, they decided to drop the subterfuge. On the theory that two minds are better than one, they decided to question Oldfield together.

Bill suggested they approach him that afternoon, if Oldfield was available. He was. As always, Oldfield's office door was open. As often, he was sitting at his desk, his computer on the left side, the right side covered with notepaper, computer paper, books, charts, graphs, and more computer paper. He was doing preliminary work on his budget request for the fiscal year after the upcoming one. To some, it seemed absurd to work on the next fiscal year budget request when the current budget had not been finalized. But Oldfield knew from experience that one could not start too soon. His short, corpulent body was bent busily over his computer as he manipulated various figures this way and that to try to present the strongest argument possible for the biggest budget possible. The more attorneys he got to do the unit's work, the bigger his empire.

Not that Oldfield did not have ample justification for budget-increase requests. The amount of prison litigation had exploded as prison inmates learned how easy it was to start a lawsuit in either state or federal court against anybody and everybody they wanted —for example, against any correctional officer, warden, doctor, prosecutor, or member of the prison litigation unit. They simply had to fill out forms that the prisons were required to provide free of charge; list the names of the people the inmate wanted to sue; order the prison officials to send the forms to court for filing; and serve the defendants. Any grievance any inmate had, real or imagined, could become a lawsuit, even a federal lawsuit, just that easily. There was no limit to the number of suits a single inmate could file; some filed them by the dozen.

In recent years the explosion had swamped the attorney general's office, which was just now effectively starting to adjust. Even frivolous lawsuits, as most of them were, required substantial work to prove to a state or federal judge that they were indeed frivolous. And then there were the nonfrivolous cases, such as Brian Howarth's *Rawlings* case out of San Quentin, which often required massive amounts of work.

In order to keep up with the ever-increasing number of lawsuits while giving appropriate attention to the major cases, Oldfield needed an ever-increasing number of attorneys and support staff. A major part of his job, which he attacked with relish, was to convince the proper authorities of his needs. To this end, he and his computer manipulated figures by the hour. Today, he was trying to show that the more attorneys available to attack a new lawsuit at the outset, the quicker and more successfully the lawsuit could be disposed of, thus saving money in the long run. He had compiled an impressive array of charts, graphs, and other visual aids to convince even the most jaded bureaucrat of the wisdom of his argument. He was engaged in the task when Bill and Beret knocked on his door.

Oldfield did not look up for several seconds while he finished entering a series of numbers into the computer. When he did look, he was surprised to see who his visitors were. The prison litigation unit offices were only one floor down from the rest of the criminal division, but they could have been in another world. Outside deputies did not often wend their way to the isolated region of Oldfield's empire. In fact, they generally avoided the place at all costs for fear of being drafted to work on a prison case. Overflow work was occasionally assigned to criminal division deputies outside the prison unit. These assignments were rarely popular. It was long rumored that Oldfield sometimes abducted stray deputies, incarcerated them in dark, drafty offices, and forced them perpetually to work on prison cases. There was no truth to the rumor, but the fear kept most appellate attorneys far away from Oldfield's domain.

What could these two want? Oldfield wondered. He had met them recently at some attorney general function or other, but could not recall their names. Then he remembered reports that two of the young deputies were supposedly investigating the murder of Rachel Brandwyn. A shocking case, that. Rachel was one of the few outside deputies who took any interest in the functions of his unit. He was so upset when he heard of her death that he was unable to work at his computer for literally hours. But what could they want with him? Surely, they did not suspect him, or anyone within his realm, of the murder. Why would *they* have any reason to want Rachel Brandwyn dead? Brian Howarth worked on the same floor as Rachel. (Oldfield did not like the arrangement. He wanted everyone in his empire as near him as possible, but he could do nothing about it. Howarth was too senior to force him to move.) But surely his unit had no connection with the murder. What could he do for his visitors?

"Hello. What can I do for you?" he asked.

They introduced themselves. Then Bill said that they "just wanted to see what the prison litigation offices looked like." He wanted to be subtle about the upcoming questioning.

Seeing Oldfield's incredulous look, Beret added, "Actually, we also had some questions we wanted to ask."

"About the Rachel Brandwyn murder?"

Bill started to say no, not necessarily. Beret started to say yes, possibly. Bill coughed. Embarrassed, Beret explained that they were not sure if there was any connection, but that Brian Howarth had been shown the murder weapon shortly before the murder. They just had some questions. "I also wanted to talk to you about my *Wakefield* and *Robinson* case," added Bill. "You know, the crack-smuggling case from San Quentin. I got it from Rachel. I believe she talked to you about it."

Oldfield started to say something, paused, looked down at the computer keyboard, then said, "No, she never mentioned it to me. I'll be happy to help you if I can, but I'm not familiar with the case."

Beret spoke up. "Then for the time being let's just concentrate on Howarth." She saw no need to disguise the purpose of their visit. It was obvious, and Oldfield had guessed it.

"Fine, what would you like to know?"

What indeed? Whether Rachel's involvement in the *Rawlings* case had given Howarth a motive to kill her.

Beret started the questioning. "We understand Rachel was as-signed to assist Brian on the *Rawlings* case. Is that correct?"

Oldfield started to light a cigarette from a pack in his shirt pocket, decided against it (*they probably don't smoke,* he thought), then nervously picked up a pen from his desk and chewed the end of it. It was already well chewed. "That's more or less right. With six or so attorneys working full-time on the case for the inmates, we thought Brian shouldn't have to be alone. Someone should be available to help him if necessary. Everybody in my unit was far too busy for another big assignment. Rachel ex-pressed an interest in broadening her horizons. Fred Olson said she could help as long as she continued to carry a full appellate load. He stressed that in light of the Backlog, she could not expect any less work from him. Rachel agreed to work nights if neces-sary. Naturally, I jumped at the chance. Rachel is, was, a fine attorney."

Bill was busy taking notes. Beret asked, "How did she get in-terested in the case?"

Oldfield put the pen down. "I'm not real sure. She used to come down here periodically to talk with people in my unit and see what we do. She seemed to want to get involved in everything the attorney general does. She told me that she might like to work on one of our cases to get civil litigation experience. When she heard about the *Rawlings* case, Rachel thought it might be some-thing she would enjoy. That was a few months ago. I told her she was welcome to do whatever she wanted, that Brian could use the help."

Bill was still taking notes. Beret continued the questioning. "What was Brian's reaction?"

Oldfield smiled. "About what you'd expect. He never wants anyone to work with him. He said that he, a lone litigator, could always beat litigation by a committee. And he might be right. He could take a consistent, unified approach; a committee is by na-ture inconsistent, not unified. So he wasn't too happy to have Rachel foisted on him. But he's also a true professional. He didn't make a fuss. Especially when I assured him that Rachel was only supposed to help him as needed, and that he was still in charge."

"Did he let Rachel look at the files?"

"Of course. He couldn't prevent that. I think she also covered a deposition or two. But not much else. She really didn't have that kind of experience."

"Did Rachel ever talk to you about Brian's performance in the case?"

Oldfield picked the pen up again, and chewed on it briefly. He put it down and looked at Beret, then at Bill. He started to take the pen apart, then spoke with carefully measured words. He knew they were now at the nub of things. "I suppose I should tell you, although you will make more out of it than you should. I'm sure it has nothing to do with the murder. One day, a few weeks before her death, Rachel came to talk to me about the *Rawlings* case. She seemed worried. She said she was learning some disturbing things about what Brian Howarth was doing. Actually, she came to me twice. Both times I was real busy, and we didn't have time to go into detail. I got the impression that what she had to say would take quite a while."

"What things did she say were disturbing her?"

Oldfield put the pen down. He smiled. Why, they could not tell. "Well, I don't really know. That is, I wasn't really listening. I was in the middle of working on my budget; I had just found a way to justify an even larger request. I'm afraid I was rather brusque with her."

Bill spoke this time. "On both occasions?"

"Well, one time. The other time I was busy, too. I don't remember what I was doing, but I'm sure it had something to do with the budget." There was a moment of silence. Then Oldfield continued. "Look here, I'd like to help you, really I would, but Rachel Brandwyn had a reputation for butting in where she didn't belong. Working on the unit budget requests is the most important thing I do. I really didn't have extra time to listen to her complaints."

"You asked her to work on *Rawlings* on her own time, and then couldn't be bothered to listen to her concerns?" Bill tried to sound as incredulous as possible.

"That's not the way it was. Of course I could spare the time, only not right then. Anyway, I know Brian Howarth. He's one of my best lawyers. I never should have asked Rachel to work with him. He was capable of taking on a whole cadre of lawyers all by himself—with a paralegal or two to help out. He was always complaining about her. In fact, it was hard to tell who complained more about the other, Brian or Rachel." Oldfield added hastily, "Not that he would ever want to murder Rachel."

"No, of course not," replied Beret. "What did Brian complain about?"

"Nothing specific. Just that she was meddling, and was not of much help. He requested, almost insisted, that I take her off the case. But I told him no-go. I wasn't going to turn down free help from Fred Olson's crew. We need all the help we can get. I told Brian that he had to put up with her and that he should try to make her as useful as possible. She had her faults, but she was a good lawyer, although her experience was mostly appellate." Oldfield began musing. "They're a strange bunch, these appellate lawyers. Always worried about the record and precedent and legal principles—things like that. I feel uneasy around them. They're too theoretical, too intellectual. They really believe that intellect and the law can mix. I like people to be more practical, less ethereal." Oldfield suddenly realized that his listeners were themselves appellate lawyers. He hastened to add, "But some of you guys are OK, like Rachel. She had a practical bent. I liked her. In moderation."

Bill and Beret ignored Oldfield's comments. Each had heard such views before. It was now Beret's time to sound incredulous. "Let me make sure I have this right. You're telling us that neither Brian nor Rachel ever said anything specific about the other?"

"Not really. I know what Brian's complaint was. He wanted the *Rawlings* case to himself. There was nothing more to it than that, I'm sure. I assume Rachel had some theoretical objection to Brian's methods. His methods were practical, not appellate-like."

Whatever that means, thought Bill.

"You must understand," continued Oldfield, "Brian took a practical approach. His goal was to build a strong case, not just to argue the law. He had a genius for finding witnesses, even inmates, to testify on his side."

"Was it common to use inmate witnesses?"

"Nobody else in the prison litigation unit has ever done it. But it worked for him. He's zealous, but he's had wonderful results. A few years ago, he won the first annual Prison Litigator of the Year Award, given to the best deputy in the unit. It's very prestigious." After a moment, he added wistfully. "At least to us."

Beret persisted. "So Rachel said nothing specific about Howarth?"

"Not that I can remember. In fact, the second time she came by, she said she would write me a memo that I could read at my leisure." He chuckled. "As if I have any leisure, with all this budget work."

"Did she write you a memo?"

Oldfield started working at the computer. "If she did," he said, "I never saw it." He became engrossed in what he was doing, shuffling paper and making computer entries with impressive speed. Beret and Bill took this as a signal that they were dismissed. They left. They had probably gotten everything out of Oldfield that they could. He did not look up as they walked out.

Bill and Beret went straight to Jeff Hines. He said he did not know anything about any memo Rachel might have written concerning Brian Howarth or the *Rawlings* case. At their request, he looked through her file cabinet and everywhere else he could think of. He could find nothing.

Bill and Beret returned to their offices to get back to work. When Beret approached her door, she heard her telephone ring. She ran inside, reached over her desk, and grabbed the receiver. The voice at the other end was muffled, yet familiar. Within a second, Beret knew what it was. The voice that gave the earlier message about Ramon Aguilar. "You weren't listening," the voice said. Beret was listening now, intently. Again, the voice was indistinct; she could not even tell if it was male or female. She heard no background noise. The voice continued. "Ramon Aguilar is the one you must concentrate on. I'm sure he did it. There's got to be proof somewhere."

"Who are you? What are you talking about?"

"Who I am doesn't matter. What I am talking about does. Very much. Ramon is lying to you. Their meeting at the Palace was not business. Rachel didn't want to talk to him about any office problem or her Supreme Court argument. They were in love. At least she was. I'm sure she told him she was pregnant. He killed her to prevent her from naming him the father."

"How do you know what Ramon told me?" Beret could think of nothing else to say, but instinctively felt she should keep the person talking. Maybe he (or she) would give himself (or herself) away. Maybe something important would be revealed. How would a real detective handle the situation? Was there some way she could have someone trace the call even though she was alone in her office? Beret had no idea. She felt helpless.

"You're not listening." (Yes, she was!) "I am not important. Ramon Aguilar is. Don't let him bamboozle you with his smooth talk. I don't know how, but somewhere you can find the proof you need, if only you look in the right place. He *must* have said something to give himself away. They always do if you only recognize it. He must have said one thing too many. Or he might yet. They always do. Think about it, investigate it."

"What do you mean?" Beret knew her questioning was clumsy, but it was the best she could do on the spur of the moment.

"I mean you've got to concentrate. Ramon Aguilar killed her. I'm sure of it, as sure as I'm trying to help you. Don't blow it! Don't let him get away with murder. Rachel was too wonderful a person to let her killer escape."

"What do you mean?!" Try as she might, Beret could do no better than to repeat herself. At least she might buy some time while she tried to think.

"I think I've been perfectly clear." The voice spoke the next few words deliberately, one word at a time. "Do—not—let—him —escape."

Two things occurred simultaneously. Beret screamed, "Wait! You've got to help me!" And she heard a click on the telephone. The line went dead.

"Hello? Hello?!" No answer. Nothing. "Don't hang up!" Too late. The voice was gone. She could not get it back.

Beret sat transfixed for almost half a minute, the receiver still in her hand. She felt utterly inadequate. She tried to fix in her memory exactly what the voice had said. When she finally hung up the receiver, she was sure of only two things. If the call was a fraud, an attempt to divert her attention, she must not let it succeed. If the call was genuine, and Ramon Aguilar had killed Rachel, she must concentrate her efforts to find the key, and bring him to justice. Which, however, was the case? She wished she knew.

Chapter 17

Wednesday night, Bill and Beret went to the ballet. Over the last two days, they had analyzed the mysterious telephone call exhaustively. Beret repeated it verbatim as near as she could remember. They even wrote down an approximate transcript for future use. Beret also tried to remember the details of her conversation with Ramon Aguilar. They analyzed all parts of it from all directions, but could find no clue. Were they missing something? What? They got no closer.

They did not ignore the larger picture. They felt the voice was right about one thing. The killer usually does give himself away by talking too much, at least according to murder mysteries, which was all they had to go by. Therefore, Bill and Beret analyzed everything they could remember that all the suspects had said, and what the inspectors said they had said. Had someone *else* gone too far, said something he (or she) should not have? Were they missing something? What? They wished they knew.

But this was a time for relaxation, not for investigating a murder. Bill had chosen the evening's festivities. They went to the Paramount Theater in downtown Oakland. Beret had never been there. It was Bill's favorite. A magnificent art-deco-style theater, originally built in the thirties and recently restored, Bill found it more impressive, almost more breathtaking, than anything even San Francisco had to offer. It was not exactly beautiful. Art deco could never be beautiful. But big, glittery, colorful, with towering ceilings, busy Egyptian decorations, and a huge stage.

The ballet was Prokofiev's *Romeo and Juliet.* Not one of Bill's favorites, but definitely acceptable. Beret had never seen it. It started promptly at 8:02 P.M. During the first half, while the two teenagers fell in love, and the dancers translated into dance the web of circumstances leading to tragedy, Bill's mind, as always during the ballet, was free to run wild. Part of his mind enjoyed the graceful movements of the female dancers and the powerful leaps of the male dancers. Another part of his mind wandered. He even dozed once or twice, again as always during a ballet. This did not mean he found it boring, only soothing.

Try as he might, the kaleidoscope of events, impressions, motives, evidence, comments, disclaimers, law cases, and emotions surrounding the shocking murder of Rachel Brandwyn swirled in his brain. Distracted by the music, the dancing, the story on stage, the awareness of who was sitting next to him, he could not focus on the kaleidoscope, he could not organize his perceptions into a whole. He could only see images, images which, in his mind, danced faster, more incessantly than the dancers on stage. Only vaguely, subconsciously, did he have the uneasy sense that he was missing something, that the key was out there, somewhere, if he could only find it. On stage, Romeo's love for Juliet was expressing itself in dance; in the audience, Bill's thoughts were rotating in a continual jumble.

Bill's perceptions of the events portrayed onstage blended into his meditation on who was responsible for Rachel's murder, indeed, on who was ever responsible for death. He wandered back and forth between contemplating Rachel's death and the suicides of the young lovers. In his reverie, he considered the role played by Friar Lawrence. The feud between the Montagues and the Capulets had always been blamed for the tragedy, but, as Bill now contemplated, the friar himself was far from innocent.

Friar Lawrence gave Romeo the drug which set into motion the chain of events culminating in the double suicide. Imagine, Bill thought, in an era of uncertain communications, giving to an impressionable and emotional teenager in love a narcotic that supposedly would give the appearance but not the reality of death. Tragedy was easy to foresee if anything went wrong. Juliet might not learn the truth in time, as actually happens in the story; the drug might be more dangerous than believed, and might itself kill Romeo; an improper dose might be taken; any of several things might occur to thwart the silly scheme of Friar Lawrence. Yes, the friar was guilty of at least criminal negligence.

Regarding Rachel's death, Bill could reach no conclusion. But regarding the young lovers, he concluded that if *he* had been the district attorney of Verona when Romeo and Juliet had died, he would have charged Friar Lawrence with voluntary manslaughter, or at least involuntary manslaughter, in the death of Juliet. The danger of the scheme causing a fatal mishap was too great to ignore. The Friar's culpability for the death of Romeo was, Bill admitted, more problematic. A jury might consider it less foreseeable that Romeo would awaken from his deathlike trance, see the dead Juliet, and then in turn kill himself. But even there, the friar was not guiltless. His scheme ultimately caused two deaths. If nothing else, Friar Lawrence was surely guilty of contributing to the delinquency of the minors. Yes, Bill thought, Friar Lawrence had gotten off to lightly in public opinion.

These thoughts filled Bill's mind until the intermission. Beret, too, could not prevent herself from thinking about Rachel's death even as she tried to concentrate on the music and the dancing on stage. She, too, felt that the key was out there somewhere, just beyond her grasp. Despite everything they had done, they did not seem any closer to solving the crime than at the beginning. What were they missing?

During the intermission, the two would-be but so far unsuccessful sleuths rose to stretch their legs and admire the rest of the theater. Each purchased a glass of champagne and strolled to a balcony overlooking the main lobby. Below, hundreds of spectators were milling about. Some were making a beeline for the outer lobby to smoke cigarettes. The two stood a while, taking in the scene. To their left, they noticed two other persons walk hand in hand through the crowd to a small, relatively isolated nook. Bill and Beret knew the two; they had, of late, increasingly been seen as a couple, though not at their place of employment. Michelle Hong and Thomas Atkins.

Almost involuntarily, Bill and Beret watched the couple approach the spot they were seeking. They silently convinced themselves that they were not merely yielding to curiosity; no, they were investigating two suspects in a murder. Tom and Michelle engaged in what appeared to be intimate conversation; at least it was soft enough to be drowned out by the surrounding hubbub. Twice they kissed, without any apparent self-consciousness. Entirely different from their behavior at work. While Bill and Beret were gawking, Tom glanced their way and recognized them. Quickly, he removed his arm from around Michelle's waist. Bill and Beret looked away, as if to pretend they had not seen Tom. But it was too late. The eye contact between them, although brief, had been too substantial to ignore. There was nothing for Bill and Beret to do but approach Tom and Michelle and join the conversation. They did.

When they got within hearing range, Bill said, a little too jovially, "Well, so we meet again. We seem to have the same social schedule."

Michelle put her arm around Tom's waist and said, "Yes, we can't seem to stay apart. As you have no doubt figured out for yourselves, at work we act as strangers, but away from work we are not strangers." She smiled at Tom. "Not in the least. You may as well know the truth. We can't keep any secrets from you."

Tom smiled (was it a forced smile?), and rather awkwardly put his arm over Michelle's. "That's right," he agreed. "We sure can't keep any secrets from you."

Or was there one *secret that you are quite successfully keeping from us?* wondered Beret. Aloud, she said, "A lovely performance tonight, isn't it?" Everyone agreed that it was a lovely performance tonight. And that the dancers were very good, especially the Romeo. And that they really enjoyed going to the ballet. And that the Paramount never looked better, and was indeed grander than anything in San Francisco. A painful silence ensued. Tom and Michelle said nothing more about their relationship. Bill and Beret did not know how to ask gracefully. Then Tom said something that surprised them.

"What do you make of the second anonymous telephone call blaming Ramon Aguilar for Rachel's murder?"

"How did you know about that?" asked Beret.

"Oh, everybody knows. It's the talk of the office. One of the secretaries told me about it. Frankly, it doesn't surprise me. I always thought it might be Ramon. I'm sure he got Rachel pregnant. The two were always talking in his office. What else were they doing? He's so secretive. As I told Michelle, you can't trust that kind." He looked at Michelle.

"Yes, that's right, you did say that."

"In fact," Tom continued, "just a couple of days before she was killed, I saw Rachel in Ramon's office for a long time in what seemed like a deep, serious conversation. When they saw me, they seemed embarrassed. Something was going on, what I don't know."

Beret reflected that recently *she* had engaged in a deep, serious conversation with Ramon in his office. Aloud, she said, "I'm sure it was all innocent."

"Not everything that has happened has been innocent," said Michelle significantly. "At first, I thought Anna Heitz was probably the killer. She was so upset when Rachel stole her Supreme Court case. Or maybe Fred Olson, because Rachel always caused him so much trouble. Now I don't know. It sure looks bad for Ramon. Anyway," she smiled sweetly, "I'm sure you two will uncover the truth."

"We'll try," Beret assured her. "But the police inspectors are doing the investigating. We are only trying to help."

Michelle took hold of Tom's right hand. "I hope you hurry up. We are waiting for the murder to get cleared up before we announce that we are getting married."

Tom looked unhappy, but the statement, once made, could not be erased. "That's right," he confirmed, "We, uh, we want to get married as soon as possible." He added hastily, "But we want to keep it secret until the murder is solved." Bill and Beret assured them that the secret was safe with them. *Surely*, Beret thought, *we won't have to tell Inspectors Petersen and Tarkov. Will we?*

"You see," Michelle explained, "we don't want to announce our engagement until just before we get married. Fred Olson is strongly opposed to intraoffice romances." This was news to Bill and Beret. They glanced at each other as if to ask what they were getting themselves into. When Michelle realized that they did not know what she meant, she added, "It all goes back to the affair between Martin Granowski and Georgette Johnson." Beret had vaguely heard of Georgette; Bill had not.

Michelle and Tom told them the story. When Martin and Georgette were young deputies, they had a "smoking" (Michelle's word) affair. They were in love and became engaged. Then something happened, and they broke up. Each accused the other of, as Tom put it, "the most vile misbehavior." Their feud lasted for months, and severely damaged their performance on the job. It split the office into two camps, one supporting him and one supporting her. "In fact," said Tom, "Rachel was the most vocal of those supporting Georgette. Michelle and I also sympathized with her. Martin seemed so unforgiving, so unyielding, so, so—" He groped for the right word. "So vindictive. Fortunately it did not harm our long-term relationship with Martin. We get along with him just fine now."

Michelle interjected that Rachel also made up with Martin; she believed they were good friends at the time of her death.

Eventually, Georgette left the office. The move did not hurt her career. She got a position as chief deputy county counsel in Santa Clara County, and later was appointed a superior court judge. "She's rumored to be in line for the next vacancy on the Court of Appeal," said Tom.

Fred Olson had been outraged by the affair. Office productivity suffered dramatically. More important, Georgette was one of his best attorneys, almost a workaholic. The number and quality of her briefs was legendary. Fred once commented in public that if one of them had to leave the office, why couldn't it have been Martin Granowski. The comment did not endear him to Granowski.

"The upshot of it all," Michelle summed up, "is that Fred is adamantly opposed to romance among his attorneys. Now that the murder has been so hard on him, we don't want to upset him further. It will be OK when we actually get married, but not until then." The logic of this last point escaped Beret and Bill, but they had to accept it. Michelle looked at Tom, and added, "But we'll show Fred that this is one love story he need not fear. This one won't cause any trouble."

Tom grinned (was it a forced grin?), and agreed vehemently (too vehemently?).

By now, the time had come to return to their seats for the second half of the ballet. Michelle's parting words were, "We liked Rachel so much, it just doesn't seem right to get married until her murder is behind us. It won't be behind us until you catch the killer."

Chapter 18

The next few days passed uneventfully. Over a month had elapsed since the murder, and Bill and Beret had no idea what to do next. They seemed to have reached an impasse. As they told themselves while pursuing their regular legal duties, which was rather a relief, they had never claimed to be detectives. The criminal division returned to a state that was, if not normal, at least acquiescent. People came to accept the murder and the idea that it would not be solved soon, if ever. The need to return to a routine eclipsed even the oppressive knowledge that a murderer was probably in their midst.

During their only conversation that week with either of the inspectors, Tarkov hinted to Bill and Beret that a possible "break" in the case was coming soon. He and Petersen were pursuing a promising lead. He would keep them informed. In the meantime, he stressed, they should be careful. Their adversary was a dangerous killer who would not hesitate to kill again.

Monday morning came. An unusual June rainstorm wet the streets and caused havoc with the traffic, but did little to alleviate the chronic California drought. BART was running smoothly, however, and Bill and Beret arrived at work no later than usual. Each found a message to call Inspector Petersen. They called in Beret's office. He answered on the second ring. The big break had finally come, he told them enthusiastically. Could he and Inspector Tarkov come by to discuss the case? They would plan how to exploit the break.

Beret assured him that of course he could come. They would be in their offices all morning. Petersen said they would be there soon. In the meantime, Bill and Beret could tell the others in the office that there would be big news later that day. But, he cautioned, they should not say what it was. That was for later.

This last directive was easy to follow. Bill and Beret had no idea what Inspector Petersen was talking about.

The inspectors arrived shortly after ten, and marshaled Bill and Beret into Fred Olson's corner office. Olson was not there. Tarkov told Elizabeth Cronin not to let Olson enter the office and closed the door.

After the inspectors hung up their raincoats, Tarkov looked around the office briefly as if checking for hidden microphones. Then he sat down in Olson's relatively luxurious chair behind the desk. Bill and Beret sat in the smaller chairs in front of the desk. Petersen paced the floor. He asked them what they had learned since he had last seen them. They gave a full report, except, in keeping with their promise, they did not mention the secret marriage plans of Michelle Hong and Thomas Atkins. They apologized about how little they had to report. Inspector Petersen assured them they were doing just fine, that they were amateurs and were not expected to do more than they were doing. "Anyway," he said, "our efforts have been more successful."

Tarkov leaned across the desk and whispered in a conspiratorial manner, "We think we know who got the victim pregnant."

The sentence hung in the air for a moment. Both inspectors gazed intently at the attorneys, who sat dumbfounded. Finally Bill broke the silence. "You mean you know who the father was?" As soon as he asked the question, he realized how silly it was. He was not good at murder investigations. "I mean," he added, "who is it? How did you find out?"

Petersen spoke. "We prefer not to say yet for psychological reasons. We don't know for sure, and we want to announce what we have learned at the right time and in the right way. But the victim herself supplied the clue, although we didn't find out until just recently."

"What do you want us do?" asked Beret.

"Tell Fred Olson to call a meeting of the entire criminal division this afternoon," responded Tarkov. "Make sure all of our suspects are there. We'll arrive during the meeting, and take it from there. With any kind of luck, we'll flush out the father, and maybe even the killer."

"That's it?"

"Also look around, pay attention to people's reactions." Tarkov stood, and walked around the table. Petersen continued pacing. Tarkov checked that the door was still closed, and whispered, "I assume everyone knows we are here." Bill and Beret assured him that their arrival had certainly been noticed. "Feel free to spread the word that there's been a breakthrough. In fact, tell people we know who the father was. We want to give the father, and the killer, time to stew about it."

Bill and Beret agreed to follow these instructions. "One last thing," cautioned Tarkov. "Don't tell anybody yet who the father was."

Again, this last directive was easy to follow. They had no idea themselves who the father was.

The meeting was held at two o'clock in the library conference room. Everybody was present. Olson had been upset that the inspectors did not communicate directly with him instead of through his two young underlings. Nevertheless, he followed orders. Actually, he told himself, it was a convenient time for a meeting, as the division had much important business to discuss. There had not been a general meeting since the announcement that Rachel Brandwyn had been pregnant. Until the inspectors arrived, he would preside over a regular meeting.

The mood of the deputies as they gathered around the central table, and once again admired the Ansel Adams photographs, was quite different from the previous meeting that now seemed so long ago. The rumor concerning the big news to follow naturally caused tension. But a quiet determination to put the murder to one side and get on with the business of the criminal division dominated.

After the meeting was announced, speculation became rife in the hallways and, more often, in the privacy of individual offices over who the father was, and how the inspectors had come to know. And why a divisional meeting was needed for the announcement. Most people had assumed that the father was also the killer; now that they were forced to reflect on it, they became less sure. But, in any event, learning who the father was would at least help. Because of the strange telephone calls, Ramon Aguilar was at the center of the speculation, but most people insisted that he could not really have been the father, and certainly not the murderer. Everyone respected him far too much. He was happily married, and had children of his own. Of course, people had to admit, *someone* had been the father. That being the case, why not Ramon?

At 2:05 P.M., after everyone had already entered and sat down, Fred made his appearance, and took his accustomed spot at the end of the long table. Everyone stopped talking, and looked at him expectantly, pens and legal pads at the ready. Except for some doodling, the legal pads were blank. Soon they would not be.

"Because of the shortness of time, and the unusual nature of the circumstances that bring us together," orated Fred, "I did not have time to prepare and distribute a written agenda. I'm sure that upsets you no end." There was strained laughter. "Instead, I'll state the agenda orally. The main thing I called you here for is to talk about the Backlog." Wrong, everyone knew. The inspectors called us together, not you. "Surprisingly, there is some good news in that department. Then we'll talk about the oral argument tomorrow in the *Jones* case before the Supreme Court. As you know, Thomas Atkins heroically agreed to bear the burden of that case after Rachel Brandwyn's, uh, untimely demise."

Atkins, in his accustomed chair opposite Fred, stood ceremoniously and bowed with mock solemnity. The other laughed. After pausing for this welcome diversion, Fred continued. "Other topics include our ongoing automation project. We hope to modernize our computer system any week now." They had heard that before. "Also, we will talk about new attorney positions we will fill when the hiring freeze ends, and about the budget for next year. Finally, and most importantly, I intend to preside over a freewheeling discussion of changes we will have to make as this office" (again, it sounded like "corps") "moves toward the next century. Indeed," he added portentously, "as this office enters, and seeks to adapt to, the third millennium."

Brian Howarth interrupted. "What about the murder investigators. Where are they? I came from San Quentin just to hear them."

"They will come later. I understand they have something to tell us about the murder of Rachel Brandwyn. As I was saying, we'll talk first about the Backlog."

"Is it true they know who the father was?" asked Anna Heitz.

"I don't know. We'll have to wait and see. As I was saying, I am very proud of the way the office came together, and put their noses to the grindstone ever since the unfortunate set of circumstances that led to the tragic demise of Rachel Brandwyn—"

"Why did the investigators have to call a meeting to announce their new discovery?" asked Trevor Watson.

"I don't know. We'll have to wait and see. Now if everyone would start acting like professionals, and please let me get on with the day's business." (In other words, stop interrupting me!) "As I was saying, the numbers have distinctly improved in the last month. Statistically analyzed, the average Backlog has actually decreased two percent over the previous reporting month. That doesn't sound like much, but my figures show that the increase in the average mean time between the filing of the appellant's brief and our office's filing of the respondent's brief has decreased forty-seven percent when compared with the average medium increase in the same time period over the average length of the filing period of the last measuring period, which is the month of May, when those figures are fully extrapolated to account for the time during the funeral of Rachel when nobody was writing briefs."

Ramon Aguilar interrupted. "Does this mean we filed more briefs in May than in April?"

"Yes, that's what I said." Fred paused while everyone made a note of this. "But we need to work even harder in the future to increase the decrease in the increase in the Backlog." He paused to let people write down appropriate notes A few attempted, but quickly gave up. "Are there any questions on these figures?" There were many, but none were voiced.

"Now," continued Fred, "on to the next order of business. Tomorrow at nine o'clock sharp in the Supreme Court courtroom, Tom Atkins will argue the *Jones* case. I urge as many of you as possible to be there to watch, for it promises to be scintillating." Bill and Beret had already agreed to go together.

"I know I plan to be there," interjected Thomas Oldfield. Although Oldfield was not in Fred Olson's department, he usually attended these meetings as the head of the prison litigation unit.

Fred thanked Oldfield, then continued. "As you know, *Jones* is the case Rachel Brandwyn was supposed to argue before her, uh, untimely demise. All kudos to Tom Atkins for so readily agreeing to take over the case." Everyone knew Atkins had had no say in the matter, but no one chose to point that out. "How are you coming in your preparations for the argument?"

"Well, um, fine, I guess." Atkins, normally at ease at these meetings, now spoke in a voice pitched much higher than usual; he drummed his left fingers on the table. "Actually it was not quite as hard as you might have expected. I had a big head start. Before her death, Rachel talked to me about the case in detail. In great detail. In fact, she discussed all her cases in great detail with me. As you know, Fred, I wanted to take over her *Wakefield* and *Robinson* case until you insisted I give it to Bill Kelly. It seemed like she told me everything there was to know about that case. But," he added hastily, "it's in good hands with Bill. I certainly didn't mean to suggest, well, you know, that Bill couldn't do it, just that I had such a good feel for the case that I, you know . . ."

Normally, Atkins did not drone on like this. Fred rescued him. "Thanks, Tom, we understand completely. And good luck tomorrow. We'll all be there pulling for you. It will be nice to get the *Jones* case behind us, and get on to bigger and better things." After a pause, "That is to say, not that *Jones* is not big, just that it will be good to be done with it."

"And now, if there are no further questions" (there were none), "let's get on to the next item on the agenda. Let's see. Ah, yes. Filling vacant attorney positions." Everyone looked hopefully at Fred, but with little enthusiasm. The lack of enthusiasm was about to be justified. "I'm afraid there is nothing new to report. The hiring freeze is still on, and there is no word on when it might end. You will not receive any help for the time being." A despondent but resigned silence. "But," Fred added brightly, "we have several outstanding applicants we can make offers to as soon as the freeze ends."

"But how many of the good ones will still be available when we finally make our offers?" asked Trevor Watson.

"Hopefully, as many as possible."

"But it's been months since we interviewed these people," persisted Trevor. "Surely anyone who's any good has already accepted another offer."

"Possibly, but we can't help it. Hopefully, there will still be good people available. In any case, there will be *someone* available, and someone is better than no one."

"But shouldn't we be trying to get the best?" Trevor again.

"Of course, and we *are* trying. Now, if I can continue." (That is, don't ask such awkward questions.) "The next item on the agenda is . . . that is, if there are no more questions." Fred paused to give the appearance of allowing further discussion, although everyone knew from experience that he would not welcome more questions on the subject.

During the pause, there was a knock on the conference-room door. A split second later, before anyone could react, the door was flung open, and Inspectors Petersen and Tarkov stormed inside. They were carrying briefcases, and walked briskly to a podium next to Fred's chair. Neither smiled. When they got to the podium, they took off their dark business suitcoats, thereby revealing their department issued handguns strapped to their waists. A Smith & Wesson revolver for Tarkov; a Colt Python .357 magnum for Petersen.

Fred Olson tried to introduce the inspectors, but they brushed him aside. Petersen spoke first. "We called this meeting so that we could inform all of you at the same time of recent developments in the ongoing investigation into the murder of Rachel Brandwyn."

Everyone listened intently, staring at Petersen. The notepads lay forgotten on the table. With one exception, all wanted the mystery solved, and the murder put behind them. The one exception was no less interested in what the inspectors had to say, although for different reasons. While the listeners concentrated on the inspectors, the inspectors concentrated on them. One of their listeners, they were confident, was the killer. Both took pride in their ability to read faces. If the killer gave himself or herself away, they were determined to observe it. So far, neither had seen anything suspicious, but there was still time.

"Although," Petersen continued, "it may not seem like we have made much progress, we have been working nonstop. I'm sure you have talked among yourselves, and you know a lot of what has been happening." A pause. Silence. "Until a couple of days ago, we seemed to have reached a dead end. Lots of motive. Lots of opportunity. Little hard evidence. But, thanks in large part to assistance from some of your colleagues," Petersen looked directly at Bill and Beret, "Inspector Tarkov and I developed an idea." Petersen stepped aside, and Tarkov took the podium. Both continued scrutinizing the members of the audience. All were transfixed. But no actions suggested anything other than intense interest.

Tarkov resumed the recitation. "With the aforementioned assistance, we learned the interesting fact that the victim once wrote a draft of a memo to officials in Sacramento complaining of sexual harassment." Several of the listeners reflexively turned to look at Trevor Watson. Watson sat stoically staring at Tarkov. Fred Olson squirmed uneasily in his seat next to the podium. "She never sent it. She apparently wanted to think it over before she did. Then we learned that the victim also wrote a draft of a memo to Sacramento criticizing the handling of a murder trial. It is called, I believe, the *Morton* case." Tarkov turned to Petersen, who nodded. "Interestingly, the murder weapon in the *Morton* case was the very same one used to kill the victim in this case." Several reflexively turned to look at Martin Granowski. Granowski also sat stoically, saying nothing. Olson squirmed even more.

"The victim did not mail this memo, either. Apparently, she wanted to think about it, too, but she was murdered first." Tarkov paused. Ramon Aguilar coughed quietly. Everyone else sat motionless. After a few seconds, Petersen spoke.

"This started us thinking. The victim appeared to be a person who habitually wrote letters or memos on important matters, then put them aside while deciding whether to send them. At least, she did that in her professional life. Mightn't she also do that in her personal life? What was the most important matter in her personal life at the time of her death? The answer is obvious. Her pregnancy, and what to do about it. Should she get an abortion? Should she tell the father? Should she make him help her? We started thinking about these matters." Petersen again paused. Both inspectors stared at the audience. Some averted their glances. Others returned the gaze. So far, no one gave himself or herself away.

Petersen continued. "We knew that the victim wrote memos about important professional matters, then left them." He spoke the next words very deliberately. "What if she did the same thing regarding her pregnancy?" He turned to Tarkov, who resumed speaking.

"We knew that she had a word processor in her apartment in the Marina district. Did she, perhaps, use it to write a letter that she never sent? Perhaps a letter to her doctor? Or to a friend, or counselor, or member of the clergy? Perhaps," another pause, then, "perhaps to the father himself?" The silence was intense. Was someone in the audience reacting differently from the others? Inspector Petersen sensed something, what he could not tell. "If she had written, might it still be on the computer? There was nothing for us to do but to find out for ourselves. We called the victim's parents, her next of kin, and got permission to search the apartment, and specifically, the word processor.

"I was able very quickly to access the documents stored in the word processor. Most of the documents were of no interest." Tarkov allowed the word "most" to linger. No one failed to notice its significance. One person in particular tensed visibly upon hearing it. Petersen noticed that person. "One document was of *great* interest." Tarkov looked into his briefcase for a dramatic moment, did not find what he was seeking, then turned to Petersen. "I believe it's in your briefcase."

With calculated motions, Petersen reached into his own briefcase and rummaged around briefly. "Yes," he said. "Here it is." He removed two sheets of paper that appeared to be a typed letter. He quickly showed it to the audience, then laid it on the podium. "We struck gold. The victim wrote a letter, but she did not send it. At least, she did not send it as far as we know. Instead, she kept it on the word processor. We printed a copy." He pointed to the two sheets of paper on the podium. The person Petersen had noticed in the audience slumped back in his chair. Petersen noticed that, too.

Tarkov took up the narrative. "Rather than keep you in suspense, we will tell you what the letter is. It is a letter to the father. That is, to the man who made the victim pregnant. It is unsigned, but states as clear as can be who the father is." Another pause. "It informs him that she was indeed pregnant, and demands that he admit to his paternity. It says that if he will not assume his responsibilities as the father, she will have an abortion. It is dated two days before she was killed."

Petersen spoke next. While he did, he looked directly at the person he had noticed reacting. "We will state who the letter is addressed to if we have to, but we would prefer not to have to. You know who you are. Wouldn't it be better to say it yourself, rather than force us to say it?" Petersen folded his arms. Tarkov reached across and picked up the letter. They waited a few seconds in silence. Tarkov started to speak. Suddenly there was a voice in the audience, quiet and deliberate.

"All right, I'll speak up. I was the father. I should have said so sooner, but I didn't have the courage."

All eyes turned in disbelief to look as Thomas Atkins stood up. Several people gasped. "Yes, it was me." He looked at the inspectors, who said nothing. "I was going to talk her out of an abortion, but she was killed before I could." He sat down. For a while it appeared as if he might cry, but he composed himself, and continued. No one interrupted him.

"You have good reason to hate me for keeping quiet all this time. It was stupid. At first, we agreed she would have an abortion, and nobody would ever know she had gotten pregnant. Then I changed my mind. As I got used to the idea, I came to realize I wanted the baby. I was going to tell Rachel when her Supreme Court argument was over, but I never had the chance. It was . . ." He stopped to bring his emotions under control. Then, "It was too late. You must believe me. I would never have hurt Rachel."

Suddenly a horrified expression came over his face. "And I certainly would never kill her." He looked around at disbelieving faces. "You must believe me," he screamed, "I didn't kill her. You don't understand. I couldn't have killed her. I loved her." He covered his face in his hands. "Yes, that's right, I loved her. I was going to be the father of her baby. I was frightened at first, but then I became ecstatic." Atkins stood up slowly. "Why would I kill her? I had no reason to. You must understand, I loved her. I didn't realize it at first, but I did love her. And she loved me. We were going to have a baby. *Our* baby! Her death was devastating. Don't you understand? I want to slit the throat of whoever shot her."

Atkins walked out of the room, saying incongruously that he had to finish preparing for his oral argument tomorrow. No one stopped him.

The meeting was over. The rest of the business Fred Olson had wanted to talk about would have to wait. One by one, the attorneys followed Atkins out of the library conference room. There was little conversation at the moment, although soon there would be much. Olson himself walked out, greatly concerned. How would this look in Sacramento? How would it affect the Backlog? At a minimum, he suspected that no more briefs would be written that day. He was right.

Bill and Beret quickly huddled, and decided they had to meet that evening to talk about the day's events. "How about dinner at my place? Six o'clock," suggested Bill. She agreed.

Inspector Tarkov placed the two sheets of paper into his briefcase, breathed deeply, and put on his coat. Inspector Petersen picked up his own briefcase, and put on his own coat. They looked at each other in quiet satisfaction as they left the room together. That had been close, their glances said. They did not know what they would have done if Atkins had not spoken when he did. There was little they could have done. Rachel Brandwyn's letter to the father had never existed.

After everyone else had left the library conference room, Michelle Hong sat silently for several minutes in her chair, staring at the blank notepad in front of her. Then she stood up slowly, and walked out of the room.

Chapter 19

Inspector Tarkov sought out Bill and Beret a few minutes later. He explained to them that the inspectors had simply invented the letter Rachel supposedly wrote, and that their ruse had succeeded. He thanked them for their help in baiting the trap. He also told them to "keep your ears open," but to continue to be "supremely careful."

After the inspectors departed, Bill and Beret, like everyone else, spent the rest of the day in frenzied discussions. If Thomas Atkins was the father, was he also the murderer? The very idea shocked everyone. He couldn't possibly have killed Rachel. It was too awful to even contemplate. No conclusions were reached. Bill and Beret heard nothing from anyone that seemed to be incriminating. They did not talk to each other privately. That was for later.

Atkins himself retired to his office and closed the door. He apparently really was preparing to argue the *Jones* case the next day. And why not? Why shouldn't he argue it? There was no proof he had committed a crime, only an indiscretion he had unwisely kept quiet. No one else could take the case and be ready to argue it the next day. Because the argument had been postponed once already—although for a pretty good reason—the Chief Justice would be reluctant to agree to a second postponement. In addition, maintaining a semblance of normality might be best for all. Fred Olson, for one, would be happy to get the *Jones* case behind him.

Bill left work early to go to the store and get something for dinner. He could cook no better than Beret. On such short notice, the best idea he could come up with was hamburgers. With frozen French fries and a small green salad. He would do better next time. In fact, one of these days the two of them would have to have a really good dinner. But not tonight. Food was the last thing they wanted to worry about now.

Beret arrived promptly a few minutes after six o'clock. She brought the same chilled Chardonnay that Bill had taken to her house the evening of the spaghetti dinner. They decided to drink it even though it did not go well with hamburgers and frozen French fries. Bill's cat, Prince, took an immediate liking to Beret, undoubtedly because his bright orange fur looked so nice when it clung to Beret's dark-blue slacks. *Oh, well, at least it's not white,* she thought.

After a quick and quiet dinner, they moved to Bill's living room for coffee and a discussion. Bill collected his notepad and the chart of the suspects he had made in court so long ago. Both sat down on his couch, where Prince promptly jumped onto Beret's lap. Bill started by asking the obvious question. "What about Tom Atkins. Is he our murderer?"

"If he is, he's a great actor," Beret said. "He gave quite a performance. His story was dramatic, but it does not prove he was the killer. On the other hand, it is quite a coincidence that Rachel gets pregnant and then is suddenly murdered. Are the events connected? If Tom really wanted to marry Michelle Hong and Rachel threatened to announce publicly that he had gotten her pregnant, that's what is called a motive."

"But there's no proof. He had access to the murder weapon, and an opportunity to use it, but so did several others. Personally, I believed Tom. Nobody could put on that performance if it were not real."

Beret scratched Prince under the chin. The cat rolled over, indicating he preferred to have his belly rubbed. She complied. "I agree with you. I think. But *somebody* killed Rachel, and Atkins is as likely a suspect as any. We can't dismiss him just because he put on a good show."

Bill made a notation on his notepad. "Atkins. Innocent? Or great actor?" He looked up. "Now I suggest we do what we did last time. Go over the suspects" (by now it seemed natural to call their colleagues suspects) "one by one in alphabetical order. Then let's see what we have." Beret agreed. "First is Ramon Aguilar. He seems to be completely off the hook. The anonymous phone calls suggested he was the father. We now know he wasn't."

"Do we? Atkins *thinks* he was the father, but can he be sure? The letter naming him as the father did not really exist."

Bill stared at Beret for a moment. "Are you suggesting Rachel was sleeping with more than one person?"

"I'm not suggesting anything. Except that we can't exclude the possibility. It seems to me that something strange was going on between Ramon and Rachel. That meeting at the Palace was definitely out of the ordinary. And it really took place. Ramon admitted it to me. He might have thought he was the father, and the stormy meeting was Rachel's way to put pressure on. Ramon acted suspiciously when I talked to him. We can't rule him out."

Bill pondered the matter for a moment. "Another idea, a rather bizzare one, has occurred to me. The whole thing might be a double reverse."

Beret looked at Bill doubtfully. "What do you mean by that?"

"Did you ever read the story or see the play, *Witness for the Prosecution?*"

"Both. Agatha Christie wrote it, didn't she? And Marlene Dietrich starred in the movie."

"Exactly. A man is charged with murder. A woman goes to the prosecution in disguise with damning evidence against him, and becomes the star witness for the prosecution. Then she secretly supplies the defense with evidence to prove she is lying. The defense uses the evidence to destroy her on the witness stand. By the time the defense attorney, Charles Laughton, finishes cross-examining her, everyone is convinced she tried to frame an innocent man. The jury ignores the rest of the strong evidence against the defendant and acquits him. It turns out the witness for the prosecution was the defendant's girlfriend. She had planned the whole thing to get him acquitted because she knew he was guilty and would otherwise be convicted."

Beret smiled. "You think this case might be similar? Ramon Aguilar kills Rachel, then makes the anonymous calls suggesting he was the father and therefore the murderer. When it turns out that someone else was the father, he is no longer suspected. How diabolical. That could only happen in fiction, never in real life."

"They say that life imitates art. I'm not saying that's how it is. Only that it might be."

"But how would Ramon have known that the identity of the

father would ever be established? After all, it only came out by luck."

"Good question. Maybe Ramon had confidence in Tarkov and Petersen."

"Or us," added Beret.

"Or us." Bill laughed. "Although that seems less likely. I admit I don't have all the answers. But I agree with you that we can't rule Ramon out. The meeting at the Palace suggests he had a motive of some kind." He made another notation on his notepad, "Ramon Aguilar—double reverse?" then said, "Let's go on. We've already talked about Tom Atkins. He clearly has a motive. Next is Martin Granowski."

"He still has to be considered a prime suspect. He had custody of the murder weapon and Rachel was threatening to publicly criticize his handling of the *Morton* trial."

"The memo she wrote was not exactly subtle," agreed Beret. "Also, Tom Atkins and Michelle mentioned that Rachel had taken the side of Georgette Johnson when she and Martin split up. That was a bitter quarrel, and hard feelings might have lingered. Maybe Rachel's interference in *Morton* was the last straw."

"He sure showed a lot of people how to use the gun and silencer. Maybe to spread the suspicion. One would have expected him to be very careful with those exhibits. We definitely have to consider Martin." Bill made another note. "Who's next? Anna Heitz."

"I don't know what to think about Anna. It's hard to believe she would commit murder merely because she felt Rachel stole her United States Supreme Court case. But she apparently was really upset. She denies it, and denies making any threats, which is all the more suspicious."

"It's also quite a coincidence that her nephew, the gardener at San Quentin, killed his roommate because he claimed the roommate had stolen a paper. That's a remarkably similar motive to Anna's."

Beret moved slightly to get more comfortable. Prince stood up in irritation, then quickly curled up again in the same spot and fell asleep. "And Anna testified on his behalf. She supported that defense, if you can call it that. Is there some Freudian subconscious element at play here? Anna testifies that her nephew killed for a reason, then later she kills for the same reason?"

"I don't know," replied Bill. "That's too deep for me. But we have to think about it. Some famous detective once said to beware of the coincidence; it might be design, not chance. I think Father Brown might have said it, or maybe Nero Wolfe. Or was it Sam Spade?"

Beret smiled. "Perhaps William Kelly gets the credit. It sounds good to me. It may even be brilliant. We must write it down for posterity just in case." She pretended to write something, then continued. "Seriously, it's hard to see a connection between this case and Joe's, but the coincidence *is* unsettling. Anyway, a motive is a motive, no matter how shaky. We can't rule Anna out."

"I agree. She is still a prime suspect. I just wish we had some evidence." Bill made another note. "Next is Michelle Hong. The last time we talked about her we could see no possible motive."

"How different things are now. She was in love with Tom Atkins, maybe still is. Did Tom talk to her about Rachel? Did Rachel threaten to blackmail him? Or Michelle? Did Michelle see Rachel as a threat she had to remove?"

Bill wrote all this down, then looked up. "And remember that Michelle asked Martin Granowski to show her the murder weapon and silencer the day before Rachel was killed. The timing is perfect. Maybe Michelle learned about Rachel's pregnancy, possibly from Tom, and then remembered talk about the gun Martin was showing everybody. It would have been easy for her to express an interest in the gun, and then use it the next day. She has to be considered a prime suspect."

"We can investigate this further," said Beret. "Tom might be able to shed light on the subject. How much did he tell Michelle? And when? Was Michelle angry?"

"We must talk to him," Bill agreed, "although I don't know how much he'll tell us under the circumstances. Or how much we can believe him. After all, he is himself a suspect, and his current relationship with Michelle has to be strained, to say the least. But we'll talk to him. Tomorrow, right after his Supreme Court argument." Bill made a note. "Talk with Atkins re Hong after *Jones* argument." He stood and went into the kitchen to get some ice cream for dessert. Prince jumped off Beret's lap to follow but was soon disappointed to discover that Bill was not getting cat food. When Bill returned, he looked at his notepad. "Next we have

Brian Howarth. There apparently was a serious conflict between him and Rachel over her role in the *Rawlings* case."

"He didn't want her involved and might have been stung by her criticism of his performance. Just like Granowski and the *Morton* case."

"Yes. She was fond of criticizing others. She also liked to have her hand in every pie. She wasn't even involved in prison litigation cases, yet volunteered to work on *Rawlings* on her own time. Why?"

"Presumably she wanted the experience," Beret responded. "In addition, her work on the *Wakefield* and *Robinson* case might have made her interested in San Quentin affairs. Anyway, she did volunteer to work on *Rawlings,* and complained to Tom Oldfield about Brian. She said she would write a memo, but apparently never did."

"Maybe she was killed before she *could* write it."

"Maybe." They both sat quietly for a moment. "All we can say now is that Brian is a prime suspect."

Bill made the appropriate note, then said, "Fred Olson. As we've said before, he's got a motive. He wants to keep his job as head of the criminal division, and Rachel was continually rocking the boat.

"Her sexual harassment charges against Trevor Watson implicitly criticize Fred. She claimed he just ignored her informal complaints. She also caused a row with Anna Heitz over the *Schultz* case. She castigated Granowski in the *Morton* case. She apparently got involved in the breakup of Granowski and Georgette Johnson. All of this might have made Fred look bad in Sacramento. It's hard to imagine Fred would believe murder could solve his problems, but we can't rule it out."

"None of the motives look that great, yet *someone* killed Rachel. I suppose Fred had as much motive as anyone. We must consider him a prime suspect."

Beret shifted her position to make room for Prince, who returned to her lap. "I have the strangest feeling that we are missing something. Something is wrong somewhere. I just don't know what."

"I have the same feeling. Someone said something or did something that doesn't fit in. But what? I've gone over everything time and again, and I can't find it. The clue is there, we just have to locate it. Any real detective would be able to. We have to think harder."

Bill and Beret looked at each other, attempted to think harder, then abandoned the attempt. "It'll come to us," said Bill. "In the meantime, let's finish what we are doing. The last of our suspects is Trevor Watson."

"I see no new development here. Rachel accused him of sexually harassing her, and was going to formally complain to Sacramento. That could have seriously hurt his career."

"He also didn't take well to people getting in his way. We have to consider him a prime suspect." Bill wrote it down.

Beret ate the last of her ice cream. "I agree. Unfortunately, that doesn't bring us very far."

"Let's do this scientifically. I made one chart a while ago. Maybe a new one will help." He walked to a desk in the corner of the room. On top were a blank piece of paper, a ruler, and two marking pens, one red and one blue. With Beret looking over his shoulder and making occasional suggestions, he drafted a chart similar to the one he had prepared what seemed like so long ago. It was artistically done. All the lines and boxes were evenly spaced, and the writing neat and precise. This is what it looked like:

Suspect	Opportunity?	Means?	Motive?
Ramon Aguilar	yes	yes	possible
Thomas Atkins	yes	yes	yes
Martin Granowski	yes	yes	yes
Anna Heitz	yes	yes	yes
Michelle Hong	yes	yes	yes
Brian Howarth	yes	yes	yes
Fred Olson	yes	yes	yes
Trevor Watson	yes	yes	yes

When they finished, they surveyed their work, and compared it to the previous chart. "Somehow, I thought this would be more helpful," Bill commented ruefully. "Find the motive, I thought, and we will find the killer. We were too successful. We found motive, lots of motive, but where's the killer? Which is the real motive?"

"If any."

"If any," Bill agreed. "And where do we go from here? I'm running out of ideas."

"Me, too. At least we can question Tom Atkins about Michelle after his argument tomorrow. After that, I suggest we huddle again and decide what to do next." Beret paused and looked intently at Bill. "Are we getting anywhere? Or are we just spinning our wheels?"

"I have no idea," answered Bill. "Everything seems so unreal. The deeper we delve, the more I feel we are in the middle of a badly written murder mystery. It's hard to believe these things could happen in real life."

Beret laughed. "If this were a murder mystery, it would definitely be badly written. Or at least boring. Nobody could make a story about appellate lawyers interesting."

Bill was insulted. "What do you mean by that?"

"People want stories about trial lawyers, like in *L.A. Law* and *Rumpole of the Bailey.* They want juries, witnesses breaking down under cross-examination, exhibits, objections, quarrels, courtroom surprises. Not transcripts, appellate briefs, and oral arguments. How dull. Could you imagine a television series called *Appellate Law?* The viewers would fall asleep."

Bill loved appellate law, and felt obligated to challenge this calumny. "But trial practice itself can be boring and routine. The exciting stuff is only on television and in the movies. In real life, trial lawyers mostly prepare for trials that never happen because the case settles, or they hang around the courthouse waiting for courtrooms that aren't available."

"True," Beret admitted. "But that part of trial practice is ignored. The public is shown only the so-called courtroom drama. What kind of drama could you show in appellate practice?"

"But this case involves a lot more than just appellate law. There is a triple murder trial in the background."

"That helps," Beret conceded.

"And the prison litigation unit."

"People would probably find that unit even duller than the appellate section. At least our cases involve serious crimes, like rape, robbery, and murder, not just living conditions in prison."

"That's true." It was Bill's turn to make a concession. "But appellate practice is law in its purest form. You're exaggerating how dull appellate lawyers are. I find them to be intellectually stimulating, even exciting."

"But that's only because you're one of them yourself."

For once, Bill had no answer.

Chapter 20

That same evening was one of contemplation, followed by sleeplessness, for another person. The days were fine, filled with confidence. But the nights were different. As during other nights, the person lay awake in bed staring at the ceiling. But this time, the ceiling was no longer shrouded in darkness. The person, increasingly terrified by the dark in recent days, bought a night-light, then a more powerful one. It was on now; although the light was dim, the ceiling could be seen. As the person moved in bed, shadows could be seen flickering on the ceiling. Other objects in the bedroom could also be seen, although only as silhouettes, dim specters of their daytime appearance. The light was comforting, although it only alleviated, it did not vanquish, the ever-growing, the ever more pervasive, terrors of the night.

The person had killed—so far only once . . . but killed nonetheless. It was necessary, and the killing had been quick and effective. The hope and, for a while, sincere belief, that no more killing would be necessary nurtured the person, and helped reduce the number of sleepless nights. But the hope was gone now. The belief had only been a delusion, never more. The events of the day proved it. What had been said had been said, and could not be forgotten. Or ignored.

The person lay on the bed staring at the dark ceiling and listening to the gentle rain that had resumed after a respite in the afternoon. The unusual rain intensified the vague feeling of unreality mixed with apprehension. *I did not want to kill, it was thrust upon me,* the person thought. *It is being thrust upon me again. To avoid killing unless necessary, that is to be expected of a human being. Only a maniac kills without necessity. But to do what is necessary, to do it efficiently and well, without hesitation and without being detected, that is the mark of the chosen few, of those who truly carry their destiny in their hands. I am one of those few. I demonstrated that a month ago. I will demonstrate it again, but only out of necessity.*

But how? The thought jolted the person into violent movement. The hands shook, the feet danced. This made the shadows on the ceiling also dance, which the person found frightening, yet paradoxically soothing. Yes, the night-light was a good idea. Especially in the rain. The shadows, visible incarnations of the necessity that governed the actions of the daytime, were comforting. But *how* to kill had to be carefully considered. The first killing (the person never thought the word "murder"—it was not murder to do what was necessary) had been easy. The weapon was at hand, the suspects many. But a second killing with the same weapon would not be wise. Besides, the person had pride. Any simpleton could use the same plan again. *Repetition is dull, unimaginative, unnecessary. I will not repeat. The necessity to kill is my fate, but versatility will be my virtue.* The logic was compelling. A new method must be found. One as quick as before, as effective, as undetectable. But different.

What method? The person lay quietly now, the shadows on the ceiling invisible, the rain slowing to an almost imperceptible trickle. How to kill again? *Who* to kill was predetermined, established by fate. It was unfortunate that he had to be killed, but was it the fault of the person staring at the ceiling? *No! I did not choose to have to kill. The choice was made for me. Why should I be remorseful? I am not at fault. Others may disagree, may criticize my actions, may even say I like to kill. But they are wrong!* The thoughts agitated the person, and the violent shaking recommenced, to be translated into dancing shadows on the ceiling. The dancing shadows in turn soothed the person, thus repeating the cycle of agitation and quiet.

The shadows stopped dancing, the rain ceased, and all was quiet. Which was how it should be. The momentous tactical decision must be made in tranquility, the plan formed with logic, not emotion. The plan must be undetectable, like the last one. Other people, if they knew who the killer was, might not understand the necessity, might not appreciate the blamelessness of the deed. They probably, almost certainly, would not. The person must never be detected. The first killing had been a masterpiece. The second must be also, but yet it must also be different. How?

The person contemplated the question for a full hour, lying on the back completely motionless the entire time. The patience, the self-discipline, this took demonstrated the person's genius. *Yes, I can outwait, I can outthink anyone! Pride! I must have pride. If I just wait, if I devise the perfect plan, I can do it.* The shadows in the room remained quiet along with the occupant. Gradually, a plan formed, inchoate at first, then clearer, finally fully visualized. Would it work? *I think so. If I do everything right. Yes, it will work! He threatened to do it to me; I will do it to him instead. How inspired! Now I only have to work out every detail.*

And the person worked out every detail during that hour. Every tiny detail. The person reviewed the plan, tried to imagine everything that could go wrong, revised it continually, always made it better. As finally conceived, the plan was perfect, and, at the same time, wonderfully ironic. The killing would be different, yet strangely similar. It would be a parallel killing. There was genius in its versatility, beauty in its similarity. Yes, the person thought, the plan was ideal. The thought was comforting, even more so than the night-light itself.

Only one minor irritation marred the satisfaction of the moment. The first killing was a work of art, as would be the second, but no one would know who the artist was; no one could ever fully appreciate the talent, the genius, that went into the planning and the execution. The killings must never be solved; but that meant the person would be cheated of the deserved acclaim. Surely there would be acclaim for the perpetration, even if disapproval of the result.

Ah, to be able to tell someone, anyone, that I did it, and to bask in the admiration, in the adulation, that is rightfully mine. The person dreamed of being able to tell someone, anyone, of the exploits, to compare them with those of other great individuals of history. That is, the person would have dreamed if sleep had been possible.

Maybe sleep would be possible now. The plan, so perfect, was soothing, a balm for the terrors that the events of the day had magnified. The person finally fell asleep, or nearly so. Then a thought penetrated the fading consciousness, a disturbing thought. Suddenly, the shadows on the ceiling danced again. The agitation began anew, the person tossed and turned on the bed.

Necessity! The person's master. Everyone's master. What if it made its appearance again? And again? Would the person kill again? Would it be *necessary* to kill again? The person had once, long ago, hoped that only one killing would be needed. That hope, the person now knew, was futile, had always been futile. Would a third killing, even a fourth, be needed? The person knew who the third sacrifice to necessity, and the fourth, might be. How would those killings be done? *How versatile can I be?* The terrors of the night returned.

But only temporarily. *I must think only of what is necessary, not of what might* become *necessary. I do not kill for pleasure, only as needed. Since killing is necessary, I might as well enjoy the pleasure. I will take the killings one at a time.* Que será será. *Let whatever has to happen, happen. I am not to blame. The next killing will be as beautiful as the first. After that, who knows? It is not my responsibility.*

By this time, the rain had stopped completely. These final thoughts brought renewed comfort, and allowed the restless person to drift into an uneasy sleep. The shadows on the ceiling—to the person, incarnations of the necessity that absolves responsibility—faded into obscurity. The sleep continued unbroken until daylight signaled the necessity to awaken and to face the day's events.

Chapter 21

Thomas Atkins awoke early the next day. The previous day's rain had turned to blue sky, with not a cloud in sight except for a few fluffy ones along the coast. It promised to be one of those lovely Bay Area days in June, cool by the coast, warm but not hot farther inland. The rain had left the air crystal clear, leaving the area's natural beauty in sharp focus.

Atkins had slept remarkably well. After the tension of the previous weeks, he found it a relief to have revealed the truth about himself. He was glad he had to be in court that morning. It took his mind off his problems. He knew he had to perform well to continue the excellent work of Rachel Brandwyn before her death. But he was an experienced oral advocate, and had so much confidence in his abilities that he was reasonably relaxed. After the argument, Atkins would begin the task of mending matters with his colleagues, but until then he was able to avoid brooding about his troubles. His relationship with Michelle Hong was uncertain, but that could also wait.

Atkins lived in Mill Valley, north of San Francisco. He usually took the bus to work across the Golden Gate Bridge. Today, however, he decided to take the ferry from Sausalito even though it took a little longer. He left home early enough to have time to go by water, check in with the Supreme Court, then go to his office for final preparations. He had originally intended to use his time on the ferry to go over his notes, but once on board he yielded to temptation and stood on the deck to admire the magnificent view.

It's good to be alive, he told himself as he viewed the San Francisco skyline in front of him—Oakland and the East Bay hills to the left, and the Golden Gate Bridge and open sea to the right, all brilliantly clear in the fresh, clean air. The air was so clear he almost felt he could see which windows on the Transamerica Pyramid had been washed recently and which had not. Even the top of the Golden Gate Bridge was free of fog. Alcatraz Island passed on the left, and San Francisco's Ferry Building, the boat's destination, drew near. For a precious few minutes, Atkins was able to get his mind off the pregnancy, the murder, the events of yesterday, and the imminent court appearance, as he felt the soft breeze against his face, still cool in the early morning, and breathed deeply of the salt air. The Bay area might have earthquakes, he thought, it might have droughts, it might have fires, but it was a great place to live. The natural disasters served only to remind us not to be too complacent about our lives.

Atkins arrived at his office a little before eight o'clock. A short time later, he walked to the courtroom to check in with the clerk, as Rachel had done a month before. The clerk said that the *Jones* case was again first on calendar, and would be heard promptly at 9:00 A.M. "And don't you dare be late! We'll accept no excuses this time." Both laughed. Opposing counsel, the same one as before, was already at his table by the podium. Atkins greeted him, then walked back to his office. There was no use returning to court until just before nine.

On the way to the office, Atkins greeted several of his colleagues. Then he closed his door, and reviewed his planned remarks one last time. Even though he had not written the brief in the case—Rachel had written it—and the record was massive, he felt he was as fully prepared as could reasonably be expected. He leaned back in his chair, placed his feet on top of the desk, closed his eyes, and meditated on exactly how he would proceed with the argument. He was confident he would do well. After that, who knew? Maybe everything would work out after all.

About a half hour after he returned to his office, Atkins's telephone rang. He picked it up on the second ring. The voice at the other end of the line was strangely muffled, as if the person was speaking through a handkerchief. Atkins could not even tell if the voice was that of a man or a woman. "If you're interested in finding out who killed Rachel Brandwyn, I can help you," the voice began. Atkins sat upright and put his feet back on the floor.

In the meantime, another person also woke early, although sleep had not come until late. The beautiful weather was encouraging;

it was a good omen for what had to be done that day. The person arrived at work shortly after Atkins, calmly greeted everyone who was passed in the hallway, then quickly took care of what few preparations there were. The portions of the building that would be used, including the escape route, were carefully checked. Yes, they would do just fine. The person was elated at how neatly everything was falling into place. The plan was perfect. It was unfortunate that no one would ever know how perfect.

Then came the necessary wait for the proper time. For the deed to be consummately beautiful, timing was everything. As always, waiting was the hardest part. But the person could be patient, could be infinitely patient, if necessary. The person sat in the chair, completely motionless, as the minutes passed. Finally, it was time, the same time as before. Oh, the irony was wonderful! The others would appreciate it, surely. The person picked up the telephone, placed a handkerchief over the mouthpiece, and dialed. When the call was answered, the person, muffling the voice, offered to help discover the killer of Rachel Brandwyn.

Atkins was astonished. The voice was offering to help him solve Rachel's murder. *Why me?* he wondered. Then again, why not? He, the father of the child she was bearing, was the most cruelly victimized among those still alive. It was fitting that he should unmask the murderer, not those two young deputies who, although they were nice enough, had no real stake in the matter. The voice obviously thought so, too. "Who are you?" Atkins asked as calmly as possible. "Or, I mean, yes, of course I want to know who killed Rachel." The question, Atkins realized immediately, had been foolish. The voice at the other end of the line clearly intended to remain anonymous. No matter. Atkins would accept help wherever he could find it.

"Good. You must do exactly what I say. Alone. I will be watching. Any variation, and we will call the whole thing off."

"You can count on me. But please speak a little more clearly. I'm having trouble understanding you."

"I will do the best I can." The voice spoke more slowly, but not more distinctly. "Listen carefully. We have to speak in person, but I don't want you to see my face. Exactly three minutes after I hang up the telephone, come to the east vestibule in the old left wing of the library." The left wing of the law library of the San

Francisco attorney general's office had been damaged in the earthquake, and was presently abandoned. The door leading to it had been closed for some time, and was not supposed to be used, but it was not locked. "Bring nothing with you, and tell no one. When you enter the vestibule, close the door behind you. Do not turn on the light until I say so. You will get further instructions at that time. If I even suspect you are not precisely following instructions, you will never see or hear from me again."

Atkins knew exactly what room the voice referred to. It was not really a vestibule but an old, surprisingly large, office for an assistant librarian. It contained high stacks of obsolete law books and a few pieces of forgotten furniture and nothing else. No one had been inside for months. "I understand, but where will you be?" asked Atkins.

"No questions. Be there in three minutes. Alone." Atkins heard a click, and the line went dead.

What did it mean? Atkins was unsure, and felt vaguely uneasy. He looked at his watch. There was just enough time to make the rendezvous, learn what there was to learn, and then go to court. The timing would be tighter than he liked. But he felt his duty was clear. He must do exactly as he was told. With the solution to the murder possibly so near, why should he take chances? Atkins noted the exact time and stepped out of his office. He looked up and down the hallway, almost expecting to see someone watching him. He saw no one and started walking slowly toward the library. He entered the library, and nodded to a couple of acquaintances inside. He was relieved that the only person from the criminal division he saw was Elizabeth Cronin. She was sitting at a carrel, flipping through a volume of Martindale-Hubbell, a directory of attorneys. Atkins passed her without speaking. Trying to appear nonchalant, he slowly approached the old wing of the library. He walked behind a stack of books that blocked the direct line of sight between Atkins and the others in the library.

Atkins looked at his watch again, then looked back in the direction from which he had come. He saw no one. He entered the old wing, and then, precisely three minutes after the speaker had hung up the telephone, he opened the door to the vestibule and walked in. It took a few seconds before he remembered to close the door behind him. The room was dark, with only a little light penetrating from a small, dirty window in the corner. As instructed, Atkins did not turn on the light. In the silence, Atkins's eyes gradually became accustomed to what light there was. He vaguely sensed that someone else was present. An indistinct noise from his left drew his attention. Turning in that direction, he saw a figure that he could barely recognize in the semidarkness. It was a friend. The friend's left hand was resting upon a massive stack of books.

"Hi, what are you doing here?" a startled Atkins asked. The person said nothing in response. Instead, the left hand pushed against the bookstack. The heavy metal bookshelves, weakened by the earthquake, suddenly toppled over onto Atkins, spilling books everywhere. It knocked Atkins to the ground, and pinned him underneath. "What's going on?" he shouted, a shout that could not be heard outside this abandoned wing of the library.

Atkins had no time to say anything else. He looked at his friend's right hand. It was wielding a knife. It looked like a butcher knife. A paper towel from the restroom was wrapped around it.

Without saying a word, the person pounced on the stunned and helpless Atkins and thrust the knife into the throat that was exposed as Atkins strained to see what was happening. The knife penetrated. The right hand pushed as hard as it could, twisted the knife, then made a sharp cut to the right. The hand then twisted the knife again and made a sharp cut to the left. Blood gushed from the gaping hole that resulted.

Atkins made a brief gurgling sound, then was silent. The assailant dexterously avoided the blood and carefully withdrew the knife. A quick examination of the body convinced the person that no further use of the knife was necessary. The knife was carefully placed on the floor next to Atkins. No one could connect it to that person, so why try to hide it? The person looked around briefly to make sure nothing was left to betray the killer's identity, then briskly walked out of the room, closing the door behind. Everything had gone according to plan.

The person quickly walked to a nearby staircase, and, following a route that had been carefully scouted a short time before, returned to the office unseen by anyone. On the way, the paper towel used to avoid leaving fingerprints was tossed into a wastebasket. Inside the office, the person, elated, took a deep breath, and tried to calm the beating of the heart.

It was 8:54 A.M., exactly as planned. *Damn,* the person thought, *no one will ever know how exquisitely, how brilliantly, I planned this.* As far as the person knew, there had been no mistakes.

Chapter 22

A sense of déjà vu quickly pervaded the crowded courtroom as everyone waited silently for Thomas Atkins to appear to argue the *Jones* case. The same people were present as a month earlier: some were literally the same; others, such as the attorneys waiting their turn to argue, had slightly different faces as before, although the same attire and briefcases. The Chief Justice had called the *Jones* case at 9:01 A.M. Once again, he presided over a deadly silent courtroom as everyone waited for counsel to appear. The empty chair reserved for the attorney general dominated the scene. When the clock on the back wall clicked to 9:03, the clerk nervously remembered his parting words to Atkins less than an hour before: "Don't be late!"

Those who had been present on the fateful day a month earlier —the reporters, opposing counsel, the justices, many of the deputies attorney general in the audience—involuntarily thought the horrible thought: Might history be repeating itself? The attorneys in the later cases waited anxiously, wondering what could possibly cause an attorney to be late for a Supreme Court argument. The reporter for the afternoon paper from the town where the *Jones* murders had occurred again grew increasingly frantic due to his tight deadline.

There was even a group of high school students on a field trip to see the judiciary in action, only this time they were juniors from Galileo High School. Like their predecessors, they had no idea what was going on, but were not impressed with the proceedings. When does it get exciting? they wondered. And, how long could they sit here in silence? So far their behavior had been impeccable.

Beret and Bill sat together in the audience, as they had a month before. They sat transfixed, almost paralyzed, as the clocked clicked to 9:04. Each thought that they surely must go upstairs to see what was happening, but they could not. It was not due to fear, but inertia. In the face of the uncertainty, it was simply easier to wait and see what would happen. They remained planted in their seats. Atkins knew his argument was scheduled, they told themselves, and surely he would appear soon with a good explanation. Or someone else would appear with an explanation. If not, they could investigate in a few minutes. The same emotions seemed to keep the other members of the criminal division in their seats.

The Chief Justice grew even angrier than he had been a month ago. As he observed the clock click to 9:05, he told himself, *I overlooked the tardiness last time. I will not tolerate it a second time. This is contemptible, and will be punished as such. Justice must not be trifled with. Who can I cite for contempt? Atkins certainly. Probably Fred Olson. Maybe even the attorney general himself? No, that was probably going too far. Atkins and Olson will be enough. But I will accept no excuses this time.* As always, such thoughts relaxed him. He would continue waiting.

The clock clicked to 9:06, five minutes after the case had been called. Suddenly a young woman burst into the courtroom from a side door, shrieking, "Tom's been murdered!"

A few minutes earlier, Elizabeth Cronin had been working in the library getting some information for Fred Olson. It occurred to her vaguely that although Tom Atkins had walked past her toward the rear of the library several minutes previously, she had not seen him return. *That's odd,* she thought, looking at her watch. *Isn't he supposed to be in the Supreme Court by now?* She had dismissed her concern and resumed her work. He probably had left the library without her seeing him. But gradually she became uneasy. Where was he? More out of curiosity than anything, she got up and walked back to where she last saw Atkins. Nothing appeared out of the ordinary. Atkins was not to be seen. Where did he go? The more she thought about it, the more certain she became that Atkins had not walked back past her, as he would have if he had gone to court.

The door to the old left wing of the library, the one no longer used because of earthquake damage, was closed. Without fully understanding why, other than somehow being drawn to that door, Elizabeth approached it and opened it. The darkness and the silence frightened her, although the feeling was silly because the lights would naturally not be turned on and there was no one around to make any noise. She turned the lights on. The place was dusty, which was to be expected, but everything seemed in order. Atkins was not there. Then she looked at the office for the assistant librarian in the corner. For some reason it had always been called the vestibule. Its door, too, was closed. But what was that splotch under the door? It seemed to be growing. Elizabeth approached to take a closer look. It was a liquid, a red liquid, seeping under the door. Just like last time.

Elizabeth did not feel any vague sense of déjà vu. She felt instead terror—stark, pure terror. But she steeled herself, and walked to the door. Careful not to step in the liquid, she slowly opened the door. She reached for the switch next to the door, and turned on the lights. It took all of her self-control to look inside. When she did, as a month before, she screamed at what she saw.

The shout about a murder jolted the Chief Justice from his reverie. *Damn,* he thought. *Not again. Well, it's not going to work this time; heads are going to roll no matter what. Atkins might be off the hook, but not everyone else. Not by a long shot.* But, he reluctantly decided, contempt proceedings would have to wait. In the meantime, he had a courtroom to run. While bedlam broke loose and the students perked up and the reporters started rapidly writing and the deputies attorney general fled the courtroom, he ordered the clerk to call the next case, an attorney malpractice case. The clerk did.

In a matter of seconds, decorum returned to the courtroom. Four attorneys were to argue the malpractice case, one each representing the two parties and one each representing *amicus curiae* for each side. Unexpectedly called upon to argue the case an hour early, they hurridly assumed their places at the front tables, all with their respective bulging briefcases. One middle-aged attorney frantically organized his notes and, with one last comment to a much younger colleague who remained behind, he stepped to the podium. He introduced himself to the court in time-honored fashion, and began his argument. It was a long time before any of the justices interrupted with a question.

* * *

Fred Olson was stunned. He had lost Rachel Brandwyn's productivity. Now Thomas Atkins's. How could he possibly keep the Backlog from becoming even larger? Could he at least replace Atkins? The only good news that he could discern was that it appeared the same person had committed both murders. If that person turned out to be a member of his staff (Olson's worst fear), then only one more attorney, not two, would be lost to him. Cheered only slightly by this thought, Olson sent a young deputy to ask the court for another continuance. Having done that, he decided that all other decisions regarding this turn of events could wait. Olson did not even begin to consider who he could now assign to take over the *Jones* case. With the first two assigned the case dead, who would be the third?

The instant they heard the shout, William Kelly and Beret Holmes got up and ran hand in hand back up the stairs to the attorney general's office. The number of suspects in the murder of Rachel Brandwyn suddenly had been reduced by one, but not in the manner they had desired. The need to solve the case, and immediately, had been driven home in no uncertain terms. Each wondered briefly whether it was his or her fault for not finding the key that surely lay out there somewhere. Each understood their unspoken but mutual determination to find the answer soon. Bill did not spare a single thought for the softball game that was scheduled for that evening but would again have to be postponed.

California State Police Officer Theodore French was the first officer on the scene, as he had been a month before. He observed a body lying on its back in a pool of blood. The eyes, still open, were looking upward. The mouth was strangely contorted; to Officer French it looked like a silly grin, as if the victim had considered the incident to be a bad joke. But it was no joke. The blood had flowed from a hideous gash on the victim's throat. Some of the blood was still liquid. Closer inspection revealed that a tiny amount of blood was still dribbling from the wound. A metal bookshelf, which had apparently toppled over, lay on top of the body, covering it from the chest downward. Old law books were scattered all about; some were now bloodstained.

French examined the body closely, although a quick glance sufficed to convince him that it was beyond medical help. All that was left was for French to preserve the scene. He was now a veteran preserver of homicide scenes, having preserved one a month before. As a veteran, he went about his business calmly and dispassionately. At least reasonably so. The knife and anything else that might contain fingerprints or other clues were carefully not touched. The curious were kept away. Within a few minutes, officers from the San Francisco Police Department arrived and took over the investigation. The search for physical evidence began.

Inspector Petersen arrived within ten minutes, followed fifteen minutes later by Inspector Tarkov. The latter had been called away from a homicide investigation in the Sunset district. Both inspectors, even the veteran Petersen, were shattered when they saw the body. Neither had ever had a second murder intrude on a homicide investigation. They blamed themselves for not bringing the culprit to justice earlier and preventing this tragedy.

For Tarkov, there was a possible consolation. He took one look at the scene, with its wealth of potential physical clues, and felt a surge of hope that maybe this time scientific analysis would solve the crime. Maybe this time the killer had left his fingerprints behind. Or, better yet, maybe a blood sample. Or something else? Petersen was less hopeful, but was willing to try anything. The criminalists performed their duties meticulously.

An hour later, the inspectors met with Olson, Kelly, and Holmes in Olson's office. Fred sat in the big chair behind the desk, Bill and Beret in the smaller chairs in front of it. The inspectors stood, with Petersen continually pacing. Tarkov began briefing the others. "The victim died of exsanguination due to extreme lacerations in and about the region of the pharynx extending to the left and right auricle regions caused by a long stabbing instrument." He paused to take a breath. Fred looked at Bill, who looked at Beret, who looked at both of them.

"His throat was cut from ear to ear," explained Petersen.

"Ah," responded the three attorneys.

"As you know," continued Tarkov after a glance at Petersen, "the murder occurred in a portion of the library that appears to have been deserted."

"Yes, what we call the vestibule," explained Olson. "That part of the library was damaged in the earthquake and has been closed until the damage was repaired. Budget constraints have prevented us from taking care of it. There are only obsolete law books there now."

"It looks like the killer was waiting for the victim to come into the room. When the victim entered, the killer pushed the shelf of library books onto him, then slit his throat as he lay pinned underneath. Do you have any explanation for why the victim would have entered that room?"

Olson thought for a moment. "I do not. There was no reason for anyone to be there. And especially not for Atkins a few minutes before he was to argue a case before the California Supreme Court." Olson explained to the inspectors about the *Jones* argument. Then an idea occurred to him. "Maybe the killer lured Atkins to the vestibule on some pretext."

Tarkov sighed, and spoke as if to a child. "That's a good point. We'll look into that possibility."

Olson smiled. "Glad to be of help."

Petersen asked the next question. "The bookshelf looks like it was very solid, and should have been screwed to the floor. Do you have any idea how hard it would have been to push it over?"

Olson responded quickly. "Not hard at all. It had been severely weakened by the earthquake. Anyone could have pushed it over. Even someone like Anna Heitz. We considered it very dangerous. We have long been planning to, uh—" As soon as Olson spoke these last words, he regretted them.

"You were planning to do what?" asked Petersen.

"Um, we were planning to take the books down and get rid of the shelf, but we never, um, never . . ."

"You never got around to it, is that what you are trying to say?" persisted Petersen.

"The room was closed off. It wasn't that dangerous. How was I to know that a mad killer would use it?" pleaded Olson. To himself, he said, *please, oh please, don't let the people in Sacramento find out about this conversation. A second murder and in a room that was supposed to have been repaired months ago.*

Tarkov took notes, then changed the subject. "The murder weapon was left behind. It is a common kitchen butcher knife, containing no fingerprints. The killer apparently wore gloves or wiped the knife handle clean before placing it on the floor. The knife has no distinctive features, no way we could reasonably connect it with anybody." He found it difficult to keep the disappointment out of his voice.

"So this time the murder weapon is not a court exhibit?" asked Fred, his relief obvious.

"No. At least there was no exhibit tag attached to it." Tarkov looked sharply at Fred. "You're not prosecuting any case involving a butcher knife, are you?"

"Of course not. Not that I know of anyway. No, I would know, and we're not. The killer probably brought the knife from home."

Tarkov sighed as if to say he was glad to have that straightened out, then said, "The time of death will have to be established by the pathologist, but it appears the stabbing occurred sometime between eight forty-five and nine o'clock. We will, of course, examine the various blood samples, but the appearances suggest that the blood all came from the same person." After a moment he added unnecessarily, "The victim."

"In short," Petersen summed up, "it looks like our killer, and it almost certainly is the same person, has again managed to leave no physical clue behind."

"So we are back where we started?" asked Fred.

"Not necessarily," responded Tarkov. "We will still analyze the physical evidence scientifically. And very thoroughly. We might still find something." Even Tarkov could not sound convincing. Bill and Beret glanced at each other. They had not really expected there would be any useful evidence. That did not seem to be in the nature of the case. "In addition," continued Tarkov, "we will interview everyone like we did before. With any kind of luck, some of our prime suspects will have ironclad alibis, maybe even all but one. Also, the killer had to walk to and from the homicide scene. Maybe someone saw him. If anyone did," he concluded grimly, "we'll find out."

There was a pause. Petersen looked directly at Bill and Beret. "We will conduct these interviews, and the rest of the investigation, ourselves. Roman and I have talked this over." Tarkov nodded agreement. "And we have to take you two off the case. It's too dangerous. Someone who has killed twice can kill again. You two would be the next obvious targets. Especially if you threaten to get too close." *There does not appear to be much danger of that,* thought Bill. "Roman and I appreciate all your help, but that's it.

We will spread the word that you are off the case, which should help shield you from danger."

"I can help in that regard," Fred said eagerly. "I'm calling a division meeting for this afternoon to discuss the day's events. I'll stress that Bill and Beret are no longer working on the case." *That will give them more time to write briefs,* he told himself. The thought cheered him.

"You do that," responded Petersen almost as an afterthought. Bill and Beret voiced no opposition. There was nothing more they could do anyway. They had tried but failed. Each thought, however, that nothing could prevent them from talking about the case and reporting to the inspectors anything they might discover by chance.

"So," concluded Tarkov, "the two of you should now leave the room while we conduct the interviews." He turned to Fred. "Since you're here, we'll begin with you. What were your exact movements this morning?"

Fred resented the implication that he was one of the "prime suspects," but could do nothing about it. While Bill and Beret walked out of the office, he began reciting his movements that morning.

The inspectors were no more successful this time than after the first murder. Nobody had seen anyone but Atkins approach or depart the area of the crime or seen anything else of any help. Further investigation showed that the killer could quite easily have walked from the area of the criminal division, taken a little-used stairway to the next floor down, walked to another part of the building, and then gone back upstairs to the scene of the crime, all without being seen. The return trip would have been equally easy, either back to the criminal division or to the courtroom. The crime obviously had been well planned.

Inquiries into alibis were equally fruitless. Fred Olson had been working in his office, but had left twice on business. He had spoken with Elizabeth Cronin a number of times that morning, but not around the time of the murder. In short, he had no alibi. Anna Heitz said she had been in her office from around eight-thirty until the body was discovered. A few people saw her in her office, but none could deny the possibility that she slipped out for a few minutes on a deadly mission. Martin Granowski, Ramon

Aguilar, Brian Howarth, and Trevor Watson were all sitting alone in the courtroom when the news of the murder came. Each said he had arrived sometime before nine. No one could supply a full alibi for any of them.

Michelle Hong, obviously distraught, insisted that she had not spoken to Atkins since he revealed that he was the father of Rachel's child. She had not known where her relationship with him stood and now would never know. She said that she did not arrive at work that morning until shortly after nine. She intentionally arrived after the oral argument was supposed to begin to make sure she did not meet Atkins. She went straight to her office, intending to confront Atkins later. Although two people saw her enter her office around nine, no one could say for sure she was not in the building earlier.

Jeff Hines, Rachel Brandwyn's former secretary who had recently been assigned to Atkins, said that Atkins had arrived sometime around eight-fifteen. He had gone to his office and closed the door. That was unusual, but not surprising in light of the upcoming court appearance. Hines had noticed that the office was empty and the door open a few minutes before nine, but observed nothing useful in between those times.

Everyone, of course, vehemently denied stabbing Atkins. No one could possibly have had any reason to want to kill him except, everyone stressed, the person who killed Rachel, whoever that was. He had been universally respected, liked, and even admired. Even more so than Rachel Brandwyn herself. He had been a fine lawyer, a sympathetic supervisor, a hard worker, a valued colleague, in short, a pillar of support for the entire criminal division and, indeed, the world as a whole. He was a wonderful person, even if he *had* been the father of Rachel's baby. He would be sorely missed by all. That is, everyone stressed, all but one.

The inspectors finished the interviews shortly before noon. They told Fred Olson that they had made little progress, in fact none, but would continue their investigation. The killer was smart, but they would catch him (or her). It was just a matter of time. And, added Petersen, legwork.

Chapter 23

At two-thirty, Fred Olson presided over an emergency meeting of the criminal division, the second meeting in two days. Everybody was there. The library conference room was deathly quiet. Those present stared at the table in front of them. None spoke. As always, the legal pads were on the table, but they would not be written upon during this meeting. Two murders! And almost certainly related. Those who had grimly hoped the murderer would turn out to be an outsider had to admit that that was unlikely now. No, the murderer was an insider, probably one of those in the room right now. Although that still couldn't be right, could it?

The chair that Thomas Atkins usually occupied was vacant. The humorous ceremony a year before in which that chair had been dubbed the Thomas Atkins Memorial Chair did not seem so funny now. Those present studiously avoided looking at the chair. It would be a long time before anyone dared to sit in it, and that person would be a newcomer, unaware of its history.

Michelle Hong sat alone in a corner of the room. Everyone knew that she and Atkins had been engaged to be married. During the day, members of the criminal division had come by her office to express their condolences. Brian Howarth had conveyed his profound feelings of sympathy on behalf of the entire prison litigation unit. Trevor Watson had started to put his arm around Michelle's shoulder as an expression of sympathy, but thought better of it, and merely murmured his regrets. Everyone felt awkward. How did Michelle feel about the murder? they wondered. How could she feel? *Was she the murderer?* No one knew, although that did not prevent endless speculation. After everyone commiserated with Michelle, they avoided her. She was alone now, with no one sitting on either side of her. A few minutes before the meeting began, Thomas Oldfield, who until then had remained in his office one floor down, approached her, and also expressed his regrets. Michelle forced a strained smile and thanked him. He sat far away.

The condolences expressed by one person were not entirely sincere. Oh, the person regretted the necessity of having to kill Atkins, and to that extent was sincere in expressing to Michelle the great sorrow that was felt. But a different emotion, secret and carefully suppressed, dominated. Elation. The sheer joy of a job well done, of everything combining perfectly to create a masterpiece. A murder rerun, but with a different means. And with perfect timing. The crowning glory was accidental, but exquisite nonetheless. Elizabeth Cronin had found the body, as she had the first one. That was unintended, could not have been planned, but was beautiful in its irony. *Yes, I am a genius,* the person thought smugly. No, not smugly. The person must never, would never, become smug. Necessity would never allow smugness. Satisfaction, yes, but a cautious satisfaction.

Fred Olson began the meeting at two thirty-two. He expressed his profound grief at the new tragedy that had befallen Atkins, his family, his loved ones and friends, and, last but most certainly not least, his colleagues in the criminal division. Everyone present would obviously be allowed to take time off work to attend the funeral. The grief naturally felt by everyone present (Olson assumed there were no exceptions) was overwhelming but would be overcome in time. In the meantime, however, he insisted that the work of the criminal division would have to continue. "Time, tide, and appellate briefs wait for no one," he said jovially. At least he tried to sound jovial. No one laughed or even smiled.

Olson gave a report of what he knew of the state of the investigation. There was little that those present had not already heard in the many private conversations that had been held that day. "As always," he stressed, "every single one of you should do everything possible to cooperate to the fullest to bring this vicious killer to justice. Bill Kelly and Beret Holmes are, incidentally, no longer working on the case. The inspectors decided it was just too dangerous." Everyone involuntarily glanced at the two. They stared in embarrassment at the blank notepads in front of them.

With these preliminaries completed, Olson attempted to turn the meeting to business. No one was interested, it seemed inappropriate even, but at Olson's insistence, they went through the motions. In order to continue reducing the Backlog, everyone would have to soon, very soon, place their grief behind them and write more briefs. The *Morton* trial would soon keep Martin Granowski busy for months, so no briefs could be expected from him. Granowski nodded. Olson said that he would probably be on his own during the trial, as no one could be spared to help him. Beginning immediately, Beret Holmes would have to work full-time on appellate cases. Granowski stated that that was fine with him, that he had never asked for or desired any assistance.

Olson turned to Ramon Aguilar. "As Beret's supervisor, try to find something for her to do now that she's not working on the *Morton* case."

Aguilar looked at Olson. Was he joking? Olson knew that Aguilar had seven new cases he had not been able to assign to anyone. Olson was not smiling. "Don't worry," Aguilar answered with a straight face, "I'll try to find something to keep her from getting bored." He looked at Beret; she smiled back. He was a good supervisor. She would work hard for him. She was sure he was not the killer . . . wasn't she?

Next, for some reason, Olson felt compelled to obtain a progress report on all of Rachel Brandwyn's cases that had been reassigned to others. Bill Kelly was forced to chronicle in detail everything he had done on the *Wakefield* and *Robinson* case. Atkins, he said, had been very helpful, and the respondent's brief was about half finished. He still had to work on some of the pretrial issues, he reported, but the case looked promising. The Court of Appeal would probably affirm the convictions.

"Splendid," enthused Olson.

Olson required those who were assigned Rachel's other cases to give similar detailed reports. Anna Heitz had one of them. Rachel, she reported, had made some mistakes in the case, but she was able to correct them, and everything looked good. Ramon Aguilar had two of them. He had them well in hand. Rachel's work had been excellent, and he had no trouble starting where she had left off.

Olson seemed satisfied that all of Rachel's cases were under control. Then came a discussion of Atkins's cases. They would obviously have to be reassigned, which would not be easy. It had been hard enough to find people to absorb Rachel's workload. Olson asked Anna Heitz to review all of Atkins's cases and determine whether he had done any work that might be useful to the new attorney. Heitz said she would do it right away. "By tomorrow," said Olson, "we should be able to figure out exactly what Atkins was working on, so we can reassign it." Nobody appeared enthused about the prospect. More assignments was the last thing anyone needed.

"However," continued Olson, "there is one matter we can take care of right now. The *Jones* case. It took all of my diplomacy, my considerable charm, and my mesmerizing powers of persuasion—" A pause to let people laugh; no one did. "But I was able to persuade the Chief Justice to put oral argument over until the next court session in September. So whoever gets the case will have plenty of time to prepare. It's a golden opportunity for some ambitious young, or not so young, deputy to argue a case in the Supreme Court. Who would like it?" Normally, a Supreme Court case, already briefed, would be anyone's dream.

Olson waited several seconds. No one spoke. "Surely, someone would like it." No one, it appeared, would. "Well, then, um, if there are no takers—" Olson waited again. There were no takers. "Then I guess we'll hold off on that for right now. But think about it. A Supreme Court argument is waiting just for the asking. A deal like that won't come around often."

Olson rambled on some more about the Backlog, about prospects for hiring new attorneys, and about salaries. No one took notes. No one was interested. Finally, after what seemed an interminable time, he ended the meeting. Everyone quickly and silently poured out of the room.

Once the meeting ended, the silence did not last long. In the hallways, in the offices, in the restrooms, small groups gathered for animated discussions about the events of the day. Why was Olson acting so strangely? Probably only shock over the murder. More importantly, who was the killer? Many theories were propounded; none seemed reasonable.

One person who *knew* the killer's identity participated fully in the speculation. The person felt compelled to participate; everyone, with no exceptions, must appear anxious to solve the mystery. The person was, however, a little disappointed that no one talked about how beautiful the timing of the killing had been. Ah, well, one can't have everything. The person contributed much to the speculation. All wrong, of course.

Only one small, troubling thought deep in the recesses of the person's mind clouded the moment. What would be necessary next? At first, the question was deferred. It could certainly wait. But the question persisted and grew and gradually penetrated the consciousness. What next? The more the person contemplated it, and considered the recent events, the more anxious the person became. Maybe the question wouldn't wait. After a while, the person returned alone to the office to pretend to work but actually to think and to brood.

Beret Holmes and Bill Kelly, although no longer expected to try to solve the case, found themselves talking about it in her office shortly after the meeting. Legal work that day was impossible, so why try? Maybe, if they gave it one last effort, they could discover what they had been missing, and all would become clear.

They went over everything. The murders, people's reactions, the alibis, the legal cases that were intertwined in the affair, the motives, their conversations with what they now routinely called the "prime suspects," the divisional meetings. Everything. Both had the vague, unsettling feeling that they were overlooking something. Something was not right, in addition to two bodies. Something did not fit. The clue was there somewhere. But where?

They got no place. The only person they could think of with a motive to murder both Rachel Brandwyn and Thomas Atkins was Michelle Hong. Did she kill Rachel as a rival or as a roadblock to the future happiness of herself and Atkins? Did she then kill Atkins after hearing him announce publicly that he had loved Rachel? Superficially, it was plausible. But they could not bring themselves to believe that Michelle, sweet, gentle Michelle, was capable of such cold-blooded deeds. In fact, they could not believe any of their acquaintances were capable of these murders. Yet, they had occurred.

"We seem to have a shortage of motives for the murder of Atkins," mused Bill.

"True, but I recall a similar shortage at one time for Rachel's murder. Before long we had a cornucopia."

"I hope the same thing doesn't happen again," Bill said wearily. "We've got to get this thing solved soon."

Eventually, shortly after six o'clock, they gave up. It was time to go home. Bill filled his briefcase with materials from the *Wakefield* and *Robinson* appeal, intending to work that evening at home. Beret was honest enough with herself to realize it was unlikely she could work that evening. She did not take anything home.

As they had the day of Rachel Brandwyn's murder, the two walked together to the Civic Center BART station. They no longer talked about the murders. They had exhausted that topic. Nor did they talk about themselves. That, they implicitly agreed, would wait. That left office business. Beret talked about the *Morton* case, even though she was no longer working on it. She, as Rachel before her, was concerned about Martin Granowski's preparation for trial.

"But I'm glad to be off the case. Granowski complained bitterly about both Rachel and then me getting involved. As you know, he was very angry at Rachel for going to Fred Olson with her criticisms. She apparently taunted Martin by telling him everything she had told Fred. He knew *exactly* what she had told him. The whole situation made me feel uncomfortable."

Beret continued talking. But Bill was no longer listening. By this time they had passed in front of the public library and reached the imposing statue of Ashurbanipal on the side. Suddenly, under the shadow of the ancient king, Bill stopped walking. He exclaimed, "That's it!" and grabbed Beret by the arm. She stopped. For a full five seconds, he looked intently into her eyes, deep in thought, concentrating on her precise words. She stood still and said nothing. Then he spoke. His voice was calm, his words measured.

"I think I know who did it. It's what you said just now."

Beret did not comprehend. "What I said just now?"

"Yes. That Martin knew exactly what Rachel told Fred Olson."

"So?"

"So, she did it all the time. She would complain about someone to their supervisor, and then tell the person exactly what she had said. And I mean *exactly*." Bill stopped, thinking of the right words to use. "But what if you knew for sure that Rachel had *not* told Fred some specific fact that Martin *thought* she had. Or what if Fred had gotten it wrong? Do you think that the fact that was wrong might be of special significance?"

"I suppose so. If Rachel did not mention something but Martin thought she did, or was *afraid* she did, maybe that something is the key to the whole case." Beret stopped to think. "But what discrepancy is there? For the life of me, I can't think of any difference between what Martin thought Rachel had complained about and her actual complaints."

"Does it have to be Martin?"

Bill looked at Beret; she returned the look, thinking all the while. Then the solution dawned on her. It had been there all the time. It was so simple. They talked about it. Their ideas coincided. Each contributed more thoughts, more insights, more facts remembered. Yes, it all made sense. There was no proof, but everything meshed together nicely. If they were right, the killer, though oh so clever, had made one mistake. One infinitesimal mistake. One mistake so small that it had escaped them until a second person was dead, and almost escaped them altogether. Almost.

In the excitement, Bill had put his briefcase on the ground. He glanced at it, then exclaimed, "We've got to get back to my office." He could not explain why. He just had an uneasy feeling that they were needed there.

Beret did not fully understand, but shared the feeling. "But first," she urged, "let's call the inspectors. Tell them to meet us there. We mustn't take any chances."

Bill agreed. They rushed across the street to United Nations Plaza. The escalator leading to the BART station was not working, so they ran down the stairs to a telephone. Beret put in her two dimes and dialed the number on the card the inspectors had given them. Neither Tarkov nor Petersen could be reached. Beret left a message, saying that they had some ideas about the murders, and could the inspectors please meet them as soon as possible in Bill's office. When she finished, Bill told her to say that it was urgent. But she had already hung up.

They climbed back up the stairs and, without speaking, retraced their steps back to the State Building. Words were no longer needed. They walked quickly. It took seven minutes. They got off the elevator on their floor. No one was in sight. That was no surprise, given the time and the events of the day. No one was likely to work late that day. They walked down the hall toward Bill's office. They could see from a distance that the door was closed. That was odd. Bill normally did not close his door when he left for the day. He was quite sure he hadn't that day, either. He took hold of Beret's hand as they approached the office. The closer they got, the quieter they walked. It seemed necessary.

They reached the office. Bill felt an irrational urge to knock. But it was his own office, so he didn't. As he stood there, Beret reached for the doorknob and, in one movement, opened the door wide. Inside, behind the desk, by the window, they could see the bent form of a person who was looking through a file of small transcripts.

Bill stepped inside. In a voice that was surprisingly firm, he said, "Hello, Unicorn."

Brian Howarth straightened up and turned around. He smiled. "So you figured it out."

Chapter 24

B eret stepped into the office. Her heart was pounding. So they *were* right. "Yes," she responded, "it took a while, but we figured it out." Her voice, too, sounded calm, almost matter of fact. How odd it seemed. She and Bill Kelly in Bill's office talking to a double murderer as if discussing the weather.

Everyone hesitated. The attorneys-turned-amateur-sleuths did not know quite what to do once they had cornered their quarry. For the moment, the killer appeared not to know what to do, either, although the appearance would soon prove an illusion. The three looked at each other. Then Howarth laughed. "It must have been the change in the weather. Come in. Let's talk about it."

Bill and Beret obeyed, and stepped further into the office. Why, they could never explain. Howarth had been their friend and colleague for so long, it seemed natural to do what he suggested. Neither felt danger, although logic would have screamed danger if logic had been present.

Bill spoke next. "Unicorn. The outsider in the *Wakefield* and *Robinson* case who smuggled drugs and weapons into San Quentin."

"Never weapons. Only drugs," interrupted Howarth sharply. "I would never have smuggled weapons inside. Too dangerous. Weapons can kill people." He reached to his right and grabbed an object. A handgun. He had placed the gun on the desk when he entered Bill's office to have it available if necessary. It was now necessary. "Like this one." Howarth pointed the gun directly at Bill, then at Beret, then back at Bill. Beret was no expert, but it looked to her like a .357 magnum. If so, it was as fearsome as its reputation. Bill and Beret stared at the weapon. Both found it hard to take their eyes off the barrel.

"Yes, it's a .357 magnum." Howarth removed all doubt. "Different gun than I used before. Same make. It's reliable." He noticed the open door. "Close the door," he commanded. Bill complied. "I'm sorry, truly I am," continued Howarth. "You two are nice kids, I like you, but I didn't ask you to learn the truth. It's not my fault. Now that you know, I can't let you live. You know that. Just like I couldn't let Rachel and Tom Atkins live. I'm going to have to kill you. It's necessary."

Beret started to try to talk him out of it but understood immediately that it was useless. All they could do was try to stall until assistance arrived. Until the cavalry, in the form of the inspectors, got their message and rode to the rescue. Had she told them it was urgent? "There is a lot I don't understand."

Howarth smiled. Without lowering the gun, he spoke in a soothing voice. "I'll bet there is. Well, we have time. The building is empty. I've been dying to tell someone the full story; now I have the chance. Relax. Just don't make any sudden moves or they'll be your last."

Howarth stopped smiling. He spoke in deadly earnest. "That last statement was melodramatic, wasn't it? I'm sorry, but I must be serious. Just be quiet and you'll hear the whole story. You might even answer my own questions."

Willingly, thought Bill. *As many as you have. Take as much time as you want.* When would help come? Had Beret told whoever took the message that it was urgent?

Howarth invited the two to sit in chairs that he pushed toward them. They did as he suggested. No point in angering him. Howarth leaned against the ledge of the window, the gun pointed sometimes at Bill, sometimes at Beret, sometimes at neither, but always at the ready. The gun looked so incredibly big. It dominated their whole field of vision. The end of the barrel, where the bullet would come if it came at all, grabbed and held their attention. It loomed large, interfering with their ability to think. Or to conduct a conversation. But conduct a conversation they must. It took all their concentration, but they had to take their minds off the gun enough to talk calmly.

"What made you do it?" asked Beret.

"Do what? Become Unicorn? Or kill Rachel and Tom?"

"Either, both," answered Bill. *Take your time*, he thought.

"Becoming Unicorn was fun. I went to San Quentin all the time on the job. I befriended some of the inmates. They're not all bad, you know. I even discussed my cases with them. You'd be surprised how unsympathetic some of the inmates are to the jail-house lawyers. One inmate offered to testify for me in one of my cases. For a little quid pro quo. When I told Tom Oldfield and the others in the prison litigation unit that I had an inmate willing to testify *for* us, I became a hero. That had never happened before."

Howarth paused to let them appreciate the magnificence of his accomplishment. "What I did not tell them was that the inmate wanted something in return for his help. Some crack cocaine. He could obtain it from sources on the street, but could not get it inside the walls. He wanted me to smuggle it in. What the hell, I thought. Why not. It seemed harmless. It was easy to bring it inside. I had been coming and going to the prison for so long that no one asked questions. It amused me when everyone later assumed the visitor's room was used for the smuggling. I just used my pockets. As easy as that. It helped that everyone's attention was focused on the wrong place."

"So that's how it started," commented Beret.

"Yes, that's how it started. Other inmates heard about it and wanted the same deal. Of course, I couldn't risk my name being used. The first inmate became my partner. I'll never disclose his name."

Bill could not help but think that such secrecy was unnecessary since Howarth intended to kill them both. He decided not to press the point.

"My partner worked with me from beginning to end. It was his idea to give me a code name. 'Unicorn' was my idea. Elegant, don't you think?" Howarth continued without giving them a chance to respond. "We put a good organization together. I got my witnesses, they got their drugs to play with." Howarth relaxed his grip on the gun slightly as he became lost in his memories. "Wakefield and Robinson were stupid and got caught. Fortunately, they didn't know anything. In fact, they also assumed the visiting room was used, which further helped to camouflage the truth. They were expendable and got what they deserved for their stupidity. Nobody caught on to who Unicorn really was."

Howarth paused to place the handgun in his left hand. Apparently the right hand was getting tired. Bill hoped Howarth didn't get so tired that he decided to simply end the conversation. The barrel still looked awfully big.

"It was a good deal for everyone. I won my cases. I became the best of the prison litigators. The inmates got their toys to distract them. No real harm was done. The claim that I also smuggled in weapons was outrageous. Weapons were out of the question. Only drugs. I wanted to sue for defamation whoever started the rumors about weapons. But, under the circumstances, I just had to ignore the rumors." Howarth paused, obviously distressed at his inability to sue.

"But," Bill pointed out, "Wakefield and Robinson were convicted of weapons charges as well as drugs."

"They free-lanced. As I said, they were stupid. They deserved to get caught."

Beret interrupted the ensuing break in the conversation. "So that's how you got your witnesses in the *Rawlings* case?" She wanted to keep the conversation going. The inspectors would be there soon. Wouldn't they?

"Exactly. That's how I always got my witnesses."

"But," said Bill, puzzled, "you told us once that the inmates testified for you because they hated Rawlings, who was a child molester?"

"That was half right. They did hate Rawlings. But obviously, without some big payoff, no inmate in the adjustment center would ever voluntarily help to defeat a lawsuit that tried to improve their conditions. They'd rather cut their own throats. You didn't *really* believe me." He looked incredulous. "Did you?" When his listeners said nothing, he added, "But, that's laughable." As if to prove the point, Howarth raised his head (not far enough) and laughed. Long and hard. It was almost a giggle. Bill and Beret found less humor in the situation. The gun was still pointed at their midsections.

Howarth suddenly stopped laughing. Just as suddenly, his eyes turned cold. Silence. Bill had to break the silence before Howarth broke it in an undesirable manner. "But why kill Rachel?"

Howarth relaxed, and smiled. Now would come the good part of his recitation. Now, finally, he could tell them everything. "It was her own fault. She was meddling. She got too close to the truth. She complained to Fred Olson and to Tom Oldfield. She threatened to send a memo to Oldfield. I couldn't allow that."

"She never wrote it," inserted Bill. "She wrote memos criticizing Trevor Watson and Martin Granowski, but she never wrote one about you."

"Oh, yes she did. She told me she had written a scathing memo about me and would send it to Oldfield if I didn't admit everything. After I killed Rachel, before I left her office, I looked for it in her filing cabinet. I couldn't find it. I didn't know she had rearranged the cabinet. When I heard from Jeff Hines that you had found the memos about Trevor and Martin in the *fourth* drawer instead of the second where she used to keep them, I slipped back into her office and found the one about me. I appreciate your leaving everything alone in her office. It was very helpful."

When the other two did not respond, he continued. "The memo was indeed scathing." He smiled at the memory. "You should have seen it. Everything I ever did, it seems, irritated her. Rachel didn't have proof, but she said she suspected me of being Unicorn. That alone justified my killing her. I couldn't afford even the suspicion being voiced. As you can imagine, I destroyed that memo but quick."

Howarth paused. He waved the gun menacingly. Beret stopped focusing on the barrel long enough to decide she had to say something to keep the conversation going. "Uh, what made you decide to kill her when you did?"

"Rachel decided to talk to Ramon Aguilar about her suspicions. She asked to meet him at the Palace, where they could talk far away from me. Ramon told me about the meeting. It seemed strange to him. He couldn't understand what was going on. I did understand. I followed her and was able to overhear what they talked about. Fortunately, she had decided to wait until after her oral argument to reveal her suspicions. That gave me time to act." Howarth's voice became higher pitched. "I had no choice. You do understand that, don't you? I had a good thing going. It wasn't doing any real harm. But no one else would have understood. It would have ruined my career if I had been exposed as Unicorn. The ingrates would have forgotten all the good I had accomplished." He almost shrieked. "You do understand, don't you?"

Under the circumstances, the two found it prudent to murmur sympathy with his plight. "That night," Howarth continued, his voice once again under control, "was torment, let me tell you. I didn't want to kill her, but I had to. I carefully worked out my plan. The gun and silencer in the *Morton* case were too convenient to resist. Granowski showed me how to use them. I knew he had also shown others. I couldn't ask for a better opportunity. Suspicion would be spread out. Like any great man, I seized the moment, and acted." He stood taller, pushed out his chest, and added proudly, "It was brilliant, wasn't it, the way I did it? With the evidence tags still attached." He stopped to see their reaction.

Even in their current predicament, neither Bill nor Beret found it possible to voice admiration. Howarth did not take umbrage at their silence. "So I did it, and I got away with it. I was a suspect, but only one of many. There was no reason to suspect me more than the others. I loved watching you two find a motive for all the suspects, one by one. Of course, I had to help with one of the motives," he added.

Bill understood the meaning of this last comment. "So you made the anonymous phone calls about Ramon Aguilar?"

"Who else?" answered Howarth cheerfully. "I figured you would never come up with a credible motive for him on your own. He's such a straight arrow. He never did anything that could possibly be twisted into a motive to kill. So I had to invent one for him. I knew about the meeting between him and Rachel at the Palace, so I could tell you enough of the truth to make my accusations sound plausible. I could count on Ramon to act suspicious when you confronted him. The whole thing was hilarious." He looked at his captives as if expecting them to share his good humor. They did not. "Imagine," he continued. "You actually thought Ramon Aguilar might have been the father of Rachel's baby, and that he killed her. Ramon, who is utterly harmless."

Beret ignored the comment. "And the second anonymous call?"

"Also from me. I wanted to add fuel to the fire." Howarth looked at Beret. "Ramon told me about his conversation with you. The naive fool. I made good use of the information he provided when I called you the second time. I wanted people to talk about the calls, to put Ramon on the defensive. So I started rumors to make everyone aware of them. That was easy. I just told Trevor Watson, supposedly in secret, that I had inside information about the calls. He did the rest. I almost burst out laughing when my secretary later told *me* in secret about the calls. It went full circle in two days." Howarth chuckled at the pleasant memory. He lowered the gun for a moment, then suddenly remembered what he was doing and again pointed it at Bill.

"Then what about the murder of Tom Atkins?" Bill also tried to keep the conversation going. Where were the inspectors? "Why should you care that he was the father of Rachel's baby?"

"Is that what you think?" No answer. "Yes, you would think that, wouldn't you? You misunderstand. I didn't care in the slightest who the father of Rachel's baby was. If Tom knocked her up, that was his problem." Howarth shrugged his shoulders. "After I killed her, I was sorry to hear that she had been pregnant, but that's the way it goes. No, I didn't kill Atkins because he was the father. His story at the meeting yesterday was touching, but it was only a diversion from what was really important." Howarth paused to let them guess. They could not.

"What was that?" Beret finally asked.

"Something else happened yesterday at the meeting. As you may recall—at least *I* recall—earlier in the meeting Atkins said that Rachel told him *everything* about her cases. Including the *Wakefield* and *Robinson* case. If she told him everything, he might eventually come to suspect, like she did, that I was Unicorn. I couldn't risk that. You do understand, don't you?" Howarth grinned. It was not a attractive grin; they could see all his teeth. "I killed once to protect myself. It was easy to kill a second time. The third and fourth will be even easier."

Beret definitely did not like the turn the conversation had taken. "How did you lure Atkins to the vestibule?"

"It was absurdly easy. I just made another anonymous telephone call. I told him to meet me there and I would help him solve the murder. The fool believed me. Of course, in a way, I told him the truth. He really *did* learn who the killer was. But only for a moment, a very brief moment." Howarth shifted the gun back to his right hand. "You should have seen the look in his eyes when he comprehended the truth. You'd have loved it." Beret had doubts on this point, but let it pass.

Howarth continued. "I worked it all out last night. He said he wanted to slit my throat; I slit his. It went exactly as planned. Rachel's murder all over again, but even more beautiful. You have to admire my artistry. And then to have Elizabeth Cronin find the second body. Exquisite!"

Howarth paused to savor the memory. Finally, he could freely give voice to the emotions of the past weeks; he could express openly the poetic, oh so poetic, thoughts that had been coming to him unbidden of late, particularly during the long nights. He voiced one especially clever epigram that he had mentally molded into perfection during one sleepless night. "You might say I am the Michelangelo of murder, the Voltaire of violence."

"Excuse us if we are less enthralled with your talents than you are," muttered Beret.

The comment did not dampen Howarth's spirits. "Consider yourself excused. I admire your courage. I don't expect you to approve of my accomplishments. I just want you to appreciate my genius before you die. The timing was particularly brilliant, wasn't it?" He did not pause for a response. "I got back to my office at exactly the same time as I did after killing Rachel. I went straight to the courtroom, and again arrived at exactly the same time. You did appreciate the beauty in the timing, didn't you?"

This last question was asked in all sincerity; it was almost an entreaty for praise. Before thinking about it, Beret interjected that they had not even noticed. "You didn't even notice? How is that possible?" Again, there was no irony in Howarth's voice. Instead, he spoke sadly, as if coming to realize that he was casting pearls to the swine. "But you must notice. You must!" Was Howarth's tone turning from sadness to anger? Beret spoke to forestall the possibility. She tried to humor him.

"We do appreciate your genius. We didn't before, but now we do." As she spoke, it occurred to her that maybe, just maybe, she could take advantage of Howarth's pride to buy some time. "And that's why I don't think you could just shoot us here like a common thug. Where's the beauty in that? You need a new plan. One even more exquisite than the first two."

Howarth laughed. Again, it was not a cheering laugh. "Oh no, you don't. Nice try, but you won't get off that easy. Maybe this isn't as pretty." He indicated his gun. "But it will be effective. And it's necessary. You forced it on me."

"But the gun will make too much noise. You have no silencer."

"True. This is just a gun I happened to have lying around the house. Silencers are illegal, you know. You'd be surprised how difficult it is to get a good one these days." Howarth laughed at his joke. His listeners did not. "But," continued Howarth calmly, "there's no one around to hear the shots. Don't worry, I worked it all out ahead of time. I have a good escape route. I will be out of here within seconds of your deaths. There will just be one more mystery for those inept inspectors to try to solve."

"And how many more 'mysteries' will there have to be?" asked Beret. "How many more will you have to kill?"

The question had been worrying Howarth more than he could let on. With an effort, he made his voice sound unconcerned. "Oh, I don't know. I suspect this will be the end of it. But if not, I'm prepared to do whatever is necessary. You might say, necessity guides me." He again laughed at his wit. Again, the others did not. Howarth, who had been slumping more and more against the window, straightened his body and made another threatening gesture with the gun.

The barrel was pointed directly at Beret's heart. Was this the end? she couldn't help but wonder. Howarth reassured her for the moment. "But not yet. No need to prematurely end a pleasant conversation. I'll tell you anything you like. I couldn't tell anyone before. Now I can. Let me enjoy myself."

They were willing to let him enjoy himself as long as he wanted. At least, until help arrived. Howarth seemed to have reached the end of his monologue. Bill came to the rescue. "How did Rachel suspect you might be Unicorn?"

"She got the idea from a transcript in her case—now your case. *Wakefield* and *Robinson.* The transcript was of a pretrial hearing on the identity of the outsider. Of Unicorn." Bill remembered the transcript. It was the missing one he had borrowed from the Court of Appeal. He had not yet read it. In fact, the copy was in his briefcase at that moment. He had intended to read it at home.

Howarth continued. "The district attorney insisted the prosecution did not know who Unicorn was." He chuckled mirthlessly. "They sure didn't know. They weren't even close. Everything was fine except for one thing. One of the defense attorneys hinted that they believed he was an attorney who visited San Quentin regularly. A lucky guess, but too close to the truth. Rachel read it and started thinking. She then started meddling in *Rawlings.* The more she looked into it, the more suspicious she became. She confronted me with her suspicions. I denied everything. I was convincing. She doubted herself. But she wasn't entirely convinced. Eventually, she decided to communicate her suspicions to others. To her mentor, Ramon Aguilar." Howarth shrugged. "You know the rest. It became necessary to kill her. I did."

He paused again to enjoy the memory. He lowered the gun a trifle, but kept it ready. Bill spoke. "So you're the one who took the transcript from the file. It was missing when I was assigned the case."

"That's right. Late the night after I killed Rachel, I went into her office, found the transcript, and destroyed it. At the division meeting today I learned for the first time that you had asked the Court of Appeal for a copy. It never occurred to me you would be so zealous. For that alone I should kill you." Howarth raised the gun and placed his finger on the trigger. Bill gazed at the gigantic barrel in wonderment. *What will it feel like? Will I hear anything? See anything?* Howarth relaxed again, and smiled. "But not yet. We have to finish talking first. You must know everything. After the meeting today I decided to see if you had gotten that exact transcript. After all, it was not relevant to any of the issues; you might still have overlooked it."

"So you waited for everyone to leave for the day, and you came to look for it," said Beret.

"You got it. I was looking for it when you so unluckily interrupted me. It doesn't appear to be here. I guess you didn't get it after all."

"Oh, I got it all right," responded Bill. "I am thorough. But it's not in my office." He decided to try to bluff. "I read the part you mentioned. I, too, got suspicious. I showed it to Fred Olson. And Thomas Oldfield. Now they know. The police are on their way right now to arrest you. Your game is up. You might as well surrender."

For a moment, doubt appeared in Howarth's eyes. But only for a moment. He quickly realized Bill was not telling the truth. What was it Bill had said that day at pizza after the softball game? That he was a lousy poker player because everyone could tell when he was bluffing? Well, he was right. Bill had never learned how to lie. His eyes gave it away. Bill glanced at his briefcase on the floor. Howarth observed the glance. *Bill is so transparent,* he thought contemptuously. He pointed to the briefcase and asked, "What's that?"

"Oh, nothing." What more could Bill say?

"Hand it to me." Bill started to reach for the briefcase. "No, wait. Push it to me with your foot. But don't otherwise move or you're a dead man." Every time Howarth spoke like this, it sounded so melodramatic Bill almost had to laugh. But he did as he was told. Howarth reached down for the briefcase. Without lowering his guard, he opened it and removed the contents. Some briefs. Some notes. A blank notepad. And some transcripts. Including *the* transcript. Howarth spoke mockingly. "How industrious. You were going to work at home tonight. Nice try, Bill, you almost had me believing you. As you said, you can't bluff. It's just your bad luck that I can tell when you're telling the truth and when you're lying." Howarth picked up the transcript, and read through it quickly. "It's right here on page seventeen."

Howarth did not offer to let Bill read it. Bill did not ask. He could only respond, "So the answer was there all the time, and I never saw it."

Silence. A dangerous silence. Bill was trying to figure out how to jump Howarth and disarm him before he could shoot. People did that successfully all the time in the movies and on television. It seemed impossible. He did not try.

Howarth finally broke the silence in a manner Bill and Beret approved of; he spoke. "And now it's my turn to ask questions." *Gladly,* thought Bill. *As many as you want.* He felt a strong urge to look at his watch, but didn't dare. It seemed like forever since they had left the message for the inspectors. Where were they? Would they come? Would they come *in time?* Howarth continued. "How did you figure out I was Unicorn?"

"You gave us the clue yourself," answered Beret. "In your second anonymous call about Ramon Aguilar. You told me that the killer must have said one thing too many—that he must have said something to give himself away."

"I remember saying that. I wanted to muddy the waters. To make you think too much and miss the obvious. I knew everyone would talk a lot and you would get lost in minutia."

"We did have plenty to think about. But finally, only one person said anything that tipped us off. You."

Despite the annoying suggestion that he had made a mistake, Howarth was enjoying himself. *Nobody's perfect,* he told himself. *Let's hear where I went wrong. I'm in full control.* He listened patiently.

Bill took up the narrative. "At pizza. After the softball game."

"I remember it. Go on."

"You complained that Rachel was 'meddling' in your case. You used the word 'meddling.' You said she criticized you to Fred Olson and Tom Oldfield."

"So? She *did* criticize me. You'd have found out anyway. I thought it best if you heard it from me. It would seem natural, and less suspicious. Besides, I didn't kill her just because she was criticizing me. Her criticism I could take; her exposing me as Unicorn I could not. That wasn't a mistake on my part."

"True. That wasn't. If you had stopped there. But you went on. You said one thing too many."

Beret spoke next. "You said that Rachel told Tom Oldfield there was some connection between your *Rawlings* case and her *Wakefield* and *Robinson* case. Wrong. She never mentioned the *Wakefield* and *Robinson* case to Oldfield. When we talked to him, he had never heard of it."

Howarth lowered the gun slightly, but not too much. He spoke next. "Rachel told me she complained to Oldfield about me. I thought she said that she told him there was some connection between the cases. But I guess she wanted to be more certain before she did. I wanted you to hear the story from me first, so you would see how unconcerned I appeared. It would seem less suspicious. How was I to know she didn't tell him?"

Beret ignored the question. "Rachel made it a habit to tell everyone exactly what she said when she complained to their supervisors—Trevor, Martin, even Anna. She would have told you if she had told Oldfield she suspected a connection between the cases. She didn't. Yet you assumed she did. Why? Obviously, it was important to you, and you assumed it was important to her. But why was it important to you? Because there *was* a connection between the cases." She paused to collect her thoughts. It was hard to think straight with that gigantic gun barrel staring at her. Then she continued. "When the discrepancy finally dawned on us, too late to save Tom Atkins"—*let us hope*, she prayed, *not too late to save* us—"we asked ourselves, what possible connection could there be between the *Rawlings* case and the *Wakefield* and *Robinson* case."

"And that gave us our answer," completed Bill. "The attorney on the one case, who got such amazing cooperation from the inmates, was the Unicorn of the other case. It all fit together. We knew."

"How ironic," murmured Howarth. He leaned back against the window ledge. "How ironic," he repeated, as if talking to himself. "I urged you to listen to everyone, and it was I who talked too much." He stood straighter, and looked closely at the other two. "But I'm not the one to suffer. Only you." Before they could decide if this was a threat, he again hastened to reassure them. "But don't worry, not yet. Not until you tell me everything. Why did you come back to this office?"

Bill himself was not sure exactly why. He explained as best he could. "At the meeting today, I told everyone, including you, what I had done in the *Wakefield* and *Robinson* case. It occurred to me you might worry that I would figure out the truth the same way Rachel did. I felt it was important to return to my office right away." Bill shifted his position. It was uncomfortable sitting motionless for so long. "And so we did," he added lamely.

"And so you did," mocked Howarth. "Wonderful. I now understand everything. And you understand everything." He stood taller, and became serious. His eyes turned cold as ice. "Which makes what I am about to do necessary. How unfortunate for you that you never thought you were walking into danger. How fortunate for me." He raised the gun menacingly. "I hate to end this nice meeting, but we have talked long enough. It's time for me to get home." He placed his finger on the trigger again, ready to fire.

"Wait!" said Bill desperately. "We did know we were in danger. We did protect ourselves."

Howarth hesitated. Bill could never bluff. But he was not bluffing now. "What do you mean?"

"We called Inspectors Peterson and Tarkov. We asked them to meet us here as soon as possible."

What was this? Howarth suddenly had doubts. He had not counted on this. Bill sounded sincere. He had either quickly learned how to lie or he was telling the truth. But the doubt passed quickly. Howarth became reassured. "Even if you did, so what? They aren't here. I can shoot you and be out of here in no time."

Silence. Bill could not dispute Howarth's logic. Nor could Beret. For a few momentous seconds, Howarth did not shoot. Why, Bill and Beret would never know. Then the two heard a welcome sound. Footsteps. Coming from the direction of the elevators. Approaching Bill's office. In the empty building, the sound reverberated up and down the long linoleum-covered hallway. Loudly. More loudly than Bill or Beret had ever thought possible. Howarth heard it, too.

"There. That's the inspectors," said Bill. "They're coming. There's no way out."

"Be quiet!" commanded Howarth. They were quiet. The footsteps came closer. "Lock the door. Quietly," ordered Howarth, although he knew that would not help if it really was the inspectors outside. Howarth was already considering what actions would be necessary if it was the inspectors. The choices were not pleasant. As always, Howarth was prepared to do what necessity demanded, and to do it promptly. Beret locked the door as she was told. Quietly. The three continued listening. It became apparent that there was only one pair of feet, not two.

"It sounds like only one person is coming," said Howarth grimly.

"That's enough," replied Beret.

"I think it's Tarkov," said Bill, listening intently. After a moment, he changed his mind. "No, it sounds more like Petersen. Or, rather, I'm sure it's one or the other." The three continued to listen in silence. Howarth's doubts increased with each passing second. Bill could not successfully lie. He was telling the truth, or at least what he thought was the truth. He really believed it was someone coming to the rescue. But was he right? How could he be sure? Maybe it was just a passerby. Well, they would know soon enough. If the person walked past the office, Howarth would be safe. If not, well . . .

The three remained as they were, frozen. Two in chairs, the third standing by the window, a gun in the right hand aimed at the other two. The footsteps came closer. Their sound dominated the building. How was it possible they made so much noise?

It seemed to take forever as the footsteps approached. *Please,* prayed Howarth, his hand tightly gripping the gun, *let them walk past the office. Please,* prayed Bill and Beret, their hands tightly gripping the chairs, *let them stop at the office.* The wait was interminable. Finally, the footsteps reached the office. The three held their breaths. The footsteps stopped. Right outside the door, they stopped. For two seconds there was utter silence. Silence that reverberated even louder than had the footsteps. Silence that stifled Brian Howarth and Bill Kelly and Beret Holmes.

Then came a knock on the door. Tentative at first. Everyone jumped. Howarth again placed his finger on the trigger. The knock became louder, then stopped. The doorknob was jiggled.

The locked door did not open. The knocking resumed, louder yet. Bill and Beret sat frozen.

Howarth was no longer frozen. Bill was right, he now realized. It was one of the inspectors! Necessity demanded that he act. That he act now. Howarth had long taken pride in doing what was necessary. Now would be no exception. He pulled the trigger.

But before he did, he jerked his hand around and placed the barrel of the gun in his own mouth. Pointing upward. When he pulled the trigger, the gun exploded. So did Howarth's head. The sound shattered the enveloping silence. Bill and Beret watched in horror as the bullet entered the brain and came out through the skull. Bits of brain spattered out. So did blood. The bullet penetrated the ceiling. Brain and blood and bone flew all over, hitting walls, window, and ceiling. Howarth fell forward, landing awkwardly on the floor alongside the desk. His arms were sprawled in front of him. The transcript that he had held to the end was partially covered by the body.

Beret jumped into Bill's arms. Bill jumped into hers. She had the presence of mind to reach over and unlock the door. The door opened wide.

To their astonishment, the person on the other side was not either of the inspectors. It was Elizabeth Cronin. She screamed at what she saw.

Officer Theodore French of the California State Police was the first to arrive at the scene. By chance, he had been on the next lower floor on a routine errand and faintly heard the gunshot followed by Elizabeth Cronin's scream. He recognized the scream; he had heard it before. He rushed to its source, arriving within a minute. When he arrived, Bill and Beret were still in each other's arms. Elizabeth Cronin was still screaming. Brian Howarth lay dead inside the office, an apparent suicide. Half his head was missing. The gun was still in his right hand. But it looked much smaller now.

A quick inspection of the body convinced Officer French that it was beyond help. There was little to do but to preserve the scene and call for assistance. Officer French had become extraordinarily experienced at that task and did his usual first-rate job. He also had to calm Elizabeth Cronin; he also had substantial experience at that task.

Inspectors Petersen and Tarkov arrived about ten minutes later. They had been investigating a homicide in the Lake Merced area and were delayed in traffic. There had been a multiple-car accident on Market Street. They did not realize the call from Bill and Beret was urgent. After carefully examining the scene, Inspector Tarkov reluctantly concluded that scientific evidence was probably not going to be needed this time.

Shortly after Officer French arrived, Bill and Beret stumbled out of the office. Before they did, Bill observed the transcript partially hidden under Howarth's body. Blood had oozed over it. Bill's last conscious thought inside the office was, *Damn, I'm going to have to get another copy of the transcript from the Court of Appeal.*

Chapter 25

Fred Olson's first thought when he heard the news was, *All right! It's an attorney from the prison litigation unit, not one of mine.* He felt a fleeting sympathy for Thomas Oldfield, who was a nice enough person and who would have endless trouble now. But Olson mainly felt exhilaration that he would not lose any more of his productive attorneys. The murders were now behind him. And the people in Sacramento could not possibly blame them on him. Not now!

Elizabeth Cronin, somewhat calmer, had called Olson at home later that evening with her story. She had stayed late at the office, doing some work that did not need to be done. Anything to postpone having to return to her lonely condominium near the Civic Center. When she finally decided to leave, she noticed that the door to Bill Kelly's office was closed. She found that odd, because Bill usually left it open. She walked down the hall to investigate. It was eerie how her footsteps reverberated in the deserted building. When she reached the closed door, she felt a sense of foreboding. She knocked a couple of times, then tried the door. It was locked. For some reason she could never articulate, she did not say anything. Probably a reluctance to break the pervasive silence.

Then she heard a thunderous bang, and the door opened. Elizabeth told Olson what she saw next.

The next morning, Olson called another criminal division meeting, the third in three days. No matter. This one was different. The morning sun had risen brightly over the cloudless East Bay hills to bathe the city in glorious light. The birds were chirping; flowers were in bloom. It was almost summer. A good time to be alive. The rain had cleared the air. And the events of yesterday had cleared the shadow that had hung for so long over the criminal division. The knowledge that a murderer had indeed been among them was shocking to the deputies, but was much easier to live with than the continual uncertainty, the mutual distrust, and the increasing fear. Now everyone could put things back together and resume normal living and working.

Bill and Beret sat apart at the large table in the library conference room. They had made reservations for dinner for two that night at Trader Vic's. Somehow, they had no desire to see each other until then. How their relationship would develop now that the mystery that had brought them together had ended, neither could say. But they would begin finding answers tonight.

Among the attorneys who attended the meeting were several who were relieved to be murder suspects no longer. Michelle Hong engaged in relaxed conversation with the others. She apparently had reconciled herself to Atkins's death and looked forward to the future. Inspectors Petersen and Tarkov spoke briefly, telling everyone what they already knew, and heaping effusive praise on Beret and Bill for their role in solving the case.

Then Fred Olson took the floor. He announced that his secretary, Elizabeth Cronin, was going to take a ten-week leave of absence. She did not say why, and he would not try to speculate. Although it would not be easy, they all would have to get along without her as best they could. Olson next tried to talk about filling vacancies in attorney positions, but Trevor Watson continually interrupted him. He tried to talk about office automation, but Ramon Aguilar continually interrupted him. He tried to talk about the Backlog, but Martin Granowski continually interrupted him.

Finally, Anna Heitz, the veteran, stood up. Turning to Beret, then to Bill, she asked the question that was on everyone's mind. "What was it like being a detective in a murder case?"

Beret looked in Bill's direction, he in hers. Their eyes met. Each understood the other's thoughts. Beret voiced those thoughts, giving an answer that greatly pleased Fred Olson, for the Backlog was not going to go away on its own.

"On the whole," she said, "I'd rather be an appellate lawyer."